Praise for Robert Asprin's MYTH-ADVENTURES series

"Stuffed with rowdy fun." —*The Philadelphia Inquirer*

"Give yourself the pleasure of working through the series. But not all at once; you'll wear out your funny bone."

—*The Washington Times*

"Hysterically funny." —*Analog*

"Breezy, pun-filled fantasy in the vein of Piers Anthony's Xanth series . . . a hilarious bit of froth and frolic."

—*Library Journal*

"Asprin's major achievement as a writer—brisk pacing, wit, and a keen satirical eye." —*Booklist*

"An excellent, lighthearted fantasy series." —*Epic Illustrated*

"Tension getting to you? Take an Asprin! . . . His humor is broad and grows out of the fantasy world or dimensions in which his characters operate." —Fantasy Review

The MYTH-ADVENTURES Series

by Robert Asprin

ANOTHER FINE MYTH
MYTH CONCEPTIONS
MYTH DIRECTIONS
HIT OR MYTH
MYTH-ING PERSONS
LITTLE MYTH MARKER
M.Y.T.H. INC. LINK
MYTH-NOMERS AND IM-PERVECTIONS
M.Y.T.H. INC. IN ACTION
SWEET MYTH-TERY OF LIFE
MYTH-ION IMPROBABLE
SOMETHING M.Y.T.H. INC.

by Robert Asprin and Jody Lynn Nye

MYTH ALLIANCES
MYTH-TAKEN IDENTITY
MYTH-TOLD TALES
CLASS DIS-MYTHED
MYTH-GOTTEN GAINS
MYTH-CHIEF
MYTH-FORTUNES

by Jody Lynn Nye

ROBERT ASPRIN'S MYTH-QUOTED
ROBERT ASPRIN'S MYTH-FITS

The DRAGONS WILD Series

by Robert Asprin

DRAGONS WILD
DRAGONS LUCK

by Robert Asprin and Jody Lynn Nye

DRAGONS DEAL

by Jody Lynn Nye

ROBERT ASPRIN'S DRAGONS RUN

ALSO BY ROBERT ASPRIN

The PHULE'S COMPANY Series

PHULE'S COMPANY
PHULE'S PARADISE

with Peter J. Heck

A PHULE AND HIS MONEY
PHULE ME TWICE
NO PHULE LIKE AN OLD PHULE
PHULE'S ERRAND

ROBERT ASPRIN'S

MYTH-FITS

JODY LYNN NYE

ACE BOOKS, NEW YORK

An imprint of Penguin Random House LLC
375 Hudson Street, New York, New York 10014

This book is an original publication of Penguin Random House LLC.

Library of Congress Cataloging-in-Publication Data

Names: Nye, Jody Lynn, 1957– author.
Title: Robert Asprin's myth-fits / Jody Lynn Nye.
Description: New York, NY : Ace, 2016. | Series: Myth-adventures ; 21
Identifiers: LCCN 2015039367 | ISBN 9780425257029 (softcover)
Subjects: | BISAC: FICTION / Fantasy / Epic. | FICTION / Action & Adventure. | GSAFD: Fantasy fiction.
Classification: LCC PS3564.Y415 R63 2016 | DDC 813/.54—dc23
LC record available at http://lccn.loc.gov/2015039367

PUBLISHING HISTORY
Ace trade paperback edition / June 2016

PRINTED IN THE UNITED STATES OF AMERICA

10 9 8 7 6 5 4 3

Cover illustration by Walter Velez.
Cover design by Sarah Oberrender.

Penguin
Random
House

To Lynn Abbey,
with affection and respect

ROBERT ASPRIN'S

MYTH-FITS

CHAPTER ONE

"When you wish upon a star, your dreams come true."

—A. EMANUEL

I looked up at the gentle tap on my door. Guido leaned in, filling most of the doorway. The enormous enforcer looked dismayed and concerned.

"Hey, boss, got a minute?" He aimed a thumb over his shoulder. "I need you to come and talk wit' dis broad."

"Sure, Guido."

Curious, I set my book down and rose to follow him. It wasn't often that my fellow Klahd and partner in M.Y.T.H., Inc., ever found himself in need of assistance or advice when it came to handling people. I presumed that he needed a "bad cop," as another of our partners, Aahz, might say, to balance his "good cop" in striking a deal. Grabbing a handful of magik from a force line that ran directly underneath our tent in the Bazaar at Deva, I put on the appearance of Skeeve the Magnificent. It was this austere, gaunt, imposing wizard that entered the office.

Guido had not, in fact, been inaccurate or disrespectful in referring to our visitor as a "broad." I had never seen someone who so resembled a wall as she did. Front to back, she wasn't that much thicker than I was, but from side to side, she was, well, broad. Her posterior took up three chairs. She had no neck to speak of. Her head sat squarely, or, rather, rectangularly on her shoulders. My outstretched arms, and I have long arms, could not have spanned her face. Brick-red skin added to the resemblance of the side of a barn. The perky hat with a small yellow bird in it tilted to one side of her head threw me a little. I recovered my wits and stalked in to loom over her.

"Miss Flowers here's got a problem wit' our pricing structure," Guido told me. "I figured you could explain it to her a little."

"As you wish," I intoned in my most sepulchral voice.

She glared at Guido and waved an angry hand at me.

"Oh, yeah, you're gonna try to put me off by bringing in a cute guy! Well, I tell you, it won't work!"

I blinked my eyes. They appeared to be set cavernously under arched black brows. *Cute guy?*

"What seems to be the difficulty?" I asked. I admit, I was taken aback at having my best disguise referred to as a "cute guy." How could she think I was *cute?* I must be slipping. I held myself even more upright and caused my eyes to withdraw more deeply under my brow ridges.

It was the wrong move to make. Miss Flowers's expression softened even more. She batted thick pale eyelashes at me, and her very wide mouth pursed itself in a heart shape. I gulped. Instead, I mitigated my demeanor somewhat, making me look less austere. That made her sit back on her three chairs.

"The difficulty, Mr. Fancy Pants, is that you want like three times the going rate to find out who's invading our pastures and taking our yakaroos," she said. "This skinny lout here quoted me a fee of six gold pieces."

I nodded slowly and deliberately as I considered. Six for a simple livestock surveillance program, with possible additional expenses if we had to apprehend the thieves ourselves.

"That is our price for a mission such as you describe it. Our organization is the top-rated institution of its kind."

"Top-rated doesn't always mean the best," Miss Flowers said. "I got a quote just the other day from another party, and they said they'd do it for two."

"Top-rated does mean the best, in our case," I assured her. "If you wish cut prices rather than effective execution of a task, go to those others." I shook my head sadly. "Very well. When you require us to correct the errors of this other party, we will allow you to return."

Miss Flowers made a fleering noise that sounded like two bricks rubbing together.

"I'll come back to this penny-ante establishment when Deva freezes over," she said. "But you can call me," she added with a wink.

She had to ease out the flap of our tent sideways. Straightening her small hat on her large head, she sashayed up the street, knocking Deveels and other denizens of the Bazaar out of her way.

"She wasn't really a good fit for us," I said, shedding my disguise. I resumed, to all intents and purposes, my normal appearance, which was that of a young Klahd: straight yellow hair, tall skinny frame, and large blue eyes that Aahz told me made me look like a deer in the headlights, whatever "headlights" were. My real face might be considered cute. The innocent expressions I could muster with my ordinary features had occasionally kept me from being beaten up by larger boys in the farm community where I had grown up.

On the other hand, my features had sometimes *caused* me to be beaten up, as when a girl in our small school decided she liked me better than her big, hulking boyfriend. By that time I had already decided to leave home.

But my memories were less important than the reality of the client who had just left.

"She ain't the first to mention this other quest-takin' organization," Guido said. It was his turn on the desk, receiving visitors and assessing potential clients. In spite of his hulking, even threatening demeanor, he was a decent soul, with a fairly soft heart. He wasn't as prone to a sob story as I admit I was, and his fib-meter worked a good deal better than mine. He didn't like M.Y.T.H., Inc., to waste its time on jobs that wouldn't turn out to be lucrative, but he wouldn't sign us up with someone whose intentions he doubted. We'd done work like that; still, better the Deveel you know than one you don't.

I sighed and poured myself a glass of wine, my one for the day. I offered some to Guido. He held up a massive hand to forestall me.

"No, t'anks. I just had a cup of coffee. Real good stuff. Got it from Jaynek's." I nodded acknowledgment. A Caffiend, a member of the sinuous species whose forms resembled Klahds but with long serpent bodies from the waist down, had set up a shop just down the street from our tent, one of many that had popped up around the Bazaar in recent weeks. "Pretty soon dere's gonna be one on every corner. We oughta buy into the business before it gets too big. Could make us a mint. I could look into it if you want. Or if Miss Bunny so desired," he added. Most of the time he remembered that I was no longer running M.Y.T.H., Inc.

"Bunny could run an analysis and see if it's worth our while. Hope it doesn't put the Yellow Crescent Inn out of business," I said. "Gus counts on those morning coffee drinkers to help keep him in the red." Or the gray, since Gus was a Gargoyle, and made entirely out of stone.

"Dere's room for more than one purveyor of ground beans in dis Bazaar," Guido said. "Gus's coffee is good, too. But when I want somethin' fancy, it's nice to have Jaynek's close by."

"There's room in this world for other groups like us, too," I said. "We don't need to take on every client. Don't worry about the ones who are looking for a bargain, Guido. When they need us, they'll come back. We have resources and experience that I think are unique. We certainly get results."

Guido smiled.

"You don't gotta convince me, boss. But I hate to t'ink a coupla lousy gold pieces stood between a potential client and a successful outcome."

At the sound of the words *gold pieces*, my dragon's head popped up. He blinked his large blue eyes.

"Gleep!" he announced, looking around hopefully. Like most of his kind, he liked to eat gold.

I leaned over and scrabbled my fingernails among the scales between Gleep's ears.

"Sorry, fellow," I said. "False alarm. We were just talking."

"Gleep!"

He slurped out with his long pink tongue. I tried to avoid it, but he left a wide trail of stinking slime on my face. I wiped it off with the edge of my sleeve. I loved my dragon, and I was glad he loved me, too. I just wished that he had a less smelly way of showing me.

"Miss Flowers probably doesn't need our special services to find out where her animals are going," I said. "I bet they're just hopping the fence in search of better tundras."

"We lost another one?"

The front flap of the tent opened, and Bunny stepped in. M.Y.T.H., Inc.'s president came from Klah, as Guido and I had, but you would be excused in thinking she came from another dimension where the people were more beautiful and ethereal. Her red hair was cut short around small, delicate ears, her cheeks were rosy apples beneath blue eyes almost as large as my dragon's, and her rather top-heavy figure attracted the avid interest of males no matter what she was wearing. Not that Bunny was flighty. She had a college degree in accounting and could keep her wits about her under almost any circumstances. That day, though, she looked worried.

"She wasn't serious," I said. "She said our price was too high, but the one she quoted from the other company sounds much too low."

"She's window-shopping," Aahz said, coming in behind Bunny with a tray of paper cups marked with Jaynek's name. Aahz was the utter opposite in terms of looks from Bunny. Hailing from the dimension of Perv, his skin was covered with green scales, his ears like bat wings, his teeth four-inch fangs. I raised my eyebrows.

"But we don't have any windows," I pointed out. Nor did most of the sellers, vendors, and hucksters who maintained premises in the Bazaar. Those who wanted their goods displayed had open-air tents.

"That's why she left," Aahz said, his expression surly. I saw it but deliberately did not take the hint. In case such expressions ever became useful, I liked to know what they meant.

"Couldn't she see that before she came in?"

"She's not looking for real windows, kid. It means she's browsing but not really intending to buy."

"Got it," I said. "Well, she couldn't be in a lot of trouble, or she'd be serious about hiring us."

"That's true," Bunny said. We followed her into her office. She sat down at her desk, her spine erect. We settled in the various chairs that had been designed for each of us. Mine was a big upholstered chair with a footrest long enough for my legs. I hoisted my feet onto the cushioned rest and crossed one ankle over the other shin. Aahz set the tray on a table near his chair and helped himself to one of the cups. "Our clientele tend to be on the desperate side."

"But we ain't seein' a lot of dose lately either," Guido said. He perched on the edge of his black leather seat.

Bunny tapped a pencil to her lips.

"I know. I don't understand it."

"Why are you worried?" I said. "We have lots of money, much more than we know what to do with."

"Kid," Aahz said, with an exasperated look on his face, "you *never* have too much money."

"But we're not getting a lot of new money," Bunny said. She looked very concerned.

"I've never heard of money going bad," I said. "I could always see about exchanging it with some of our neighbors, or trading it at the Even Odds." The Even Odds was the local casino in which we had a partial ownership.

"Dat would be money laundering," Guido said. ". . . Not dat I have a particular objection to the process thereof."

"Well, you'd have to launder it," I pointed out. "Some of those coins have gotten pretty disgusting by the time the Deveels let go of them."

"Kid . . . !"

"And it wouldn't help," Bunny said with a sigh that tore at my heart. "In the end we'd have only the same amount we started with."

I exchanged looks with Aahz and Guido. I sat down on my chair and scooted it close to her desk.

"Bunny, what's wrong?" I asked. "We've been doing well. Half of the partners are out on jobs. At least one of the clients is an old friend, and we know he's good for the money."

She nibbled at a fingernail. I noticed that her fingertips were a little ragged. That was unusual. Bunny normally projected the most polished and professional of appearances, in contrast to, say, me. I had had to learn at her knee, and a very attractive knee it was, the importance of sartorial perfection.

"I know, but I was hoping we would show more profit this quarter."

Guido stalked out of the office and into our anteroom. Through the door I watched him wrench the top off the low table in the center. He had had exactly the same thought I had. To the average visitor it would look like a fairly ordinary piece of furniture, but underneath the polished slab of wood lay a box about five feet square that was filled with coins, most of them silver or copper, many of them gold. They came from dozens if not hundreds of dimensions, profits not only from successfully completed missions, but our investments in several places, including the aforementioned casino. We used it as a slush fund. Any of the partners could grab a handful or a sackful of coins, no questions asked. Guido kicked the box. It let out a fat jingle as if it were too full to move.

"It's all here, Miss Bunny," he said. "How much you need? I can arrange to convey it all to anyplace that is to your desirin'."

She smiled, but it was a wan expression.

"Thanks, Guido, that's all right. I guess we have plenty."

"Okay, Miss Bunny."

Guido reassembled the table and stalked back to the office.

Aahz tipped me the kind of look that meant it was up to me to try to coax more information out of Bunny, but later on, if we were alone.

BAMF!

A whirlwind of green appeared out of nowhere and attached itself to me, lips first.

"Hello, tiger," Tananda said. She was a Trollop, a female denizen of Trollia. She was curvaceous as Bunny but taller, and had long green silken tresses. Her costume consisted of the briefest, tightest trews and the lowest-cut jerkin possible, yet she still managed to pack an astonishing array of weapons and lock-picking devices within them.

"Hello, all!"

Behind her was her brother, Chumley. Unlike Trollops, Trolls were huge, lumpen, and covered with thick purple fur.

Chumley possessed an intelligence that vied with his looks for which was the most fearsome.

"Is that mearcat back home again?" Bunny asked.

"Yes, although he took some persuading," Tananda said.

"Which Little Sis was all too happy to provide," Chumley said, proudly. He felt within the thick pelt of fur over his breastbone. "And I am reminded . . ." He produced two gold pieces and a silver piece, which jingled when he tossed them onto Bunny's desk.

"Thank you," Bunny said. She drew one of her ledgers to her and wrote a notation in one of the line items. "Would you like some coffee?"

"Meanwhile, back at the ranch . . ." Aahz said, waving his coffee cup.

"You visited a ranch?" I asked, eagerly. "Here? In Deva? What do they raise there?"

"Figure of speech," Aahz said, cutting off my questions. I shrugged. We lived in the same dimension, but I often felt as if Aahz had a much more interesting life than I did. "There's a new Pervish restaurant in the Bazaar."

"I know," Guido said, wrinkling his nose. "People was wonderin' exactly what died. And how many hundreds of 'em."

I had sampled Pervish cooking in the past. The *better*-smelling dishes gave off an aroma like dragon's dung. You had to stun some of the food with a spoon to keep it from crawling off the dish. Needless to say, the restaurants weren't popular off Perv. When one opened in the Bazaar, it had to keep changing locations because of complaints it was driving customers away from nearby businesses.

". . . I finally caught up with it near Lucky Mo's Pawn Shop," Aahz said, his brows lowering dangerously. "They make some pretty good vulopteroid soup. I had two or three bowls. If it doesn't get chased out of the Bazaar completely I'm gonna make it my regular lunch stop." He patted his belly and let out a hearty belch.

My stomach turned.

"What has dis got to do wit' us?" Guido asked, the same thought in his mind as mine. "You're not gonna ask us to dine out wit' you. I don't wanna hafta earn hazard pay."

"Nah, it's the guy I met when I was coming out of the café," Aahz said. "Said he's looking for help locating a fancy cup. He called it the Loving Cup."

Bunny's delicate red eyebrows lowered on her forehead.

"A cup is a small item," she said. "Doesn't he realize an interdimensional search for something like that would cost a fortune? Can he pay our fees?"

"Sounds like it. He's got a few hundred gold pieces on him."

"He wants you to look for a *cup*?" I asked. "Is it magikal?"

"So he says," Aahz said, dismissively. He leaned back and put his feet up. "To do what he says it can would make it more than magikal. More like miraculous."

"And what is that?" Bunny asked.

"It's supposed to make the two people holding it come to permanent agreement. He needs it back for peace talks in his own dimension. His country and the five others surrounding it have been at war for hundreds of years. His king got them to the negotiating table, but the Loving Cup was the ace in the hole. He was going to use it to make the two biggest enemies swear eternal peace, but it was stolen right out of the conference chamber. Without it, things there are going to deteriorate in a hurry. In fact, he had to go back to his dimension and get back to the meeting. I took the job. I knew you'd want me to." He fished in his pocket and came up with a handful of gold pieces. He stacked them on the arm of his chair. I counted ten coins, and my eyebrows rose. "I made him give me a deposit against expenses. Five percent."

"That's wonderful, Aahz!" Bunny said.

"Two hundred gold pieces?" I asked, my voice rising to a squeak. "He must be desperate. Or maybe crazy."

Aahz grinned, showing all his teeth. "Desperate clients are

the best kind. We negotiated for a while. He said it would be worth it if his country could stand down from a constant state of Defcon Two."

"It's too much! Especially for finding one little item like a cup."

"If he's ready to spend that kind of dough, I'm not going to say no."

"Aahz, we'd be cheating him out of a small fortune."

Aahz looked at me as if I were the crazy one.

"And you don't think we're worth it."

"Not that much!"

"It does sound like a lot," Bunny said, warily. We were allowed to accept assignments on behalf of M.Y.T.H., Inc., if we thought our skill set was up to the task. "And you're sure that it would be something we can accomplish?"

"We stand a better chance than anyone else," Aahz said.

"But looking for something small could take forever," I pointed out. "Why are you interested in helping this guy?"

Aahz grinned.

That expression I knew, from playing cards with him and the others. It meant that he had at least one ace, if not Elves high.

"He said it was last seen in Winslow. That'd make it worth taking a look, anyhow."

"Winslow?" The others beamed at Aahz.

"Winslow?" I echoed, bemused.

"The whole dimension's a resort," Aahz said. "A luxury establishment. Everything's first class, especially the service. The concierges are trained never to say no to any request."

"Tananda and I went there for a girls-only weekend a few months ago," Bunny said, smiling. "Our tanning steward was a seriously cute guy." She wriggled her shoulders, sending my heartbeat into a frenzy. "And pretty good with a tube of sunscreen."

"Mmm-hm!" Tananda agreed. "Even at night."

"I chased a perpetrator dere once," Guido said, with an expression that spoke of fond remembrance. "If I wasn't sentimentally attached to M.Y.T.H., Inc., I might've looked for a job there myself when my errand was completed."

Brushing aside strange concepts like "tanning steward" and "sunscreen," I tried to draw everyone back to the proposal at hand.

"How do we locate something like a cup in an entire dimension devoted to pleasure and indulgence?" I asked.

Aahz smirked.

"Just look for people getting along a little too well," he said.

CHAPTER TWO

"If you gotta ask, you can't afford."

—D. TRUMP

"People getting along a little too well" was not as useful a description for locating the Loving Cup in a place like Winslow. In Deva, accord would have been obvious, if not openly suspect. In Winslow, however, it seemed as if everyone was happy to be together.

We arrived just a couple of paces above the high-water mark on a white sand beach that stretched off toward the horizon in both directions. Though some people frolicked in the tossing waves of the turquoise-blue sea, couples from dozens of dimensions lay all around us on colorful squares of cloth. To the eyes of one brought up in a very small and rather parochial town, they appeared to be wearing the briefest of colorful underwear. I had encountered such swimming costumes before, naturally, when Bunny had participated in a beauty pageant.[1] A Deveelish pair staring deeply into one another's eyes had on garments of matching green floral pattern that actually complemented their natural red complexions. The same went for the Impish couple in red plaid that clashed violently with their pink skins, the Kobold duo exchanging tender emoticons who wore pristine white, and the Trollop who had on three tiny scraps of ivory cloth that did nothing to hide her very obvious charms, commanding the undivided attention of three enormous Trolls, a Pervect, and a Titan who towered over all the rest. None of those five males were shouting or trying to kill one another. They ought to have been trying to pound one another into the sand, but they were behaving in an unnaturally polite manner, even refilling each other's drinks from a huge barrel within easy reach of the Pervect. I could not help but gawk. When I fell behind, Bunny reached back and seized my arm. I stumbled after her.

A very small Wyvern boy packed sand into a coral-colored pail with a tiny yellow spade and turned it upside down on top of a pillar consisting of several other cones he had already created. The whole mass shifted slightly, and an enormous slitted green eye larger than my head peered up at me from the sand only inches from my foot. I jumped backward, almost into Aahz's arms. He set me on my feet, put one hand into the middle of my back, and pushed me forward. I tripped in the sand.

"Did you see that?" I exclaimed, as I regained my balance.

"Don't draw attention," Aahz said. As he passed the Wyvern child, he patted it on the head.

"But he's burying a full-grown dragon!"

"It seems to like it," Aahz said, showing his teeth in a massive grin. "I told you, this place does things to people."

---

1. Bunny's experience is recorded in "Myth Congeniality," a short story featured in *Myth-Told Tales*.

Gleep had already succumbed to the blissful mood permeating the atmosphere. At times he galloped along beside us, other times falling back to roll ecstatically in the sand or to nudge his head underneath the hands of people sitting on the beach. He thundered back to me and slurped me with an enthusiastic tongue. Then he hurtled up the beach again.

As I often heard in our desert home in Deva, it wasn't the heat that was hard to take, it was the humidity. My clothing was much too heavy for the Winslow climate. I tugged at the sodden collar of my shirt as I trudged up the incline of white sand from the sea's edge. I felt downward for the nearest of the force lines I could sense under our feet. It was a hugely powerful, yellow-white line as sinuous as a strangle-snake. Better to fill up my internal supply of magik in case we needed it. Enormous though the source appeared to be, I could drain only a small amount at a time, as if the whole river of power were already spoken for. I did what I could. Once I had some magik on board, I was able to cool myself off. Only then could I appreciate the real beauty of the dimension.

Not surprisingly, once the rest of my partners heard that we had a mission on Winslow, every one of them volunteered to help seek out the Loving Cup. Pookie, Aahz's cousin, and Spyder, her Klahdish colleague, were on another job and had to opt out. Guido and Nunzio, to their open disappointment, had to do a follow-up on a mission they had completed the previous week.

"The client has, sorta, forgotten to complete his financial obligation to us," as Guido put it, with admirable delicacy. "It therefore behooves us to remind him a little."

Tananda and Chumley, on the other hand, had no previous engagements. The sister and brother from Trollia raced one another up the beach, laughing and throwing handfuls of sand at one another. Tananda wore a tiny swimsuit that matched her marvelous tumbling green tresses. As much as

I admired and trusted Tananda as a partner in M.Y.T.H., Inc., I could never forget that she was also an accomplished thief—far better than I had ever aspired to be—as well as a retired (I hoped) assassin. Chumley, in his nom de guerre of Big Crunch, tended to loom threateningly in public. Not difficult, since he was an eight-foot behemoth with odd-sized moon-shaped eyes. Yet in Winslow, he seemed free to enjoy himself. His huge laugh echoed over the sound of the waves. He had described his attire as "board shorts," though I couldn't see where the board fitted in the flower-printed cutoff trousers.

A further addition to the party was Markie. Her pink suit was trimmed with an abbreviated skirt of lilac. She carried a pail and a spade to match. A denizen of Cupy, she resembled a small and immature Klahd, a useful disguise in many cases. In fact, her diminutive appearance had fooled me and my partners.[2] Though she would never be a full partner in M.Y.T.H., Inc., she had helped us out on some occasions. Her elemental powers were good to have in a pinch. Though, considering what the others had said about Winslow, I doubted if we were going to need them. Winslow was just too . . . nice.

A blue-scaled male with a very round head and tiny round ears wearing only a white waistcoat flapping open over his narrow chest, a white bow tie, and white shorts came running up to me and brandished a small circular tray. On it were balanced stemmed glasses filled with liquid about the same color as his skin. He wore a name tag that said *Filup*.

"Cocktail, sir?" he asked.

The drinks looked inviting. Condensation on the surface of the beakers just cried out to tell me how good they would feel clutched in my hot and sweaty palms.

---

2. Read the whole sordid though exciting story in *Little Myth Marker*, available from your better booksellers, now in physical, ethereal, and audible form.

"Uh, how much for a round for me and my friends?" I asked.

The waiter seemed shocked. "There's no charge, sir! This is an all-inclusive dimension."

"But we haven't paid anything yet."

He smiled at me. His eyes were round and lidless like those of a fish but somehow still expressed friendliness and deference.

"Our rates are very attractive, and you'll be delighted to know that we have several specials running right now. In fact, there is a promotion for parties of seven! Three gold pieces per person per day!"

"Ouch." I winced. I had done jobs on behalf of M.Y.T.H., Inc., that paid a single gold piece for several days' work. "That's awfully high. Could you do any better for us? We are a large group, as you noticed."

"Sir, that is a very fine deal," the waiter said, looking a trifle hurt. "Our usual rates are quite a bit higher."

"Sounds good to me," Aahz said.

I turned to look at him in shock. Aahz never let go of a coin unless he was forced to. I wondered if the atmosphere of Winslow was affecting his brain. He didn't seem impaired, but I wasn't sure I would be able to tell.

"Aahz, he said three gold pieces a day! Each!"

"The client's picking up expenses, remember?" Aahz said, pushing me aside. "We'll take your deal, my good man. Now, how about that cocktail? If you have something to drink from that's larger than a thimble."

"But of course, sir!" the waiter said, looking even more pleased than before. He snapped his fingers. A being of the same species but shorter and stockier came running up. Dangling from his hand was a glass pail. It was filled with the same brilliant blue liquid. "The Pervect aperitif," our server explained.

"That'll do for a start," Aahz said. He took the bucket in both hands and glugged down the contents. When he lowered the container, it was empty. He wiped his mouth with the back of his hand. "Aaah! My compliments to the mixologist! But that just barely wet my whistle . . ."

Before Aahz had finished voicing the thought, yet *another* small fish-scaled waiter ran up and swapped the empty for the sloshing pail in his other hand. Aahz gave a broad grin that showed all of his teeth. He accepted the fresh drink and took a healthy swig. The first server offered Bunny and me glasses brimming with blue liquid, then trudged up the beach to serve Chumley and Tananda. Yet another server materialized to put a bowl in front of Gleep. My dragon began to slurp happily at the contents. Markie got a tall glass with a bright red cherry clinging to the rim.

I sipped from the glass. The beverage packed a wallop, but only in flavor. It tasted spicy, fresh, and fruity all at the same time, yet I could sense only a touch of alcohol. I could have several of this cocktail without my judgment becoming impaired. I wondered whether Aahz's bucketfuls were similarly harmless, but I doubted it. He hated watered-down drinks and would have told the waiter off for trying to foist any on him. It seemed that the powers that oversaw Winslow were able to tailor their offerings on a personal level. Perhaps we were going to get our three gold pieces' worth in thoughtful attention. I was deeply impressed.

With my drink in my hand, I looked around. The sand was full of sunbathers. Though a number of the blue-skinned servers plied the crowd with beverages and snacks, I couldn't see a bar or inn that provided them. I kept an eye on one waiter until his tray was empty. He stepped away from the last patron and vanished silently. It was a nice trick. I wondered if I could learn how to do it. The only disappearance spells I knew were noisy. For what we had agreed to pay per day, I was pretty sure I could leverage some magik lessons from the staff.

"Isn't this nice, Skeeve?" Bunny asked. Her eyes sparkled over the rim of the glass.

"I can see why you like it here," I said. "Where should we start looking for the Loving Cup?"

I heard a gasp. I turned to look around.

A girl in a rather modest blue sun costume sat on a towel only a few feet away. I noticed her legs before I noticed anything else. The part of their length that was revealed below the midthigh pantaloons was shapely. I followed the line of her body upward, past the stout book she held clutched against her chest. She had long, wavy hair the color of syrup and large blue eyes with long, thick brown eyelashes. I couldn't stop myself from staring. She had high, prominent cheekbones and a little pointed chin, so her face resembled an inverted triangle, one of such perfect proportions that my mind demanded I take the time to marvel at it. She was very pretty. Her lips were parted over small and very white teeth. I couldn't stop staring at her. I realized that she was staring at me, too.

I felt I had to explain myself.

"You have eyes just like my dragon," I blurted out.

Her lips closed, and she turned the beautiful eyes away from me. She looked so unhappy. I felt my heart sink. Quickly, I tried to think of something else to say. A heavy hand clapped down upon my shoulder.

"Smooth, partner," Aahz said, laughing as he hauled me away. "You have a lot to learn about pickup lines."

I kept glancing back as we walked toward the crest of the hill.

CHAPTER THREE

"Here's looking at you, kid."

—THE NSA

On the other side of the slope, a small city seemed to be waiting for us. Each building, low or high, large, small, round, square, peaked, or crenellated, had been painted in pastel colors trimmed with white or pale gray. Flower gardens with hovering butterflies and bees filled almost all the land in between the structures. I had visited numerous places that felt unwelcoming, even hostile. The majority of dimensions and cities I had been to were indifferent as to whether I came or went. Winslow was different. The very buildings had an air of anticipation, even eagerness. They were eager to please. I felt as if it were impossible for me to live up to their expectations, even if I understood what they were.

Over the tops of the buildings near us, I could see towers and other structures created out of metal girders. While I watched, a train of carts ascended along one of the artificial slopes of metal. It was filled with people. All of them threw their hands in the air and screamed happily as the carts crested the top and began a rapid descent. I lost sight of them.

A female of the local species came out to meet us. She wore a loose robe of the usual gleaming white and had a bow in her puffy, light-pink hair. A plain white tablet and a blue metal pen hung from a broad belt around her tiny waist. Around her were a group of her fellow Winslovaks, all of them holding square, covered baskets in their arms.

"Greetings, visitors!" she exclaimed, shaking our hands. "I am Fedda, your personal concierge during your stay. Anything you want, anything at all, please ask me. Here are your welcome gifts! Please enjoy them."

Her companions stepped forward. I steeled myself. Now came the sales pitch. I shook my head as a petite blue-skinned girl offered me her basket.

"Please take it," she said, with a winning smile. "It's just a gift."

"No, thanks," I said. "I really don't want to buy anything else."

"Come on, Skeeve," Bunny said. She had already opened her basket. Inside were colored glass bottles, a folded fuzzy cloth of brilliant pink, and a gizmo that looked like a cross between a bath brush and a multilashed whip. I winced and held out my arms. My greeter plunked the container into them. It clanked and rattled, and I felt its center of gravity shift as if something sloshed inside.

"Can I ask what this costs?" I asked.

"It is all included in your resort fee, Mr. Skeeve," the girl assured me.

"Don't be a stick-in-the-mud, kid," Aahz said. He had flipped the lid on his gift and was rooting among the contents. The fuzzy thing in his basket was a full-length bathrobe of ochre yellow that just about matched the veins in his eyes. "Just play along, all right?"

"I suppose so," I said, uncertainly. The basket felt as if it weighed as much as I did.

Fedda beamed at us.

"Now, if you would like to follow me, I will show you your suite."

"Gleep!"

Gleep, the fastest of us, zipped right up beside Fedda and put his head underneath her hand. She patted him as she padded down the slope toward the cluster of buildings. She wasn't afraid of him at all, even though dragons were one of the fiercest species that existed across the dimensions.

I noticed that every one of the buildings had been freshly painted, and the flagstone walks that led through the trees and flower beds to each was swept clean. Not a leaf or a speck of dust was evident anywhere. I felt even more uncomfortable than I had before. I was used to a much more casual way of living. The thought that an invisible army of workers, even if they were magicians, spent all day doing a host of menial chores for me made me feel, well, unworthy.

Fedda came to a halt at a two-story, round building that had been painted lavender. Its peaked roof was overlapped shingles of light gray. A pair of clean but worn blue shoes stood beside the white-painted door. Fedda looked down at them with a frown creasing the smooth blueness of her face. Suddenly, the shoes vanished. I glanced around for the invisible magicians. Somewhere, someone was going to get in trouble for that lapse. I felt sorry for them.

"Look at that," Bunny said, beaming.

She pointed to the upper panel of the door. A small brass plaque had been affixed, I suspected in the last few moments, with the words *Welcome, M.Y.T.H., Inc.*

Even though the door had a shiny brass knob, Fedda touched the plaque, and the door swung open.

"Please, come in," she said.

I almost gasped at the extent of the interior she revealed. The Winslovaks, like the Deveels, were experts at using interdimensional space to make the best use of an area. When we passed inside the door of our suite, we found ourselves in a castle. To either side were two sets of massive double doors of translucent white that opened onto beautifully decorated rooms that would have held a thousand people. The enormous blue marble staircase that met us just inside the antechamber rose to a gallery fifteen feet above our heads, then split into six curving or spiraling flights that led off in different directions.

"Your bedrooms are upstairs," Fedda said, gesturing gracefully upward. "Let me show each of you where you'll be."

"Gleep!" exclaimed my dragon. He took off running up the set of steps that was third from the right and vanished along a landing.

"No, Gleep!" I shouted. I dropped my basket and sprinted in his wake, but no Klahd on foot can catch a galloping dragon. Drawing on my supply of magik, I pushed off the ground and took to the air.

Gleep thundered ahead of me, throwing playful glances over his shoulder occasionally to let me know he was teasing me. He flicked his tail from side to side, smashing vases and statues on stands as he went. I dodged shards of priceless porcelain. The longer he stayed out of reach, the higher my temper rose.

"Come on, Gleep! We're here for business! Don't destroy everything!"

Corridor after corridor opened up before us. Myriad doors to either side stood open to chambers set up for a multiplicity of purposes: bath, massage, bedrooms, sitting rooms, torture chambers, dining rooms, music rooms, libraries, and so on. It could have held hundreds, maybe thousands of guests, instead of the seven of us.

Gleep turned right or left as further passages appeared. He

wove down hallway after hallway. The only way I could guess which way he had gone was to listen for the destruction of crockery in his path.

I flew above a couple of wooden pedestals that had lately held plaster busts, now strewn across the floor of the corridor, and spotted the end of his tail going around the corner ahead on the right. Fuming, I put on a magikally enhanced burst of speed. As he galloped down the middle of a red-patterned carpet strip that buckled under his charging feet, I caught up with him. Before he could dash down a flight of stairs that appeared on his left, I threw myself at him. I landed on his back with my arms around his neck. Gleep tossed up his head and crashed into a newel post. We tumbled head over heels down the hall, narrowly missing the bumpy drop.

When we came to a halt, we were rolled up in the hall carpet and he was lying on my chest. He raised his head on his long, sinuous neck and slurped me with his pink tongue. I gagged at the smell.

"Gleep!" he proclaimed, his round blue eyes shining.

"Why did you do that?" I panted. I was out of breath.

"Skeeve . . . have fun . . . here," Gleep said. He looked worried. "Be . . . careful."

Did I mention my dragon can talk? None of my other friends know it. I looked down the hall that we had just dashed down, in case any of them had followed us.

"Why did you run away?" I whispered.

"Felt . . . listeners."

He *felt* listeners? I opened my mouth to ask how he could feel someone hearing him, when Tananda came hurtling through the air toward us. She landed lightly on our roll of carpet and peered down at me.

"Starting the fun without us?" she asked.

"Yes," I said. I tried to disentangle myself from dragon and rug. Tananda levitated neatly a few feet higher. Gleep flipped over onto all fours. He shook mightily. The length of rug unwound itself, flinging me into the air. I caught myself with a handful of magik and settled to the floor on my feet.

"Aren't you cute?" Tanda said, kneeling down beside Gleep. I had to admit he did look kind of cute, with the strip of carpet draped over his head and looped over his back.

"Gleep!" he exclaimed, slurping for her face with his tongue. Tanda avoided him nimbly but kept scratching.

"I guess he wanted to see the place on his own," I said. If Gleep suspected someone was overhearing us, I would have to find a secure location where I could tell the others.

"I say, Little Sister!" Chumley's stentorian voice rang in our ears from somewhere in the labyrinth we had just left. "Where have you gone?"

"Over here!" Tanda called. She put both little fingers in her mouth and blew a shrill whistle. The sound provided enough of a guide for the rest of our party to find us.

"That stupid dragon of yours made one unholy mess," Aahz grumbled.

I hung my head.

"I know. I'll pay for the damages," I told Fedda.

"Not to worry!" she assured us with a blithe expression. "It's all included. Please, let me show you your rooms. I am sure you would like to get out and enjoy the beach. Or the music center. There is a Snoonian concert in the pavilion during lunch."

"I can't think of anything I would rather miss," Aahz said.

Fedda smiled.

"There is also Wyvern wrestling in the mud pits just before sunset. Listen for the horn to let you know it's about to start. You are also welcome to visit our casino. All chips and drinks are free! We have a guided safari of beasts from ninety-nine dimensions, balloon rides, cliff diving, the finest water park anywhere, and riding trails for every level from beginner to expert."

"That's more like it," Tananda said, with a slow smile.

"This way, please!"

* * *

I'd barely had time to look around in the sumptuous rooms that I shared with Gleep before Markie shoved her way inside. Gleep galloped up to her and rolled on his back, waggling his feet in the air. She tickled in between his toe claws. He kicked at the air, his eyes rolling with bliss.

"This is awesome!" she said, her eyes bright. "I love those tapestries! And the bed!" She flounced over to the six-poster and plopped down on it. She kicked her short legs against the edge of the mattress. "It's big enough for a party! Everything here is big!"

"I know," I said. "Do you think it's deliberate, to make patrons feel, well, small?"

I knew Markie well enough to understand she wouldn't consider my question a comment on her diminutive size.

"Didn't you see the doll's house I'm staying in? Everything's exactly to scale for me, from the personal facilities down to the books on the shelf. The management must just think you like huge rooms."

"How would they know?" I asked.

Markie shrugged her small shoulders. "No one asks how they do it here in Winslow. The fact is, they're successful at it. All the visitors seem to like it. I think it's against the rules to be unhappy."

Her words made me think of the pretty girl I had seen on the beach. She had been unhappy. I wondered why.

Too-too-too tooooooo!

A brass trumpet appeared in the air between us and blared out a fanfare. From it, a scroll dropped and unrolled. I leaned forward to read it.

"Pleafe fee our activitief director at once to create a cuftom program for your ftay!"

As soon as I had read it, the scroll snapped up into a roll again, and the trumpet arrowed toward the door. When I did not follow immediately, it halted and beckoned to me. Gleep growled at it.

"I got one of those, too," Markie said. She put out a finger. A small lightning bolt shot from the tip. It caught the trumpet in the bell. The horn exploded in a shower of brass shavings. I threw up a defensive shell of magik to protect us, but all the shards vanished before they hit it. "The only thing I don't like about this place is that they like to organize your fun for you."

"Well, we're not here on vacation," I said. "We're on a job. You've been here before; where should we start to find the Loving Cup?"

"Asking around, of course," Markie said. "Best place to try is the main tavern near the reception center. The others are already there. C'mon."

CHAPTER FOUR

"Always read the fine print."

—FAUST

We located the Rusty Hinge by its sign. On the outside, it looked no different than the countless pastel buildings in the complex: bland, boring, and pleasant. The white shutters on the windows framed boxes of pink flowers. I hesitated.

"This isn't an inn," I protested.

"It is," Markie said. She took hold of my hand and towed me over the threshold. I felt a momentary pressure, as if I were penetrating a magikal barrier. "You can't stumble in here by accident. You have to know what it is. It's an inn. A real one."

When I looked around, I felt completely at home.

"Hark, card shark!"

A huge Troll rose from a rickety wooden table and threw down the cards in his hand. His chair flew backward and hit a pair of Deveels in the tail. They rounded on him, eyes flashing with anger. One pointed a finger at the chair. Its legs came to life. It flew at the Troll and threw its limbs about him.

"Aaarrggggh!" the Troll bellowed. He flexed his limbs, and the chair burst into pieces. A rung hurtled end over end at my head. With a wisp of magik, I caught it before it struck me. The Troll thundered toward the Deveels, grabbing one in each furry arm. They vanished from his grip, only to reappear behind him. One of them raised a shiny hoof and booted him in the rear end. The Troll staggered forward, slamming into a pillar. The room shook. The Troll steadied himself and tore the pillar loose. Showered with pieces of plaster from the ceiling, he advanced on the Deveels. Suddenly, the pillar shrank to the size of a toothpick. The Deveels laughed and slapped one another on the back. The Troll growled.

"Odds on the Deveels!" shouted a pink-faced Imp, waving a silver piece in the air. A Hag on a bar stool flipped him her coin.

"The Troll can take 'em!"

Even if they had been cheating him, the others at the card table came to the Troll's defense.

"Hey, leave my friend alone!" bellowed a gray Gargoyle with a curved nose and chin that nearly met in front of its stone mouth. It threw a roundhouse punch at one of the Deveels, catching it in the jaw. The red-skinned male flew flat on its back into a tableful of Kobolds who had been exchanging some nice, quiet code over glasses of beer. They rose, spewing characters, and joined in the fray.

I smiled. Nothing like a nice brawl to give a tavern some character. Maybe Winslow wasn't so stuffy after all.

Markie pointed and tugged at my arm. Tananda sat at a high, round table near the serving door with the rest of our friends. I followed her around the perimeter, dodging flying crockery and hurled insults.

"Look out!" a voice shouted.

I ducked just in time. A stoneware wine pitcher splattered

against the wall. Chunks of pottery exploded outward. I got sprayed in the face with wine. I ran my tongue over my lips. A cheap vintage, but drinkable. I wiped my face with my handkerchief. Waving Markie and Gleep ahead, I went to lean over the bar and speak to the man in the apron polishing glasses with a dirty towel. Over the business of pouring me some of the local vintage, I asked him to inquire about the Loving Cup for me. I handed over a tip—not too generous but high enough to be memorable, then joined my friends.

I clambered onto a bar stool beside Aahz and set my glass on the table.

"Pretty good floor show," Aahz said.

"Nice place," I said, holding up my glass. "The wine's a little thin, though."

"Fewer additives," Aahz said. "If you knew what was in a typical bottle of Deveelish wine, you probably would never drink again."

I winced. "Don't tell me," I said. "Have you gotten any leads yet?"

"Haven't asked. Too thirsty," Aahz said, draining his bucket of beer. He caught the eye of a barmaid, who hurried over. I didn't complain. What was another moment or two in what could prove to be a lengthy search?

A small, brown-skinned fellow in a high-necked robe appeared beside him. I couldn't place the style of the puffy, illustrative embroidery, but it was of high quality. Gold and silver thread had been couched among the more ordinary silks.

"Hey, Looie! Skeeve, I want to introduce you to Looie. He's the client I told you about."

"*This* is Skeeve the Magnificent?" Looie asked, bald brow ridges rising on his forehead. "This is a boy!"

"Looks can be deceiving," I intoned in a sepulchral voice. "Would I have gotten friendly information from the innkeeper looking like . . . this?"

With that, I spread out my arms and assumed my elderly-wizard disguise. Looie backed up a pace.

"Er, no . . . I suppose not." He whipped his hand in a deferential circle and inclined his head. "Duke Looistankos de Mishpaka, at your service."

I tilted my head an inch. "Your Lordship. A pleasure to make your acquaintance. May I introduce the rest of our company? Tananda and Chumley. Markie. Gleep . . ."

"Gleep!" said my dragon, snaking his head up on his long neck. He shot his tongue out to lave the face of our visitor. I whipped a fragment of magik in his way, and Gleep licked the air. He dropped his chin with a look of deep disappointment toward me. I gestured sharply. My dragon slunk to my side and set his chin firmly on my foot. I favored our visitor with a wintry smile.

"And this is my employer, Bunny."

"Your employer?" Looie asked. I had no idea that somebody could pour so much scorn into a single word. Then he gasped.

Disguise magik can conceal, but one of the things it's really good for is enhancement. Digging deep into the thick blue force line running along just outside the inn, I gave the spell all I had.

Bunny normally wore her hair cut short around her ears, but I gave her the flowing, waist-length crimson locks of a fairy-tale princess. Her skin, though very nearly perfect, now had a literal inner glow. She exuded light. The diaphanous silk dress of the same pale blue as her real clothes hugged curves I did not need to enhance in any way. I did tweak the appearance of the neckline down most of the way to her navel. I drew on my memory of how Bunny had looked in an abbreviated bathing suit to get the, er, details right. Precious stones gleamed from her ears and wrists, but those only emphasized her beauty. I could tell by the breathless expression on Looie's face that I had succeeded in impressing him.

"Dear lady," he said, unable to keep his eyes from sweeping up and down Bunny's form. "I had no idea that such a vision as you was behind this, er, company." He stumbled closer, almost dazed. Bunny stuck a perfect hand into his face, stiff-arming him at a distance.

"Put your eyes back in your head and sit down," Bunny said. A glance from her told me I had better show her later how she looked. I was not afraid that she could handle Looie. She was the niece of Don Bruce, leader of the Mob, as well as our president, and was used to dealing with difficult people.

Looie felt for the nearest empty bar stool and pulled it close, all without taking his eyes from her.

"If I may say so, my beautiful maiden, I would not have believed that such a marvel as you would be found in this ersatz wonderland."

Bunny smirked.

"Charmed, I'm sure," she said, extending a delicate little hand. Looie reached for it and planted a smacking kiss on the back. He turned it over and pursed his lips for another kiss on the plump palm. Bunny snatched her hand back, wiping her skin with a handkerchief. She dropped the now-soiled cloth to the floor.

"Wait until we know each other better," she said.

"I hope that's soon," Looie said, a dreamy look on his face like those of the Mooncalfs of Olwinnie. He cleared his throat and regained his composure. "My lady, I hate to sound disapproving, but your representative here said you would find my treasure for me immediately. I am paying top coin for your services. It has been the better part of a day already. I want it back now!"

Aahz growled.

"I never said we could whip it together in one day, pal," my partner said. "I said we'd start *looking* for it immediately."

"That's not acceptable!" Looie exclaimed, bounding up and down impatiently. "You have to find it before someone uses it! It disappears the moment you invoke its spell! I want it now!"

"Come on over here, Mr. Looie," Bunny said, patting the bar stool next to her. He hurried to hop up on it, never taking his eyes from her. She signaled to the barmaid, who hurried over, carrying a tray laden with glasses. "Now, just how long have you been looking for this Loving Cup?"

"Two months!" Looie exclaimed. He gulped half the beer the barmaid set down in front of him. "I must have it back at once! The future of my kingdom depends on it!"

Bunny reached out to where his hand rested on the table and touched the back of it with one fingernail. He quivered visibly. She flicked the nail back and forth. Looie sat mesmerized.

"Now, you know things don't happen that quickly, especially when it comes to important magik items like that," she said, in a purr that I would normally have associated with Tananda. "If someone stole it from your treasury, then we can't just march in and demand it back. It just doesn't work that way. The thieves would protect it with their lives, wouldn't they? If it vanished of its own accord, then we have to follow the trail. Why do you think it's here?"

"Because my oth—I mean, I traced it here!"

Bunny shook her head, making the lush tresses sway from side to side, and clicked her tongue.

"Tsk tsk! You have another agent seeking it? Have you terminated that contract?"

Looie's face turned purple.

"I don't have to tell you who else I have on its trail!"

That didn't sound to me or my partners as though there were only *one* other concern out there.

"How many agents do you have working for you?" I asked.

"It's none of your business if I have other agents!" Looie hissed.

"Sure it is our business," Markie said. She took a large green lollipop from her child-sized handbag and licked it, looking more like a Klahdish child than ever. "If we're competing for the same prize, you're paying multiple specialists for the same mission."

"I never said that," Looie said, with a vicious smile. "I only pay the one who brings the Loving Cup to me."

We all turned to Aahz.

"That ain't what you told me, bud," Aahz said, in a low, dangerous voice. The ochre veins in his yellow eyes began to throb. Looie pursed his lips in a smug smirk.

"Didn't I? Maybe if you had listened to my conditions more carefully, you wouldn't be spending so freely. A private suite!"

"Is there any other kind in Winslow?" Tananda said.

"Of course there is! They have staff dormitories, and tents, and cabins, and birdhouses, and . . ."

"I ain't plannin' to pop out of a birdhouse like a Cuckoo every morning just because you want to save a couple of bucks, pal," Aahz said. "And sleeping bags are for the infantry."

Looie folded his arms. "Then come and go from your own dimension. Great magicians like you purport to be can do that with a wave of your hand! I . . . I mean, other visitors have often come here on day trips."

I put on my most austere expression. "And miss the whispers that the night breezes bring to us?" I intoned. "You wish us to locate this object for you? Do you not consider that to be a day-in and day-out task?"

He was no more impressed with my logic than JR Grimble would have been while discussing my expense report in Possiltum.[3]

"You refuse to be reasonable?" Looie asked, his eyebrows high on his balding forehead. "Then I withdraw my commission. Go

3. This pusillanimous pencil-pusher is described in minute detail in *Myth-Conceptions*, worth your while to peruse.

back to Deva. I'll use other means to locate the Loving Cup. I don't need you! Give me back my deposit!"

"Sorry," Aahz said, leaning back into the corner. "We'll need it to cover our expenses to date."

"Not a chance! No cup, no coin! I'll call the authorities! Winslow has very strict laws. You'll be thrown in jail for years! All of you!" He glared at us but regarded Bunny with longing tinged with regret.

"Now, Duke Looie," Bunny purred, leaning close to him. "Let's be reasonable. If there was a misunderstanding, it sounds as if it was on both sides of the agreement. I employ Aahz because of his deep perception and shrewdness. If he thought you promised expenses for the search, then that was the deliberate impression you gave him. We took the job on good faith."

Looie shook his head. "Your Pervert didn't understand my terms. I said nothing about expenses being separate from the reward!"

"That's Per-VECT!"

Bunny took a deep breath. It made her chest heave. Looie couldn't resist following every movement of her body. She reached over and tilted his chin up with a cocked finger.

"Don't you think it would be a good idea to renegotiate the whole deal?" Bunny asked. Looie gazed into her eyes, almost panting.

"Eh, maybe. Perhaps we can go somewhere more . . . *private* and discuss the terms?"

"Perhaps we can," Bunny said.

Looie grabbed her wrist and hopped off his stool. "Let's go!"

I swooped in and loomed over him. Bunny and I had decided that we were better off friends than potential mates, but I felt a swell of anger at this male's casual possessiveness.

"Unhand the lady Bunny," I boomed, reasserting my Skeeve the Magnificent disguise.

Looie looked at me with undisguised scorn.

"Madam, would you have your minion withdraw?" he asked, sounding pained. "It seems he doesn't know his place."

Bunny turned to me and flicked her free hand in my direction. "You may go, Skeeve," she said. She tucked her arm through Looie's. "Where to, big spender?"

"Bunny!" I exclaimed. She deliberately turned her head to avoid my gaze.

Looie almost bounced as he led her toward the door.

"This way, dear lady. This way!"

CHAPTER FIVE

"One must be relentless in pursuit of one's goals."

—INSP. JAVERT

I watched them go with my heart in my shoes. Tananda came up and curled herself around me. Her teeth nibbled on my earlobe.

"She can take care of herself, Skeeve," she assured me. "Remember that she used to be a moll in her uncle's Mob. She isn't helpless."

But *I* felt helpless. "How could she even think of throwing herself at that worm? He's not worth it!"

"It's just for show," Markie said. But even she looked uncertain. "Looie is clearly a guy who likes to think he's important. She's letting him think so. As soon as we hand over the item, she'll drop him like a hunk of rotten meat."

"But what about . . . ?" I stopped. I guessed that what she did with Looie was none of my business, but when she came to work with us full-time, part of the deal was that she didn't have to, well, give it all for the job. Her mind was her best tool. The fact that she was beautiful was a bonus, but it also caused a lot of males' minds to stop short with her appearance instead of seeing through to the intelligent woman inside. Normally she played on that weakness. This time she had thrown herself into the perception. I worried about her state of mind.

"Don't make assumptions," Tananda warned me. "There's a thousand ways to make a man feel like a king that have nothing to do with *that.* Even if she does, though, you don't have to worry about it. It's her choice."

"It's too much, though," I said, very worried now. "He's just one client. We just don't need this mission that badly."

"Maybe she thinks we do," Aahz said, with a thoughtful look on his face. "And I'm going to find out why."

"All right," I said, slamming my fist into my palm. "I guess we start looking."

The man behind the bar signaled to me with a raised eyebrow. I sidled over casually, resuming my normal appearance—no one in the bar seemed to notice me changing back and forth—and leaned over as if to get a refill of my drink.

"Fancy magikal items are all over this dimension," he said. "Tough call. There's thousands, you know that?"

"I can guess," I said. "So, how do I find out if this Loving Cup is one of them?"

He shrugged. "I'll put the word in to the Central Help Desk that you're looking for it, sir." I reached for my belt pouch. "Oh, no, sir. Everything is included. Your previous gratuity was *much appreciated.*"

I couldn't miss the emphasis on the last two words. "There will be more if you help me find it. How long will it take?"

"Couldn't tell you, sir," he said, picking up an already spotless glass to polish. "It could take months."

"Months!" I squawked. A few of the patrons turned to look at me. "We don't have months."

He looked apologetic. "I am really sorry, sir. This isn't

something I normally do. Couldn't I just tell you tales of guts and glory? Listen to your troubles? Fix you up with a pretty girl? There's a couple been giving you the eye since you came in. They like magicians." He raised his eyebrows suggestively and nodded toward the side of the room, the one away from the ongoing brawl. Two girls, one with long blond hair and the other with midnight-black tresses, waggled their fingers at me and giggled.

"No, thanks," I said. I turned away with a sigh.

"'Scuse me," said a voice at about my knee level. I looked down. A big black-and-tan creature on four legs looked up at me from bloodshot brown eyes. "Couldn't help but overhear—with ears like mine it's an occupational hazard, you might say—heard you mention that you were lookin' for something. Wonder if I can help? Name's Haroon. From Canida. Haroon." He stretched out the second syllable of his name until it overwhelmed the sound of breaking glass. I winced. I extended a hand, and he offered his right front paw.

"Nice to meet you, Haroon," I said. I didn't try to emulate his pronunciation. "I'm Skeeve."

"Heard that, too," he said. "And your friends. Aahz. Gleep. Tananda. Chumley. Markie."

"Nosy, aren't ya?" Aahz asked, glaring at him. Haroon touched his large black nose with his paw.

"Yep, goes with the territory. But I keep everything under my hat. Confidential investigator, that's me. You ask for references, I can't give 'em to you. My client list is private."

"Then how do we decide if you can do what we need you to do?" I asked.

"Give you a free sample," Haroon said. He stood up on his hind legs and sniffed me all over. "You're stayin' in the Round Castle," he said. Another thoughtful sniff. "Room 208. Pinky gave you your gift basket."

"You could have found that out from Fedda," Markie said.

He dropped down from my shoulders and sniffed Markie

all over. She stood still but wore an expression of undisguised annoyance. Haroon licked his jowls with a long pink tongue.

"Y'all are in 215, but you went into that fellah's room, there, afterward." He aimed his nose at me. "You got its scent on your shoes."

"You know all the rooms here?" I asked in amazement. Haroon glanced modestly to one side.

"I know every square inch of this place. Come here on all my vacations. Love the smells, and I like the people. I help 'em out with a little problem or two once in a while. Don't need to do it too often, but the management knows it can count on me. M'fees are reasonable. Love to sniff out the truth."

"Party tricks," snarled Aahz. "You're good at reading people, that's all."

"Just with my nose, friend," Haroon drawled. "Happy to help you."

Tananda reached over to fondle the Canidian's floppy jowls. "Well, I think he's cute. We ought to give him a chance."

Haroon wagged his tail. I had never met a male of any species who could resist Tanda's charms.

"Much obliged, ma'am. It'd be my pleasure."

"What can you do?" I said. "We've never seen the Loving Cup. It could be anywhere in this dimension, if it's still here."

"Wal, you might not have seen it yourself," Haroon said, "but your cranky li'l friend did. He's been where it was, likely held it a mite himself. So, I'll just mosey up and take a good sniff of his scent." The Canidian levered himself up and ran his large black nose around the wooden top of the bar stool. He took a further deep sniff at the beer glass that Looie had briefly held.

"Got lots of magik back where he hails from," Haroon said. "Luckily he don't wash his hands any too often." I grimaced at the thought. Haroon tipped me a wise look. "Poor hygiene helps my kind a lot. Can't say I like a bath myself, but we Canidians keep clean so we don't get confused with other people's scents."

Aahz looked bored.

"So, now you're going to pretend to follow his trail? Then you'll conveniently say you lost it, but we still owe you a fee?"

Haroon looked up at him with open contempt.

"Lissen, Pervert, I been working trails for longer than you been around, and I can smell how old you are to within about a day. Why not give the old guy a chance? That's what your Klahd friend here would say."

"That's Per-VECT!" Aahz bellowed. The chandelier danced on its ceiling chain.

Haroon squinted up at him.

"What's that? Mite hard of hearing, you might say. Ne'mind. I just calls 'em like I smells 'em." Haroon investigated my partner. "Hm. Well, I take that back a little. Call you what you like, then."

"What?" Aahz boomed again. Then he met the Canidian's warm brown eyes. "Just don't say that again."

Haroon put on an air of innocence.

"Who, me? Don't take no offense, don't give none. So, do we have a deal? One gold piece for a successful find. Half if I pick up this trail but can't make a strike. What do ye say?"

"Sounds fair," I said. "It'll give us more to go on than we had before."

"Right, then," Haroon said. He raised his nose high. "Harooooooooon!" Then he applied it to the bar stool one last time. "Gotcha!"

The stumpy-legged creature shot between my legs and made for the door. I was so surprised by his rapid departure I just stared after him.

"Well, come on, sonny!" he called. "Harooooooon!"

He disappeared out into the twilight. Tananda kissed me on the cheek.

"Chumley isn't much for chase scenes," she said. "You follow Haroon, and we'll investigate some more leads from here."

"All right," I said. "We'll meet back at the suite later."

"Good luck, tiger," Tananda said, winking at me. I grinned at her and patted my dragon on the head.

"Come on, Gleep!"

"Gleep!"

"I'm coming with you," Markie said. She swung a leg over my dragon's back and put both arms around his neck. To my amazement, Gleep let her mount.

The baying receded in the distance. I started toward the door. A Troll at the table close to me stood up and flung down his hand.

"Hark, card shark!" he bellowed.

His chair flew back and hit some Deveels at the table behind him. Two of them sprang up and threw magik at the chair. It waved its legs and wrapped them around the Troll. I watched with an air of bemusement, wondering if I had seen exactly the same thing happen before, or if my memory was playing tricks on me. Aahz grabbed my arm and thrust me out of the door.

CHAPTER SIX

"I thought you filled the tank!"

—A. EARHART

I **ran down the avenue, which was lined with tiny white** shells that crunched under my feet. Gleep galloped behind me, Markie clinging to his back. He was rapidly pulling ahead of us. My two legs, long as they were, couldn't match the speed of his four. Aahz, whose legs were shorter than mine, would be left even farther behind. I lifted us both into the air and sped after Haroon.

Only by his baying could I tell where he had gone. We flitted up the near side of the headland, hoping to catch sight of him. The trees were too thick on this side of the beach.

Soon, I spotted the Canidian. Even with his nose to the ground, he was able to emit deafening whines and bays. I put on a burst of speed and caught up.

"There you are," Haroon said over his shoulder. "Thought you'd never get here."

"Where are we going?" I asked.

"Wherever the scent leads me, boy. Always a mystery. I love a mystery."

Haroon snuffed at the air, then took a sharp left turn to run down a long path in between hotel buildings. Surprised holidaymakers gawked at the sight of a large Canidian running, a Klahd and a Pervect flying, and a dragon with a Cupy on its back thundering down upon them. They jumped to one side or the other, snatching their children up to get them out of our way.

"Sorry!" I called as we passed.

"Forget it, kid," Aahz said, lying back on the air as if he were on his favorite chair. "We'll be the most exciting thing to happen to them all day."

Up hill and down slope we rushed in Haroon's wake. I did my best to keep my internal supply of magik charged up from the force lines, but though they seemed to my mind's eye to be large and powerful, I had trouble extracting magik from them.

"Hold on, Haroon," I called. "I've got to set us down!"

The Canidian lifted his nose to the air.

"Harooooon!"

"I don't think he heard me. Markie!"

But she and Gleep had hammered out of sight in Haroon's wake.

"What's the matter, kid?" Aahz asked.

"The force lines are blocked!" I said. "Or it's me. I can't get any power from them. I'm running out of magik."

He frowned as we dodged a rose-covered hedge and a fairground ride full of laughing children.

"How close are you to running out?" he asked.

Just then, the image I kept in my mind of a tank full of magikal power tipped over. The last drop dripped out of it, leaving the vat empty. I felt myself losing control of my flight spell. Immediately, I threw what tiny bit I had left into forming a soft cushion for Aahz and me to fall on. We dropped out of the air, hit the cushion, and kept rolling down a short incline. We tumbled into a sand pit where three small Deveel children were throwing handfuls of wet sand at each other. I fell on top of a clumsy sand sculpture with a wet squish. Aahz landed on top of me.

"Really close," I said, apologetically.

"Why didn't you say something sooner!" Aahz shouted.

"Waaaah!"

The children started crying that the big, mean Pervect and the lanky Klahd had destroyed their sand castle. The father, a huge red-skinned Deveel wearing a pair of plaid knee-length shorts, dropped the crystal ball he was reading and stalked over to us. His barbed tail lashed back and forth in annoyance.

"Who the Erebus do you think you are, disturbing my children's serene play?" he demanded.

"Look, I'm sorry," I said, getting up and brushing myself off. I patted the nearest tot on its horned little head. It stuck its tongue out at me. "I was just trying to follow a scent. I'm on a job . . ."

The Deveel looked outraged.

"You're *working*? You don't belong here! What are you doing in Winslow? Get back to Klah and leave the rest of us alone!"

Aahz shouldered in between the two of us and poked the Deveel in the chest.

"Listen, pal, don't pick on my partner, or you're going to have to take a piece out of me, too!"

The Deveel planted both hands on his hips and glared down at Aahz, who was a good head shorter than he was.

"Listen, Pervert, I could bury you headfirst in the sand so far you'd be standing on an upside-down mountaintop."

"I could use that pointy tail of yours to spin you around until you took off," Aahz said.

"You try it, you sawed-off excrescence."

"Overgrown faun," Aahz leered. "Where's your panpipes?"

"Heap of rotting scales. Dung-eater!"

"That's no way to talk about your mother's cooking!"

By now, they stood nose to nose, staring into one another's eyes. I held up a finger.

"Uh, fellows, there's no need to start a fight. All I want to do is apologize for scaring the kids," I said. They ignored me.

"How dare you even mention my mother!" the Deveel snarled at Aahz.

"Why not? Her name's on the lips of everybody in the Bazaar. Just like her lipstick."

"Jealous? Just because *you* sprouted from fungus?"

"Please, guys," I said. "Let's just back away and keep calm. How about a round of drinks? My treat!"

"Shut up!" they both bellowed at me. I edged around them, trying to slip in between them. Aahz never backed down from a confrontation he thought he could win. The Deveel had more at stake: His children were watching him. Aahz knew it. But rescue came from an unexpected quarter.

"What's going on here?" a shrill voice split the air.

Aahz and the Deveel jumped apart as though a lightning bolt had struck between them. A wrinkled female Deveel bore down on us like an approaching avalanche. She was elderly and very small, standing no higher than the middle of my chest, but she managed to reach up and grab the Deveel's ear. She dragged it down to her level. His head, naturally, came with it. She tilted the ear so he had to look her right in the eye.

"This is a fine kind of family vacation, sonny boy! You're supposed to be relaxing! Tonka Sue went to get her nails done. What will she say if she comes back and finds out you've been fighting?"

"Mom . . ." the Deveel began, weakly.

I thought it wise to intervene on his behalf. After all, we had been the offending parties.

"I'm so sorry, ma'am," I said, assuming a respectful pose. "We accidentally crushed your grandchildren's sand castle . . ."

Quicker than I could have reacted, she reached up and

grabbed my ear, too. She pulled my head down so she could scrutinize my face up close.

"A Klahd? I should have known! They just let anyone into this dimension, don't they?"

I freed my ear from between her pointy fingertips and stood up.

"Ma'am, I'm sorry. Look, would this help?"

While we had been speaking, I started gathering energy again. My internal stores were still nearly depleted, but I had enough to do a small trick. I gathered imaginary sand between my hands and patted it into shapes. Before me, the real sand in the sandbox whirled in a miniature windstorm. When it settled, it formed an elaborate castle complete with a battlemented shield wall, turrets, a drawbridge, and a moat.

"Hurrah!" the children yelled. They threw themselves on it, demolishing it in seconds. Just as before, they began throwing handfuls of sand at each other.

"All right," the old Deveel woman said, dragging her son back to his deck chair. "Just don't do it again!"

"No, ma'am. Thank you, ma'am," I said. We retreated hastily over the next rise. Haroon was nowhere in sight. I tried to listen for his cries.

"Listen, kid," Aahz said, "next time do you think you could give me a little more notice before you dump us like that? It's a little more inconvenient than if I just need to hurry up and find you a place on the side of the road to tinkle."

"What's tinkle?" I asked, bemused. "Is that a magikal term? Do I have to let you know before I make a sound like a Fairy?"

Aahz gave me an exasperated look.

"No, it's . . . never mind! I thought I trained you better than that!"

"You did!" I said. "I didn't expect to run out of magik. There are plenty of force lines here, big ones. It's just that when I try to reach into them, I can't seem to pull up any of the magik."

Aahz stroked his chin.

"That's different. Describe one to me."

I closed my eyes. It was easier to concentrate on the unseen if I didn't have to cope with the distractions of the visual.

"There's a really big blue line beneath us. It's wavy, not jagged, and about as thick as my leg."

"Sounds like nice, clean water magik," Aahz said. "You can fill up from that without a problem."

"Yes, but when I reach for it, it seems to wiggle away from me. Not wiggle, I guess, but my touch misses it every time."

"Sounds like it's overcommitted," Aahz said, stroking his chin thoughtfully. "There are some powerful magicians drawing on it in this dimension. Take in what you can. You can economize if you make me fly. I'll carry you. It'll save some of the magik." He picked me up. I tried to kick free, but Aahz held on. A Pervect is a lot stronger than a Klahd. "Hold still! That howler is getting away from us. Let's move it!"

I subsided and let myself be carried like a baby, my long legs dangling over his arm. I felt foolish, but I had to trust my partner. Aahz's plan didn't *sound* as if it would save me any power, but he was right. Making two people fly consumed more of my internal storage. One did use less.

With Aahz doing all the heavy lifting, I could concentrate on finding viable lines of force. As I had noted before, Winslow was full of them. The blue line had given me all the magik it had to spare. I spotted a spiraling yellow line overhead that gave off sparks. The line itself was blocked, but those sparks were free for me to pluck and save. With my mind's eye, I could see my supply of magik increase slightly with every yard. It was half-full when I spotted Gleep's long green body and Haroon's shorter black-and-tan coat off to the right of the path we were on.

"There he is!" I shouted, pointing. Aahz did a three-point turn and followed.

Haroon slowed to a halt at a round building similar to

the one in which we were staying, though it was painted pale yellow instead of lilac.

"Help me!" a feminine voice cried from the other side of the door. "Oh, won't someone help me?"

Somebody was in danger!

Haroon leaped up and scratched at the door with both front paws.

"Lemme in!" he howled. "The scent's in there!"

I tugged the door latch. The metal tongue inside didn't move at all. I put my finger into the enormous keyhole and hit an obstruction.

"Locked!"

"Open it, kid!"

I threaded magik through the keyhole and wrapped it around the wards. Every time I tried to take hold of a ward and arrange it so the slot was facing downward, another wisp of magik spun it again.

"It's bespelled," I said.

"Then *dis*pell it," Aahz said.

"I'm trying!"

Gleep added his strength to the Canidian's. He shook Markie off and butted the door with his head.

BAM! BAM! BAM!

Aahz and I arrived a moment behind them.

"Stop that!" I told Gleep. "You'll break it!" He backed away, his head low. I scratched between his ears. "I'm sorry, fellow, but I feel bad every time we damage something and the management says it's all included."

"Nice of you to be concerned about that," Aahz said, dryly, "but the management jacks up the fees so we *do* cover every breakage, whether we cause it or not."

"True," said Markie. "Might as well get our money's worth. One side, boys. Let the little lady through."

I jumped hastily to one side. I had experienced Markie's form of elemental magik a couple of times and didn't want to get caught in the backwash. No sooner had Gleep, Haroon, and I cleared the way than Markie rolled up a huge ball of crackling magik in her hands.

CA-ZAAP!

An enormous lightning bolt flashed from her pudgy little fingers. The door burst into pieces. We jumped over the burning remains of the threshold and rushed into the room.

"Intruder alert! Intruder alert! Intruder alert!" howled the magik mirror above the chest of drawers. "Oh, why is no one listening to me?"

The spirit of the mirror, its face contorted in horror, was not looking at us. Instead, it stared down at a slight figure that was ransacking the drawers, throwing their contents onto the floor. The spirit turned its hollow eyes to us as if beseeching us for help.

"Hey, stop!" I shouted.

The figure looked up. Its eyes met mine and widened. The mouth dropped open in shock.

To my amazement, it was the girl from the beach. I started to speak, but she threw up a hand.

BAMF! BAMF! BAMF!

CHAPTER SEVEN

"A nasty place to visit, and you wouldn't want to stay there."

—D. ALIGHIERI

We were surrounded by cold blackness. I opened and closed my eyes several times, but I couldn't see a thing. I reached out blindly. My hand came to rest on scaly skin. I patted it.

"Gleep, are you all right?"

"That's me," Aahz growled, throwing my hand off impatiently. "Your stupid dragon landed on my chest."

In the darkness, my dragon stated his agreement.

"Gleep!"

I felt my way over toward the cheerful sound. This time I found the right ears to scratch between. A stinky tongue somehow found its way in the darkness and slimed my face. I wiped off the goo. The breeze was cool and clammy, as if we weren't far from the sea. I smelled nothing but cold stone.

"Where are we?" I asked. "Is this Limbo?"

"I sure as heck hope not!" Aahz snarled.

Haroon sniffed around suspiciously. "Don't like this place. Full of dangerous smells. A lot of fires going on."

"Fires? Where?" Aahz was suddenly concerned. Pervects are tough. They're invulnerable in so many ways. You could hardly drive a knife into Aahz's skin, but fire was dangerous to him. We were nearly burned at the stake once.[4] It was only through chance and a lot of magik that we survived. He had avoided the place ever since.

"Oh, my hierarchical imaginary friend," Markie moaned, close to my hip. I patted my way down and helped her to sit up. She slumped against me. "Where is this?"

"No idea," Aahz said.

"Smells old," Haroon's voice said. "Lots of old bones around here. Lots of blood's been spilled. Rusty iron. Limestone gravel."

"How come we can't see anything?" I asked.

"Cause it's night, sonny," Haroon said. "Starless, though. Not anyplace I been before. Your girlfriend there has a nasty streak."

"She's not my girlfriend!" I protested, with more heat than I intended.

"Well, she's a magician," Aahz said. "Pretty powerful, too. A magician turned thief."

"Why do you say that?" I asked.

"Because she was robbing the room we were about to, er, investigate," Aahz said. "Must be looking for the Loving Cup, too."

"Why do you say that?" I asked. "She could have been looking for anything!"

"Occam's razor, kid," Aahz said, wearily.

---

4. See the situation described in *Mything Persons*, another fascinating account, available from your reputable and even your disreputable booksellers.

"Was he a barber?" I asked.

"Could have been. I never met a barber who wasn't a philosopher. Occam believed that the simplest explanation was the most reasonable one. Look, Haroon followed the Loving Cup to that spot. Your girlfriend was there. She was looking for something. Did you see anything else of value in that room?"

"A magik mirror," I said.

"Hah. Two silver pieces at the Bazaar, tops. Forget the furniture. That was an ordinary hotel room, not a storage facility or a treasury for collectible artifacts."

"That doesn't mean she is a thief!" I exclaimed.

"You give me another good reason why she was throwing everything on the floor."

"She wanted something at the bottom of her drawer."

"All the clothes in that room were for a man. A tall man."

"Uh . . . her husband?"

I heard sniffing sounds near me.

"Haroon, what are you smelling?"

"I ain't doin' the smellin', son. Somethin' else is smellin' *us*."

I'm not very proficient at many forms of magik, but making light was something I was good at. I reached for some power from a dark red force line deep below us and made a globe between my hands. With a mere thought, I illuminated it. I had meant only to create a candle flame, but instead I got a ball of light half as tall as I was.

Dozens of pairs of red eyes glowed back at us.

I dropped the globe. It flickered, but I lifted it again. Whatever the eyes belonged to began to growl low in their throats. More threatening rumbles rose from behind them. There must have been hundreds, if not thousands, of beasts surrounding us. The creatures near us lifted their front lips, revealing long, sharp white teeth embedded in black gums. Those teeth weren't as impressive as Aahz's four-inch fangs, but he and we were completely outnumbered.

"This," Aahz declared, "*this*, kid, is why I told you that dimension traveling was dangerous!"

"What do we do?" I asked, trying not to panic.

Aahz stood up, moving very, very slowly. He turned his hands palm out toward the creatures of the night.

"Not trying to hurt anyone," Aahz said. "We're strangers here. We come in peace. I want to talk to whoever is in charge."

GRRRRRRR! came the sound from a thousand throats.

"Are you growling at *me*? ME?" Aahz demanded, thrusting his face into the nearest cluster of red lights. "Do you know who I am? I'll tear your faces off and glue them into my scrapbook! Now, back off and take me to your leader!"

To my amazement, the glowing eyes did recede slightly.

"Good," Aahz said, folding his arms.

Then they charged.

There was nowhere to run, since the beasts surrounded us completely. I struck at the bodies that leaped on me, finding them covered with wiry, greasy pelts too thick to land a punch. The beasts bit and tore at my arms, my legs, and my face. I howled with pain. They rammed me with their skulls. My ribs were bruised, but I couldn't get out of their way. Gleep practically wound himself around my body to protect me, but we were overwhelmed.

"Use the force, kid!" Aahz bellowed.

I reached for the line of magikal power not far below the ground. It was jagged and deep purple, the kind that Aahz had always warned me against, but it was the only one within reach. I filled my internal reserves. Unlike Winslow, this magik flowed freely into me. I felt powerful and dangerous, like an evil overlord. Imperiously, I willed the creatures to go away from us and stop biting me.

Immediately, they all flew backward. Yelping, they vanished into the darkness. I picked myself up from the ground, feeling the sting of ripped skin underneath the shredded sleeves of my favorite tunic. I dashed blood off my cheek with the back of my hand. Those cuts hurt. I hoped I wasn't going to catch something from them.

Of the five of us, I was the most scratched up. My left arm had been bitten several times, though it didn't feel as if anything was broken. One of Haroon's ears had a half circle of puncture marks along the edge. Aahz's tunic had been half torn from his back. Markie looked almost entirely untouched, though her hair was mussed up. Gleep seemed unmarked and unperturbed. He licked my face. I ruffled his ears and tried not to wince at the smell of his breath.

Markie glanced at me with respect.

"You've come a long way since I saw you last," she said. "I was ready to toss those creatures into next week, but you beat me to it."

"It wasn't me," I said. "I mean, I threw a spell at them, but it was a dozen times more powerful than I expected. I thought I'd gain us some space, not clear the whole area."

"Really?" Aahz said, tugging the rags of his shirt up over his shoulders. "Where'd you get the magik from?"

I described the line of force. Aahz's scaly eye ridges rose.

"I warned you about those lines for a good reason, kid," he said, "but if you can control the megalomaniacal impulses, or if they don't poison you outright, the power shouldn't amp you up any more than magik from other force lines."

"But it does," I said, pointing to my light globe. "That was supposed to be a candle."

Markie turned away from us and thrust her small hand outward. A lightning bolt shot out. It lit up a bleak landscape before exploding into a grove of trees at least a mile away from us. She looked up at me with shocked eyes.

"Don't try any spells," she said. "Not a thing. Don't use any magik at all unless it's a matter of life or death. I was at the top of my class in Elemental School. That," she added, aiming a small thumb over her shoulder, "was the Dancing

Sparks demonstration I did to earn my Fairy Tales badge in Magik Sprouts. It shouldn't have tickled a fly's behind. There's something about this dimension that amplifies power to the nth degree."

I gulped. With magik flowing freely, I had filled up my internal reserves. I was a walking arsenal.

"What do I do?" I asked.

"Control," she said. "Try not to get into a situation where you have to use magik at all until we can get out of this dimension."

"That might be easier said than done, little missy," Haroon said, one ear cocked high. "We're about to get some company."

"Let's get out of here," Aahz said. "Markie, can you hop us back to Winslow?"

"I don't dare, without a whole lot more experimentation," Markie said, worriedly. "A transference spell could shoot us all the way through the dimensional vortex, or blow us to pieces right here."

"What about your D-hopper?" I asked Aahz.

"Same problem, kid," Aahz said, reluctantly. "Two problems, in fact: It's not that great a model to start with. This place could overload it like a Christmas shopper's husband."

"And the second?" I asked.

"It's back in the hotel room," Aahz said, sourly. "It's too big to keep on me all the time. It never occurred to me that I would need it exploring a luxury resort!"

"Then let's start runnin'," Haroon suggested. "I'm in no hurry to meet any more locals."

"Me, either," Aahz said. "Come on!"

With my globe of light bobbing ahead of us like a drunken Fairy, we ran. The plain ahead of us was fairly level, though the ground was a scree of small, loose stones that made running tricky. Gleep galloped ahead, then doubled back to run with us, covering twice the distance the rest of us did.

"Here they come!" Haroon announced.

The Canidian's ears were as keen as his eyes. Soon, even I could hear the clink of bridle tack and the distant hammering of hooves on the stony ground. Within moments, a line of black-coated steeds appeared to either side of us and cut off our escape route. We thudded to a halt. The riders trotted around us in a circle. I readied a wisp of magik—all I hoped I would need.

"Who are you?" the lead rider asked. His voice was deep and gravelly, laden with menace and power. A scarf hid the lower part of his face, as a wide-brimmed hat concealed the upper. All I could see was a pair of burning silver eyes.

"Just travelers," Aahz said, casually, gesturing to me to keep silent.

"Gleep!" added my dragon, refusing to be suppressed.

Swords crackling with blue energy zinged as they were swept out of their scabbards. One nudged toward my throat.

"You don't belong here."

"We know!" I said. "We'll get out of here just as soon as we can. Please, just let us go."

"You're trespassing," the lead rider said. The swords drew close enough to us to nick flesh. "And trespassing in Maire means death."

CHAPTER EIGHT

"Welcome to my nightmare!"

—H. P. LOVECRAFT

It did no good to try to reason with the dark strangers.

"We came here by accident," I said, hopping along behind the leader's steed as best I could in the pitch darkness. His minions had tied ropes around our wrists and the necks of Gleep and Haroon. My foot hit a rock and I stumbled. "All we want to do is go back to our dimension. If you'd just help us, we wouldn't be trespassing anymore."

The rider on the dark steed didn't reply, but a whip lashed out and flicked me on the cheek with deadly accuracy. The sinister clink of metal hooves striking the stones was the only sound. He had extinguished my candle-globe with a single pinch of his gloved thumb and forefinger. No one else spoke to us, either. Any time I tried to speak, I got another lash to the face.

The riders seemed to have no trouble at all in the blackness. I kept imagining I saw darker shapes in the darkness. None of them were real, though. I tripped over things I couldn't see, and those that I thought I saw had no substance.

A faint amber glow arose on the horizon. I thought for a long time I was imagining that, too, until a jagged line appeared beneath the glow. Buildings. Big ones, from the look of them. Not a city, but perhaps a citadel.

We crested a stony rise and began a descent into a broad valley. Small cottages, which we could see by the lamps and torches that burned in their windows and at their doorposts, dotted the landscape. The area was dominated, though, by an immense castle surrounded by a circular shield wall. Flaring torches burned on the signal towers. It looked as though there was only one way in—and we were heading toward it.

The silver-eyed man towed us all through the high portcullis. I peered up inside the arch and saw more glowing eyes looking down at me. Our captor rode up to the stone keep and around to the left side, where the main door was situated. Guards in full plate armor breastplates and chain-mail trews crossed their spears in front of the door. The rider dismounted and swept off his hat. The guards shouldered their spears and stood waiting. The rider tugged on a braided rope that hung down beside the massive iron-bound timber door. In the distance I could hear the ting-a-ling-a-ling of a bell.

The portal creaked open. More guards on the inside flanked a silent woman with a pale oval of a face and long black hair that flowed over the shoulders of her long black dress. The sockets of her eyes looked as if she had been weeping ink. In fact, everyone in this dimension had the same marking. She beckoned to us, then turned to glide gracefully toward a hallway that opened to her right. We stumbled in and followed her.

I could see the resemblance to Limbo in the style of construction and decorating. Though sturdy, the iron bolts and thick wooden pegs holding together the furniture seemed crude. The ceilings of the corridors were pointed archways, ornamented with gruesome battle scenes picked out in mosaic tiles. The pointed shape was echoed in the doorways and window slits, each of which had a mailed archer standing beside it.

"Whoever lives here doesn't like surprises," Aahz said.

The guards must not have cared for sightseers; they poked us in the back with their spears to get us moving faster. The woman glided to a high doorway. Inside the room, I could see a vast, slate-lined fireplace containing a huge fire large enough to immolate a small village. The enormous room contained oversized settees and chairs, the largest and most striking of which was arranged before the fireplace. The posts and legs of this throne were carved of a dark red wood and gilded at the feet and tips. Chains were fastened from the top of the posts to the front edge of the arms, where I swore I saw manacles. Thick, black leather formed the back and seat. As we entered, a man rose from the chair. He stood about my height, but narrow of build, with long, shoulder-length black hair that looked as if it had been shocked into its current style, but in an artful manner. He wore a leather jerkin and tight leather trousers. A chain encircled his waist, and more chains jangled around the wrists of his fingerless gloves. His long fingers stuck out like white worms attempting to escape.

The most striking thing about him was his face. It was pale as the woman's, with high cheekbones that stuck out like knobs. The pits of his eyes dripped with black. The irises, like those of the riders and the guards, gleamed silver from the depths of the hollows. I was repulsed yet fascinated at the same time. He smiled, making his cheeks look yet more gaunt. He resembled my Skeeve the Magnificent disguise, though altogether more impressive. He just had the aura. It came naturally to him. He loped over to us.

"Hey, welcome to my humble little hovel."

"Hovel? If this is a hovel, I'd love to see someplace you really like," Aahz said, looking around admiringly. "I'm Aahz." He held out a hand. The man took it without hesitation and shook it enthusiastically. "This is my partner, Skeeve. Markie. Haroon."

"Gleep!" my dragon interjected, with an annoyed stare at Aahz.

"Oh, yeah," Aahz said, resigned to the inevitable. "And Gleep."

"I am Wince," the man announced, throwing his arms out. He waited, still poised. "Ahem."

He seemed to expect a reaction. I wondered if we were supposed to show obeisance.

"Oh, *Wince*!" I said, as if the memory had struck me.

I bowed deeply. Haroon immediately followed suit, planting his two front paws ahead of him on the floor and lowering his head to meet them. The rest of my friends followed our example. Wince beamed.

"Come on in," he said. "I was just about to have dinner." He gestured toward a long, rough-hewn table on which enormous iron candelabra, also hung with chains, blazed. At the end, one place had been laid with a bloodred plate and a cut crystal goblet. A chair, similar to the throne before the fire, hulked behind it. "Join me. I love company."

As he spoke, gaunt males and females, dressed in black, began to stream in, carrying platters and pitchers. Two males carried in a massive oval dish covered by a high silver dome and placed it with a THUD! in the center of the table. I sniffed the air, appreciating the aromas of cooked meat, roasted vegetables, melted cheese, and other delicious ingredients.

"We don't want to impose," I offered, though my stomach rumbled happily.

"No problem," Wince said. "I like a feast, so there's always plenty. Would you like wine? I never drink it myself, but I keep it for guests."

Aahz leaned close to Haroon.

"Is this guy a Vampire?" he whispered.

"Nossir," Haroon said. "He's warm and he's got all his own blood, though I can smell plenty from a whole bunch of other people who came through here."

"Whew!"

"All right," I said. "We would be glad to join you."

"Terrific!" Wince said. He snapped his fingers. "Minions!"

The black-clad servants hurried out of the room. They returned immediately, with armloads of china, linens, silver, and crystal. Floating behind them was a quartet of chairs much like Wince's but smaller and less ostentatious. They set four places on the table, two to either side of their master's seat, and one on the floor for Gleep. My dragon had a big bowl instead of a plate and cutlery. The chairs thumped down at the table. Wince waved a hand, and they screeched outward as if awaiting us.

"Let's eat!"

We waited for him to seat himself, then took our places.

"So, who sent you here?" Wince asked. He signed to the servers, who moved back to the table and lifted the dish covers all at once. The biggest dish concealed a roast boar, its skin crackling and golden. It had its jaws clenched around a fruit in its mouth and an expression of terror in its eyes. It made me uncomfortable to look at it, so I kept my gaze moving. The room impressed me. It alone was larger than the inn that I owned and occasionally occupied in Klah. Even the royal chambers that I had visited, such as the throne room of Queen Hemlock of Possiltum, were smaller.

"Um, we're kind of here by accident," I said. "We're just travelers. Harmless ones. We didn't mean to come."

Wince shook his head. "No one gets here by accident. This country's got magikal barriers you just wouldn't believe around it to prevent accidental arrivals. The laws are really strict."

"We noticed," Aahz said.

Wince's servants brought the food around to each of us, except the roast boar, which he carved himself onto a silver platter. I had never seen anyone so deft with a knife. Every slice was exactly the same width. The platter slid to the edge of the table, where a female minion received it and brought it to Markie's side. Wince took a few slices for himself, examining them as if checking his own work.

"You seem like really nice people. So, who'd you tick off?"

"A magician," I said, not really wanting to go into details. I took a bite of meat. It was delicious. "She transported us when we, uh, surprised her."

"You fell afoul of a fellow magician?" He looked apologetic. "Sorry. I couldn't help but notice the air of magik about you and this little lady here. One of my little talents. And she sent you *here*? Whew! Do you happen to know her name?"

"Never had the chance to ask," Aahz said.

"Well, since you can see it was just an accident that we came here," I continued, "we'd appreciate it if you'd help us out."

"We usually don't get walk-ins," Wince said, shaking his head. "Normally interlopers are brought here by local law enforcement. But we can cope," he assured us, waving his hands in excitement. "I'll make the experience spectacular for you. You can rely on me. I'm famous across the dimensions."

In my experience, transportation spells weren't painless, but they weren't spectacular, either. I shrugged. If he said he'd help, then I was happy to let him.

"Thanks," I said. "We really appreciate it. By the way, everything is delicious. Thanks for inviting us."

Again Wince paused, as though he expected a stronger reaction.

"You *sure* you've never heard of me?"

Aahz shook his head. "Sorry, but I still can't place you."

Wince seemed taken aback by that. He dashed his palm against his forehead.

"Man, just when you think you've made it to the top, when you think the world's your oyster, someone comes along and knocks your feet out from under you. You've really never heard my name? Wince?"

"I'm sorry," I said.

"No, no," Wince said, with his hand to his forehead. "I've got to thank you. A humility lesson's good for you once in a while. No problem." He pointed at me. "Thanks for trying to make me feel good. I really appreciate that. I've got to prove myself. Trust me, all right?"

"Uh, all right," I said. I exchanged glances with the others. What choice did we have?

I stuck my fork into another piece of meat, and a heart-rending howl rose to the ceiling. I jumped back, my fork clattering to the table. More howls joined the first, and I realized it wasn't coming from my food. Outside the castle, I could hear baying and shrieking sounds like thousands of damned souls, or a typical day in the Bazaar at Deva.

"Uh, what's that?" I asked.

Wince smiled and sprang from his seat.

"It's just the villagers gathering. Come and take a look."

He strode to a set of iron-bound shutters that were as sturdy as the doors and flung them wide. We followed him and gazed down.

Outside, I saw countless small fires blazing and spitting. As my eyes grew accustomed to the darkness, I realized they were all torches being shaken by people milling around in the courtyard. Six-legged animals that resembled Klahdish dogs or wolves prowled among the crowd, snarling. The villagers were chanting furiously. I couldn't make out what they were saying.

"What does the mob want?" I asked, horrified. "What are they angry about?"

"Oh, they're not angry!" Wince laughed. "They're all here for the spectacle. The torches are an old custom. You wave the fire around to show that you approve of the music. I've got the most amazing backup band. You'll love them. But they're all here to see me!"

"In my dimension, concerts are usually held in the daytime," Markie said. "Why wait until after dark?"

"We have a really short day," Wince explained, "so most of our activity is at night. All the major entertainment comes on after the sun sets. The nightlife here is pretty good. It keeps people's spirits up, you know? There are some other popular performers, but I think I draw the biggest crowds."

"You must be some kind of rock star," Markie said.

I looked around. Apart from the stones that made up the castle walls, I saw no rocks but thought it better not to ask. Wince lowered his eyes modestly.

"I am, in a manner of speaking."

"So, what kind of ax do you play?" Aahz asked.

Wince smiled. It was a triumphant, yet sad smile. He pointed to the wall.

"Not usually an ax, but a sword. It's traditional, you know. Still, I don't like to limit myself. You never learn if you don't try anything new. My favorite's the one in the middle."

We all turned to look. I felt my skin crawl.

I had seen the wall full of weapons while we had been dining, though I had not paid much attention to it. I had been in plenty of castles since I started hanging around with Aahz. The deadly cutlery that most castle dwellers put on display was usually only for show, though there was almost always a piece or two that the lord high master favored as the last line of defense in case of sudden invasion. The rest was almost always dusty and rusted in place. Wince's collection, on the other hand, seemed to have been well used, and recently. Every piece, and there were hundreds, was sharpened and well oiled.

To either side stood ranks of pole arms, each with a different, deadly-looking head. I had had a number of weapons pointed at me. These looked as though they were meant for more than just skewering an opponent. The six-pronged spiraling monstrosity appeared designed to inflict the maximum amount of pain before it dispatched its victim.

Within the brackets of spears were axes. My father had had a number of different ones on our farm for different purposes, such as cutting wood, butchery, and breaking ice on the pond in the winter. Wince had all those plus a dozen more, ranging from a little hand ax that I'd have used for chopping straw up to a massive curved blade that could have sliced through a rain barrel in one swipe. In between the larger hardware were arrayed steel pincers, wrenches, knives, corkscrews, probes, and all sorts of horrible things I could never imagine anyone making, or using. Some the items had their own power. A knife with a curved blue blade like a wriggling snake leaked magik like a cloth sieve. At the center, the sword that Wince had indicated was long, heavy-bladed, and squared off at the tip, a design I had never seen before. I shuddered.

"That is a lot of heavy metal, my friend," Aahz said.

"It's my milieu," Wince said, with a modest shrug.

The service door creaked open, and an elderly minion with shriveled skin and a painfully misshapen back limped in.

"Tradition," Aahz said. I was baffled, but then didn't seem the time to ask what tradition he meant.

The ancient man bowed deeply to Wince.

"The band's here, Master."

"Thanks, Needles. Is my stuff on stage yet?"

"It will all be there, Master."

"Hey, set up five more places near the band, okay? These guys are going to be with us tonight."

Needles bowed again. "Of course, Master. I will instruct the roadies."

"Thanks, man."

Wince clapped his hands together and rubbed the palms vigorously.

"So, enjoying your dinner? The last meal in this dimension is always a feast. You're going to be part of the show tonight. I thought it was just going to be Isha, but since you showed up, you're going to be part of the act."

"No, thanks," I said. "We'd rather watch."

"Uh, no," Wince said. "Really, you have to. No choice. It's the law."

I exchanged glances with my fellows. "What part do we play?"

"It's really easy," Wince assured me. "Just go with the flow. You'll figure it out."

"But what do you do?" Markie asked. "Are you a musician?"

"No, they're my backup. I'm an executioner," Wince said.

CHAPTER NINE

"Everybody's dying to get into show business."

—THE PHANTOM OF THE OPERA

"You're a what?" I asked, disbelieving my own ears.

Wince ducked his head modestly.

"Executioner. Famous. Throughout at least eighty dimensions. Hey, Needles, are the others ready?"

The ancient retainer shook his head.

"No, Master. One of them is refusing to eat her dinner."

Wince waved a dismissive hand.

"Fine. Let her stay one more night. Make her comfortable. We've got plenty of victims for tonight."

On his way out, Needles limped on the other side.

"Victims?" I asked, my voice rising to a squeak.

"You're a what?" Markie asked.

Wince sighed. "There's always one who isn't listening. Executioner."

"Executioner? But I thought you were going to help us get out of this dimension!"

Our host regarded us with hurt eyes. "I never said that."

"But . . ."

Wince looked thoughtful.

"No, I'm pretty sure I never said that. Let me think about it." He put his chin in his palm and drummed his fingers on his face. "Nope. I'm pretty good at remembering what I say. I said I'd make the experience spectacular. I never said anything about letting you get away. Sorry."

"But we don't want to die!" I said.

"Aw, man!" Wince exclaimed. "I thought you guys understood! You asked about my ax and everything! It's the law!"

"But we didn't know about your law," I pointed out. "We were sent here against our will."

"*Everyone* who comes here comes against their will," Wince said. "Like I said, I assist law enforcement. I am the final stop on the justice train. People get sent here all the time for torture and death. Normally I send out the invoice first, but like you heard, I'm short of victims tonight. You guys are a blessing for me. I'll figure out who to send the bill to later. I hate to disappoint the crowd, and now I know I won't. Five more subjects will flesh out the show really well. Wow, what a range of techniques I can use tonight! You guys are really helping me out."

I had dealt with insane logic like his when we faced Isstvan,[5] but Wince wasn't insane. In a literal sense we had broken his country's laws, even if we could not possibly have known about it. It was within his rights to kill us.

"I am going to tear that blue-robed bimbo into little pieces," Markie snarled. "We're leaving!"

She sprang up and whipped her finger around in a circle. An immense whirlwind roared up from the floor. It sucked me into the vortex. The gale whipped me around and around

---

5. See *Another Fine Myth*, the first in the series of these must-have volumes.

until my stomach rebelled. Lightning crashed near enough to me to singe my eyebrows. I bumped into Gleep and held on to his collar. Markie grabbed for Aahz and Haroon as they swept past her, and pointed her finger at the door. It banged open. We were drawn toward it like water pouring down a drain. I knew she was a powerful magician, but I had never really experienced the full range of her talents. Furniture lifted off the floor and caromed off the walls. Even the gilding started to peel off the ornamental carvings. Stones loosened in the walls. The foundation began to rumble.

With the least possible magik, I tried to protect myself and my dragon so we wouldn't be torn to pieces. The funnel cloud squeezed us together. Aahz's scales rasped my face.

Though he was flapping around like a scarecrow caught in a thunderstorm, Wince looked unconcerned. With one hand, he patted the air.

The tornado vanished. I had a split second to realize it and tried to use magik to cushion my fall. Nothing happened. I landed with a thud among my friends. In my mind's eye I could see that my internal tank was full of magik, but I couldn't use it. Somehow Wince was suppressing my abilities. From the look on Markie's face, he had done the same thing to her. We were helpless.

The tables and chairs hovered in midair for a moment, then floated back to their original places. Wince smiled down at us.

"Okay, that was fun, but I've got a show to get ready for. Minions!"

He clapped his hands.

"Try again, kid," Aahz said. He hung by his wrists from iron manacles attached to the dank, stone dungeon wall. I had been pinioned next to him, both of my arms clamped high over my head inside a single metal ring. Gleep and Haroon were nowhere to be seen. I could hear Markie, but I couldn't see her. She was yelling her head off in a faraway cell. She didn't sound as if she were being tortured. She sounded as if she was having a tantrum.

"When I get out of here, I'm going to tear you into little pieces, Wince!" she shrieked. "Your reputation is going to be so pathetic that you won't be able to deadhead daisies!"

If I could free us, we could go get her and look for the others. I summoned up all the magik I could reach. There was more than plenty at hand. The force lines that ran under the castle felt like raging torrents. Normally, I would have avoided ones that looked like these as I would have a Pervish restaurant, but I had no choice. We didn't have much time left. Outside the single window of our cell, I could hear hammering and banging, alongside the howls and wails of the crowd.

It was a matter of life and death now. No matter what the overload of magik did to us, it was better than having any of those implements on the great room wall used on us. I concentrated harder than I ever had in my life.

With so much power inside me that I felt my eyeballs must be glowing, I threw the magic into the chains holding us. *Burst,* I thought at them. *Explode. Begone!*

In my mind I saw the manacles shattering into tiny pieces. My whole body shook with the force of the explosion.

I opened my eyes. The cell was covered with a fine layer of soot. Aahz glared at me. His clothes, already ruined by the night monsters, hung in tatters. I looked down. Mine were in a similar state of disarray.

"Forget it, partner," Aahz said. "Stands to reason that if magik is so powerful here, the local fuzz would have stronger countermeasures in place than in other dimensions. We can't affect any of the local dungeon hardware."

"What can we do?" I asked.

"Wait until we have a chance to make a break for it," Aahz said. "Then you transport us back to Winslow."

"Me?"

Despite my fears, I was stunned. While Aahz had taught me the basics, my skill at moving people between dimensions was not one of my best. I was confident in my ability to travel from a place to which I had been taken by someone else, such as Tananda, or by using Aahz's D-hopper. Aahz had terrified me against trying it myself on a random basis with a series of stories of what had happened to unwary travelers he had known. The list of dangers involved could have filled a library—a very scary library.

"You've always warned me against jumping to or from unfamiliar points," I said. "I don't know where we are. With the way the magik behaves here, I could blow us out to the very ends of existence. I could kill us all."

"Do we have a choice?" Aahz snapped. "It's either you or him."

"Get away from me, you has-been!" Markie shrieked. "When I get out of here, I'm going to julienne your insides! I'll show you torture!"

"Oh, yeah!" Wince's voice said. "Keep that defiance up. The crowd is absolutely going to love you."

I gulped.

We heard the creak and slam of a door with a lot of metal on it. Eerie footsteps echoed hollowly on stone. I heard a key rattle in the lock of our door.

"Let me do the talking," Aahz whispered to me out of the corner of his mouth.

"But . . . !"

"Just zip it!"

I had no idea how or what he wanted me to zip, but I fell silent.

Wince came in and looked us over. His long hair looked wilder than ever. He had donned a long brocade coat with tight-fitting sleeves adorned with bright silver buttons. At the cuffs and throat he wore elaborate lace frills. His boots were polished so brilliantly I could see my own reflection in them. It was not a pretty sight.

"I like the smudges," he said. "Nice touch! The more miserable you look, the better. The programs are all printed up with your names on them. This is going to be a historical night! You guys ready?"

"You bet," Aahz said, showing all his teeth in a cringeworthy grin.

Wince smiled encouragingly.

"Remember, let it all out. Don't keep anything back. I promise I won't. I'll give you guys the best sendoff anyone's ever had!"

"Looking forward to it," Aahz said.

"You guys are going to be great. Thanks a million!"

"Don't worry about it," Aahz said.

As soon as the door shut behind Wince, I could contain myself no longer.

"He's insane!" I said. "He's completely crazy! We're going to die!"

"Kid . . ."

"How could we have fallen into a trap like that? He's going to kill us! He'll tear us apart!"

"Kid . . ."

"Stop calling me kid! If I'm going to die, I want to be called by my name!"

Aahz shook his head.

"All right, *Skeeve*. You can stop worrying. The guy's not going to kill us."

I yanked at the ring holding my wrists in place, throwing all the magik I could at it. I succeeded only in singeing the hair off my arms. I glared at Aahz.

"You could have fooled me! Talking about sending us off as if he's waving us good-bye on a trip? What about all those torture devices?"

"For show," Aahz said, confidently. "You start to believe

it, then you're as crazy as he is. Just play along. I'll win over the crowd, and we'll get out of here. You concentrate on getting us back to a dimension we know. It'll be no problem."

I stopped pulling at my bruised wrists.

"No *problem*? How could it be no problem?"

Aahz hung in his chains as nonchalantly as anyone could in that position.

"Trust me. You'll see."

CHAPTER TEN

"If the entire city had not turned out, I would gladly have passed on the honor."

—LOUIS XVI OF FRANCE

I did not share Aahz's confidence. Within the hour, a troop of Wince's guards came in and unlocked us from the wall but left the chains weighing us down at neck, wrists, and ankles. Just to add to our state of wretchedness, a female with ink-stained eye sockets came in with a bucket and sloshed mud all over us. The guards pointed their spears at us and prodded us out the door. Squelching in my damp boots, I felt every bit the condemned man walking out to his doom.

Aahz, on the other hand, was as relaxed as though he were going to a dinner in his honor. We were led out of the dungeon and along a gravel path into an enormous torchlit arena lined with tiered seats filled with people and animals, all with gleaming silver eyes. Aahz loped behind our guards, waving and smiling to the crowd.

"Look, a Pervert!" someone in the stadium cried.

"That's Per-vect!" Aahz called back, showing more good humor than I would have believed possible. "Read your program!"

We were shoved, pushed, and pulled up a ramp to a curtained area out of sight of the mob. Wince was already there, pulling on a fresh pair of fingerless gloves.

"Hey, guys, are you ready?"

"We certainly are," Aahz said. "Listen, when you're ready, take me first. I want to tell the crowd my story. Plead my case. I've had a pretty amazing life. They'll eat it up."

The executioner tilted his head. His silver eyes glittered.

"Sounds good. They love backstory. It makes the session more, I don't know, *poignant*. I'll get back to you."

"Let me go, you escapees from a B-picture!"

Two more guards clumped up the ramp. Between them, they held a small iron cage with Markie inside. It was just big enough for her to crouch in. It did nothing to dampen the sound of her voice. The Cupy female hammered furiously at the bars.

"Let me out of this crate! You're going to be sorry! I'll rip your head off!"

Haroon trotted dejectedly behind a guard who held an iron ball in his arms. It was attached by a chain around the Canidian's neck.

Gleep was tied down to a rolling platform. He wore a muzzle on his nose. I noticed that his normally razor-sharp talons had been clipped short. When he saw me, he whimpered. I pushed away from my guards to get close to him. They wanted to stop me, but their master waved them away.

"No problem," Wince said. "You can't unlock these chains, so it doesn't matter if you're all together. Get ready for your entrance! Make it a good one, huh? The crowd loves cries for mercy."

He pushed aside the curtain and strode out onto the stage. The audience wailed and cheered.

Gleep leaned against me.

"Skeeve . . . scared . . . ?"

"No, I'm not afraid," I said. I was lying, but if it helped him feel brave, I would lie until Wince tore my tongue out. "Aahz said it's just a show. We'll go along with it, for now. I'll protect you."

No muzzle ever made could stop a dragon's tongue. Gleep slurped me through the leather straps. I gagged at the smell of the slime.

Markie pushed at the little box, then slumped, defeated.

"This is not the way I saw myself shuffling off the mortal coil," she said.

"Don't worry about a thing," Aahz said, grandly. "Just enjoy the show."

Beyond the curtain, fresh shrieks and howls as if from a thousand Furies' throats arose. The sound of twanging wires and frenzied pounding accompanied them.

"How horrible!" I said, holding my palms to my ears. "What terrible pain those people are suffering!"

Aahz grinned.

"That's music, partner. They're singing."

"That's music? It sounds like terrible torture!"

A single loud scream pierced the air. Aahz held up a finger.

"Now, that's torture. Staged, of course."

"And we're next." I gulped. We peered through the curtain.

Wince took center stage, now with a long, blacker-than-black cloak that looked like a hole in reality draped over his shoulders. From it, Wince removed knives, swords, and a massive poleax that could have cut through a castle gate. The crowd cheered with every deadly piece of iron that appeared. Finally, he hauled forth the square-tipped sword. Wince whirled it around in a figure eight, then handed it off to one of his assistants. I gawked.

"Where did all that come from? Another dimension?"

"Foolyagain cloth," Aahz said, admiringly. "Only the real executioners have it. It's where they carry the tools of the trade. This guy's the real deal."

"Small comfort," Markie said. "But at least it'll be fast."

"Only if he wants it to be," Aahz said. "I've heard of torture sessions that last for days. One of them went on so long the crowd left before it was all over."

"I ain't too young to die," Haroon said, lifting his chin in a stalwart manner. "I'll ask him to take me first. I'll try and distract them so's the rest of you can get away."

"No!" I said, smashing my fist into my palm in spite of the chains. "We all leave together."

"That's the spirit," Aahz said.

"How?" Markie asked.

"Simple," Aahz said. "Wince is a showman. He likes things to flow. I'll volunteer to be the first victim. Since everyone thinks we're condemned prisoners, I'm going to tell our story to the crowd. It'll add to the tension. Then Wince will do his thing. I'll keep him busy. He won't be paying attention to you, so he won't dampen your magik. At the right dramatic moment, you"—he nodded to Markie—"kick out everything you've got. When you have them distracted, Skeeve's going to yank us out of here."

Markie grinned fiercely. "I'm in."

"I'm still not sure I can do it, Aahz."

"Sure you can, kid. Didn't I teach you everything you know?"

I couldn't reply, because at that moment, the guards prodded us out onto the stage. I blinked in the blinding light of hundreds of torches. The band played an enormous crescendo, and the audience broke into applause and cheers. We all stayed close together. I kept my arms around Gleep's neck. Haroon leaned against my leg.

Wince strode over to us and spread a hand in our direction.

"Behold! Lawbreakers who have trespassed on our domain! What do we DO with lawbreakers? We break *them*! Yeah!"

The crowd screamed their approval. I gazed out at the sea of frenzied faces and shuddered. Aahz cringed.

"The guy could really use better scriptwriters," he said.

"None who pass our borders ever pass out again!"

"No!!!" the crowd yelled. Some of them waved farm implements and ancient swords.

"Really?" Aahz commented, looking at his talons. He picked an invisible piece of mud from underneath one of them. "That was pitiful."

"Aahz!" I hissed. "He's stirring them up against us."

"All part of the show."

"And now, we must take our awful vengeance against lawbreakers! Are you with me? Are you ready?"

"YEEESSSSSS!" the crowd shrieked.

"Here we go, partner," Aahz said. "Are you ready to get out of here?"

Even with my arms around Gleep, I was shaking hard enough to vibrate down through the boards of the stage. I looked out into the bloodthirsty eyes of the mob. They were slavering for blood—*my* blood.

"Aahz, is this really all just an act?"

In spite of the clanking manacles, Aahz swept a casual hand in an arc.

"Sure it is. Now, pay attention. You're going to get just one shot. Otherwise, if the audience loves us, we'll end up on the playbill every day for the next month. Make sure you collect all five of us when you get the spell working. No matter where we end up, it's got to be better than here."

"All right," I said. In the center of the stage, Wince was dancing, sweeping that dark cloak of his around in a circle as the band played more of its bloodcurdling music. The black-clad servants carried a heavy wooden table out into the center of the stage. At each end were hoop-shaped clamps of steel polished to a gray sheen. The table's ancient planks were stained with dried blood in dozens of colors, some of it red. Like mine. Aahz grabbed my chin and yanked it so I was looking at him instead.

"It's all up to you," Aahz said, looking me square in the eyes. "Picture where you want to go. Be absolutely focused on your goal. Make certain that your mental image is as accurate as you can make it. If not, you could transport us to someplace that is similar but still not right. You got that?"

"Got it," I said, concentrating hard.

"Every detail, down to the smell. Be careful. If you picture the scent of roses, but we left a vase of dahlialions on the desk, we could end up in a curio shop somewhere on Brinny."

"I understand," I said.

"And don't forget, everything has to be three-dimensional. I might survive a trip into Flatland, but you won't."

"I got it!" I cried.

"Stop it, Aahz!" Markie scolded him. "You're going to throw him off!"

They glared at one another. Aahz lifted a lip in a sneer.

"Listen, shortcake, if he can't do magik under pressure, then he's never going to be much of a magician!"

"Aahz, face it," I said so calmly I surprised myself. "I'm never going to be much of a magician. But I'll do my best."

"You can do it, partner," Aahz said. "I know you can."

I wasn't so sure, but I nodded.

"Pick just one place," Aahz said. "We can cope with it no matter what. Just use enough power to get us out of here. I'm going to start my speech, then Markie's going to throw her whole bucket of weather magik at Wince to distract him. You have to be ready."

"All right," I said. I drew a deep breath and tried to focus my thoughts on the office.

"Keep your mind on the details. The smallest thing can throw you off."

"Okay."

"We could even get tossed back in time if you picture something that isn't there anymore."

"Aahz!" Markie said.

"What?"

She put on her very sweetest expression. "Please be quiet and let Skeeve concentrate."

Aahz looked abashed.

"Uh. Yeah. Sorry, partner. Just try not to beam us into the heart of a rock."

I moaned. Now I couldn't picture anything *but* the center of a rock. Gleep snaked his long head up and fixed his large blue eyes on mine.

"Gleep!" he said. His long pink tongue darted out. I tried to avoid it. Gaaaah! A trail of slime covered my face from ear to ear.

But his distraction had worked. He reminded me of home. Our office in the Bazaar at Deva was like nothing anywhere else in the dimensions. It smelled of dragon slime, Guido's aftershave, Bunny's perfume, the spicy scent that was unadulterated Tananda, candle wax, ink, scrolls, and the smell of well-handled gold coins. It was all ours, and I knew it better than I knew my own name. I nodded again.

They were all counting on me. I had never gone from such a hostile location on my own before. The crossing from Winslow had been a strange one, with at least two or three bounces involved. I had to take us to Deva in one, because I couldn't count on recalling the details of the intermediary stops. It was tricky, but I had to do it.

The music rose to a crescendo. Wince stopped his wild whirling and stalked toward us with a purposeful gleam in his silver eyes.

"I'm ready," Aahz said, his back straight and his chin high.

"That's great, man," Wince said. "But we're gonna take the Klahd first."

"What?" I squawked. "No!"

"You can't do that! I've got my whole speech ready!" Aahz protested. Wince waved a hand.

"Yeah, I know! I'm saving you for the grand finale. Minions!"

"Hey, wait, no!" I shouted, as Wince's guards dragged me toward the torture table.

"Let him go!" Aahz bellowed. "You're ruining my timing!"

I fought hard, but the guards pulled my arms above my head and tied them down to one end of the bloodstained boards. My legs were fastened to the other end. I kicked and writhed, trying to get free.

Wince looked down at me. He ran a thumb along the edge of the rounded blade of the knife in his hand. A thin line appeared on his skin where it had passed, and a drop of ink-black blood rolled down into his frilly cuff.

"Ready?" Wince asked.

"No!" I growled, my chest heaving. The executioner regarded me with disappointment.

"Come on, man, scream. Let it all out, or people will think you're not getting the whole Wince experience. Okay?" He glanced up at a sudden roll of thunder. A fork of white lightning crackled across the sky. "Hey, look, it's going to rain! This will be the best show I've had in years!"

A spark of hope kindled in my chest.

Markie!

Within seconds, the winds whipped up, and cold sleet began to pound down on us. Lightning shot down, illuminating the whole stage in blue. Wince loomed over me, the knife in his hand. He lowered it toward my throat. The blade caressed the skin under my chin. Lightning crashed!

I had to separate the various sensations I knew would be

waiting for me at the other end. The office was a tricky one. The furniture was moved around frequently. The waiting room was no good. There might be people waiting in it. What if Pookie and Spyder came back? We could land right on top of them!

Wait! I knew the perfect place. I filled myself with all the silver-white power from the lightning crashing overhead. It would take everything in me. If I was wrong, we could be stranded in the middle of nowhere with nothing, helpless to defend ourselves against enemies and malign magik. I wished Aahz had his powers back, so he could do this. He'd probably made a jump like this a thousand times in his long life. But this time the onus was on me. We were going home. I was *taking* us home. I could not be scared. Must not be scared.

Wince raised his arm on high. The blade glinted.

Lightning crashed again! A blue-white bolt shot down and struck the knife, sending it flying. Wince glanced back over his shoulder. He snapped his fingers, and a minion sprang forward, a replacement knife in hand. Wince reached for it. I felt his attention leave me free. This was my one and only opportunity.

I screwed my eyes shut and threw all of the power inside me into the spell.

BAMF!

CHAPTER ELEVEN

"Fame is such a burden."

—CALIGULA

It was cold, colder than I had ever anticipated. And wet. My feet were wet to the knees. I couldn't move. My arms and legs were pinioned by many bodies pressed against me.

"The bathtub?" Aahz asked. "You transported us into the bathroom?"

I opened my eyes. The five of us stood jammed foot-first into the white, claw-footed fixture. Normally, I thought it was more than large enough for long, hot soaks with a book, and deep enough to immerse myself thoroughly if I needed to scrub off an encounter with dragon dung, Pervish cooking, or some other unpleasant substance. I'd just never calculated what it would be like to share the facility with four other people, one of them a half-grown dragon. But I now remembered that I had given Gleep a bath the morning we left for Winslow. I must have forgotten to drain it after I washed him. The cold water in which we stood had a layer of shed dragon scales floating on it.

"Well done, Skeeve," Haroon said. He jumped out of the tub and shook himself. His long ears flapped around his head. Drops of water scattered from his brown coat. "You're a pretty darn fine magician, whatever you say."

"Crazy," Markie said. She disappeared from Gleep's side and reappeared two feet away on the mat, emerging dry and scaleless. "But we're back and we're intact."

"Nice storm, by the way," Aahz said. "Really artistic lightning."

"Yes, I think I might go into the weather biz," Markie said. "Just as a sideline."

"Aahz, Wince was going to torture me!" I said, interrupting them.

"I know," Aahz replied. He reached for a towel and started rubbing soot and dried mud off his face. I sputtered.

"But you said it was all just for show! You were playing along with him! He was going to kill me!"

Aahz wound the towel into a point and inserted it into his ear. "Yeah, he was."

"But you said he wasn't!"

Aahz removed the towel. He looked at me with an impatient expression I knew all too well.

"Partner, if I hadn't convinced you that it was all just a show right up to the last minute, would you have been able to concentrate enough to get us out of there?"

"Yes!"

"No! You were panicking. You couldn't have shown us to the exit if it was marked with red neon lights."

"Yes, I could!"

Haroon raised large, brown, sympathetic eyes to me.

"My friend, I saw what this big galoot saw. Y'all were pretty darned distracted, from this old fellah's point of view. I couldn't think of anything myself 'cept what my first encounter with any of those devices would feel like. You think you felt any different than me?"

"Uh . . ." I considered the thought in all honesty. "Probably not."

"Then deceiving you was for the common good, right?"

Honesty compelled my answer, though I had to haul it all the way up from my toes.

"I guess so."

"Then my plan worked." Aahz slapped me on the back. "Would I ever steer you wrong?"

"Well, once in a while . . ."

"Well, that's that," Markie said. "Nice job, Skeeve." She rubbed her hands together. "Now I'm going to go back to Winslow and blow away that magician that poofed us off to Maire."

"No, don't do that!" I protested. I stumbled out of the tub, scattering scales as I went. Aahz stepped out behind me, in evident distaste, and sat on the edge to wipe off his feet.

"What do you care?" Markie said. "She tried to kill all of us. Might have succeeded, too. You're not going to tell me you like that in a girl?"

"Why not?" Aahz said. "Some of the longest-lasting Pervish marriages started when one of the couple took out a contract on the other."

"Yes, but he's not a Pervert, like you!"

"That's Per-vect, Short-and-Squashy," Aahz snarled.

Markie went into a crouch and beckoned to him with both hands.

"Hit me with your best spell, pal. Oh, I forgot—you don't have any powers!"

"Cheap shot," Aahz said.

Markie's mouth twisted into a rueful knot. I knew she was trying to reform, but it couldn't have been easy.

"I know. Sorry, Aahz."

Aahz waved a hand magnanimously.

"Forget it."

"Come on back with me. I'll buy you a drink after I bump off Miss Fancy Pants."

"Don't!" I pleaded.

Markie put her small hands on her hips.

"Why not? That trip could have been a death warrant for us, and I don't take that from anyone."

"Why wouldn't you want to kill Wince instead? He was about to take us apart, piece by piece!" I shuddered at the memory of the knife that had touched my throat.

Markie tossed her golden curls, which had miraculously regained their bounce and shine.

"He was just doing his job. In fact, I was pretty impressed by him. Unlike your girlfriend. Overkill is the sign of an amateur."

"I don't think she wanted to kill us," I protested. "I think she was surprised."

"By what?" Markie demanded.

"She recognized us," Aahz said. "She recognized Skeeve, anyhow."

"But why would she send us to a dangerous dimension?" I asked. "I haven't done anything to her. I've never seen her before."

"She wanted us out of the way, maybe permanently. You're famous in magikal circles now, kid," Aahz explained. "I put the word around myself when you were just getting started, but I've heard stories since then that I didn't let out. Pretty impressive stories, too. Along with a few tales about me." He grinned, showing his four-inch pointed teeth. "Those grew pretty well, too. Nothing like a game of Telephone to really blow things out of proportion."

"Tele-what?" I asked.

"Forget it. Think of a crystal ball with perpetual connection problems."

Markie shook her head impatiently.

"If we're not going to go kill Miss Quick-on-the-Trigger, what are we going to do?"

"Go back and keep looking for the Loving Cup," I said. "But we have to find the others first. I'm worried about Bunny. Looie might have . . . taken advantage of her. He was sure trying."

"Say no more," Haroon declared, shaking himself once again. He spattered the rest of us with bathwater and dragon scales. "Take me back to Winslow. I'll just put my nose down and find the young lady's scent."

"But what about her disguise?" I asked.

"Huh! That illusion you put on her doesn't change the way she smells, Mr. Skeeve. No more than making yourself look like a dried-out old prune changes you from being a young Klahd."

Since I'd been to Winslow before, I created a spell that would transport us back to my hotel room. For a moment, I hesitated, afraid I might fail. Then I realized I could do this without any trouble. I could relax. With a smile, I drew up enough power for the transference.

BAMF!

We appeared inside our suite. Haroon applied his big black nose to the floor and started sniffing his way around. We followed him up the stairs and down the long corridor. Gleep stayed shoulder to shoulder with him as though curious about how Haroon did his job. I planned to ask my dragon what he had learned, later on when no one could overhear us.

Sniff sniff sniff sniff sniff!

He stopped in front of one of the bedroom doors.

Markie snorted.

"No points for finesse," she said. "This is Bunny's room."

"Scent's old," Haroon said, walking in small circles. "At least a night's worth. But over here's different."

"Shhh!" I said.

I put my ear to the door. Aahz followed suit. What we heard made both of our eyes go wide.

ZZZZ hawnk! ZZZZ hawnk! Fuf fuf fuf *snort!* ZZZZ hawnk!

"That's not Bunny!" I said.

Aahz didn't wait to hear more. He twisted the knob and marched in.

Bunny's room was fancier and frillier than her bedroom in our tent in Deva. All the walls were painted with brilliantly colored frescoes of gardens and mythical animals. A shimmering cream-colored stone dressing table was topped with triple mirrors of the finest crystal. No fewer than three carved and gilded wardrobes lined the wall opposite the windows, with a cheval glass mirror on an oval swivel frame before them. But the main object in the room was a tremendous bed with pink ruffled hangings. Puffy feather quilts and enormous down pillows covered in white, silver, and pale pink lay scattered on the floor on both sides. A large mound lay under a rucked-up hot pink counterpane in the center of the round mattress. It was heaving and twitching.

"I wouldn't have believed it," Aahz said, scratching his ear in bemusement. "I guess you can take the girl out of the Mob, but you can't . . ."

"Gleep!" announced my dragon. He slipped past me and charged toward the bed.

"No, Gleep!" I whispered loudly.

"Gleep!" he admonished me, with reproof in his large blue eyes. He jumped up on the canopy bed and pawed vigorously at the large lump under the blanket.

It unrolled and disgorged its contents. I averted my eyes to avoid embarrassing Bunny. A sharp finger poked me in the ribs.

"You can look," Markie said. "It's not her."

Snork WHONK!

Puzzled, I glanced up. A figure lay on its back, belly heaving. To my relief, the sole occupant of the luxurious bed was Looie. He was wearing pale blue embroidered long johns that reminded me of the one-piece outfit in which my mother used to put me to bed when I was a tot. I could tell by his flaccid muscles and bad breath that could freeze a Cockatrice at fifty paces that he was drunk. Once I had recovered my wits, I noticed that his clothes were neatly folded over the back of the chair that stood before the dressing table. Bunny was nowhere in sight.

"Where is she?" I asked, torn between relief and worry.

"What I bin tryin' to tell ya, sonny," Haroon said, patiently. "I tole ya her footprints was some hours old. Come on. I'll lead you to her."

I locked the door behind us so Looie couldn't go wandering around through our quarters if he did wake up, and followed Haroon.

He sniffed up and down the hallway, stopping first at one of our assigned doors, then another. Finally, he sat down before one.

"Right here," he declared.

"But this is my room," I said.

Aahz smiled. He rapped on the door.

"Bunny? It's us."

The door opened a crack. Bunny peered out, a large metal club in her raised hand. As soon as she saw us, she dropped the metal pole. It clanged on the stone floor. She threw herself into our arms.

"Oh, you can't believe how glad I am to see you!" she said.

"We, uh, found Looie," I said.

Bunny pursed her lips. "I hope he has a headache the size of a mountain," she said, sourly. "That rat took me out to every watering hole and inn within five miles. He kept knocking back drinks and trying to get me drunk. What a cheapskate! He drank Wyvernian whisky and bought me Poulta Girl cocktails."

"I hope he didn't try anything on you," I said, severely.

"Oh, he *tried*," Bunny said, "but he's about as smooth as a wood rasp. I was deflecting passes from men like him before I started wearing short skirts. I took a sip from each glass and dumped the rest into the centerpieces. Anyhow, he's the client. I didn't want him to get robbed or hurt once he was incapable of taking care of himself, and I didn't want to end up carrying him, so I suggested we come back to my room. He jumped at the opportunity."

"I'll bet," Aahz said.

"He chased me around the room for a few minutes, then passed out. I threw his clothes over a chair and got out of there. I wasn't going to stay in there with him in case he came to."

"You chose my room," I said.

She gave me a shy little grin.

"I felt safe in there. Besides, Tananda and Chumley are back in their own suite. Markie's bed is too small, and Aahz's room, uh . . ."

"Pervect luxury," Aahz said, with a grin. "But you Klahds never appreciate the finest. Too bad I didn't get to sleep in it."

"I didn't really get any sleep, either," Bunny said. "I kept thinking he would come through the door. I'm so glad you're back!"

"We'll move your things to a different room," I promised her. "But did you get him to agree to pay our expenses?"

"No!" Bunny said. She looked glum. "We'll have to find the cup, or eat the loss."

"We don't need him," Aahz said. "I took the job; now I'm declining it. It would give me great pleasure to go in there and tell him to take a hike."

Bunny put a beseeching hand on his arm. She looked as desperate as she had when Aahz first mentioned Looie's commission.

"Don't," she said. "We've had a lot of trouble getting lucrative contracts lately."

"All right," Aahz said, looking as puzzled as I was. "I'm not going to argue with you now. Let's just get the job done."

Bunny's shoulders sagged with relief.

"Thanks, Aahz."

CHAPTER TWELVE

"One picture is worth a thousand words."

—L. FLYNT

No matter what the time of day, Winslow's staff was happy to oblige with whatever meal its guests wanted to eat. Chumley, normally so mild-mannered, was aroused from a deep slumber with a ferocious appetite for breakfast. As a result, after those of us who had been to Maire had had a speedy bath, all eight sat down to a table sagging under platters of what each of us liked for our morning meal.

"Give steak, no take!" the Troll demanded, pointing at a heaping plate of meat near me.

He spoke in the manner of his stage name, Big Crunch, because of the presence of two aproned servers. Whether or not Winslow's employees were aware that Trolls' uncouth behavior in public was usually subterfuge, Chumley did not want to be the one who revealed his fellows' secrets.

The waitress close to my end of the table reached for the

serving dish, but I waved her back. Happy to be back in a dimension where my powers worked as I expected them to, I levitated the platter and sent it floating toward him. Aahz speared a slab of meat from it as it went by. Chumley growled and grabbed the plate out of the air, curling one massive arm around it while he tore into the heap of steak. With lightning reflexes, Tananda stabbed over the mighty furred limb and speared a piece from her brother's plate with her belt knife. She chewed the meat off the point of the blade.

Gleep lay on the floor at my side, chewing on a roasted orange-scaled reptile that had been thoughtfully garnished with a sprig of parsley. Bunny breakfasted from a rectangular porcelain platter on which were placed four small square dishes of food, each a different color. Markie's idea of a morning meal involved individual bite-sized items each skewered with slivers of wood. She picked up a small round of savory-smelling meat and nibbled at it.

I went back to the plate of golden-yolked duckhen eggs, over easy, in front of me, my second helping so far. They tasted as good as any my mother ever cooked on our farmhouse's ancient stove. After our experience in Maire, I could have eaten a whole coop's worth of omelettes, along with toast, porridge, juice, fruit, pastries, and plenty of coffee on the side. I couldn't face red meat. Not for a while to come. Thankfully, there was no Pervish food on the table, either.

"We now know at least one of Looie's other hires on the trail of the Loving Cup," Aahz said. "Miss Fancy Pants being so quick on the trigger suggests that there are more agents out looking for it than just us."

"Why didn't she use a death spell to start with?" Tananda asked, reaching over the table to spear one of my pastries. "It's so much more trouble to transport your rivals than kill them. She had plenty of power, so why take the trouble?"

"Not kill? No thrill," Chumley surmised, chewing thoughtfully on a roasted beast leg.

"She might not get a kick out of doing her own killing," Markie replied, "but a trip to Maire is one-way."

"I think it was an accident," I said. "I'm not very good at transference spells. Maybe she made a mistake."

"There was no way that was a mistake," Aahz said. "I felt a magikal barrier hit us as we landed, which means she forced open their border spell to dump us there. That shows intent."

"I have never heard of Maire before," I said.

Tananda leaned back in her chair, displaying a memorable expanse of her cleavage, and addressed our two servers. "Would you two mind giving us the room for a little while? We have business to discuss."

"Of course, Miss Tananda," the male said. He and his fellow Winslovak vanished at once.

"I know all about Maire," Tananda said, returning her attention to me. "In assassin circles, it's a byword for a long and painful exit. Not our thing at all. A knife in the ribs, or a pellet of poison in the wine, make sure the mark is terminated, and out. A trip to Maire is punishment."

I gulped. It wasn't often that Tananda discussed her previous job so openly. She saw my discomfort.

"But enough about that," she said, blowing a kiss my way. "Chumley and I did a little research about standard operating procedure here in Winslow."

"What's that got to do with the Loving Cup?" Aahz asked. Tananda smiled at him.

"Everything. You just have to ask for it."

"We did ask for it," I said.

"No, tiger, we asked how we could find it. We asked for clues to lead us to it. At no time did we make a direct request to have it given to us."

"That sounds too easy," Bunny said.

"It's Deveelishly clever, what?" Chumley said. "Winslow has gained its not inconsiderable renown by fulfilling one's whims, even before one has voiced them. Most of its visitors are content with endless cocktails and attractive companionship, both easily managed. Otherwise, its magik, which as you have already noted is pressed to its limits, would constantly run out, if the staff were forced to grant half-formed wishes to everyone who paid its all-inclusive fee. An item of great power is unlikely to be on the lips of a guest who is only here for the liquor and sunshine."

"Pretty smart," Haroon said, looking up from his bowl. "I never thought about that before."

"Do they really try to grant special requests?" I asked.

"I've seen them just about turn themselves inside out for guests," the Canidian said. "They take their jobs mighty seriously here."

Aahz snorted.

"Is that how the Loving Cup got here in the first place? Someone just requested it?"

"It is possible," Chumley said, with a vigorous nod that shook his shaggy fur. "In fact, it is more than likely. Such items usually occupy a recess in the deepest, most well-guarded of treasure chambers. It would take stealth and magik to remove it without detection. One would assume it would remain where it was until called for."

"And that's why Looie is so angry," I speculated. "Maybe it was stolen from him in the first place. Why didn't he request it himself?"

"Maybe he's tried, and it got taken again. Someone here knew about the unwritten law of Winslow's hospitality customs and exploited it."

"So we exploit it back," Aahz said. "Hand me the steak sauce. Wheedling always makes me hungry."

Haroon led us to the Central Help Desk, which was housed in a palace of its own on the manicured grounds. The eight-sided building's walls gleamed pearl white. In every wall was an open door, and before every door was an enormous mat that said *Welcome!* I noticed that people on their way in wore expressions of deep gloom, pique, or just mild disappointment. Those leaving the office looked happy, some even ecstatic. As soon as we entered, I felt a wave of peace settle over me. We joined a line of guests waiting to be served. Suddenly, I didn't feel very much like complaining. I wanted to go out to the beach again and get one of those tasty blue drinks.

"Don't let the calm spell get to you, big guy," Tananda whispered in my ear. "We're here to demand."

I steeled myself as our turn came.

"Mr. Haroon, how lovely to see you again!" the perky young Winslovak behind the desk said.

"Nice to see you, Turista," Haroon said. "Hope you're doing well. You look mighty pretty today."

She colored a lovely shade of royal blue.

"Very well, thank you so much! And Mr. Skeeve! I hope you are enjoying your stay?"

"Mostly," I said.

A tiny wrinkle marred the perfectly smooth blue forehead.

"Only mostly, sir?" she asked. Her voice quavered, but she brought it under control. "What is wrong? Is our service lacking in any way? Your quarters? The grounds?"

"Uh, no. Everyone is really nice. I like it here."

"Then, our food? Have we prepared something for you in a way that is not perfection itself?"

I shook my head. "I've only had one meal here so far. It was delicious."

"But was it perfect?" Turista seemed truly concerned.

I thought about it. "Yes. It was perfect."

Turista sighed. "Good. We would never want to serve you food that was below our very exacting standards. Then please tell me what problem I may solve for you?"

"Well," I said, trying to keep in mind the precise

phrasing that my partners and I had discussed over the second half of breakfast. "I want something."

Turista lost the sorrowful expression and beamed at me, her small white teeth gleaming.

"We would love to get it for you. What is it?"

"I want the Loving Cup," I said. "I would really enjoy it if you brought it to my room."

"Loving Cup?" Turista asked. She reached out into the air. Her hand returned with a small blank scroll. She took a pen from the inkwell on her side of the desk. "Loving Cup, for Mr. Skeeve," she said as she wrote. She rolled up the small square of parchment and thrust it back into the air. It vanished. "Coming right up, sir. It should be there when you return to your suite. In the meantime, would you like a drink? A Hex on the Beach? Specialty of the house." She nodded to my left. I turned to see one of the male beach bartenders appear with a tray bearing two glasses and a bowl. He handed the first glass to Tananda and the other to me.

"Thanks!" I said. I took a drink. It was decidedly non-alcoholic. They really knew how their clientele thought.

"And one for you, Mr. Haroon?" the server asked, offering the bowl to our guide. "May we make you a reservation at one of our bistros for lunch? As you know, the one next to the Reflecting Pool specializes in Canidian food."

Haroon lifted his lugubrious brown eyes to her.

"No, thanks, just finished breakfast. Got to go water a tree already. 'Scuse me. Thanks a lot, Miss Turista!" Haroon sauntered out of the building.

"So, you think the cup will be in my room soon?" I asked Turista.

"Oh, yes, sir!" the girl beamed. "Please enjoy it, with our compliments!"

Tananda and I walked out sipping our drinks.

"That seemed too easy," I said.

"It certainly did," she said. "I wonder why."

Bunny met us at the door of the suite. Her face was alight with excitement. She beckoned to us to follow her.

"A box came for you. I've tried to open it, but it's bespelled in some way."

"Box" was a distinct understatement. The package that stood on a hall table beside the door to my hotel room stood on a crystal pedestal. Tiny lights danced around it, shedding specks of color onto the perfectly smooth, pale blue gift wrap. It was not only tied with a ribbon but festooned with tasteful bows and tied with a variety of tiny toys shaped like musical instruments. A large card on the top was engraved with the most superb calligraphy I had ever beheld. It read *To Mr. Skeeve.* Aahz stood over it with a stick.

"It hit me with an electric shock when I tried to touch it," Aahz said, his yellow eyes touched with peevish ochre.

"What's the stick for?" I asked, puzzled.

"If I had my powers, I would blast it into next week," Aahz said. "It's a pain having to rely on brute force."

"He has been attempting to open it in advance of your arrival," Chumley said, amusement making his odd-sized eyes twinkle.

"I just haven't got the right angle on it," Aahz said, a little defensively.

"I fancy it won't open because it is not addressed to you."

"Let Skeeve try," Bunny agreed.

When I took the card, the miniature musical instruments rose in the air and began to play a peppy melody. They concluded with an infectious fanfare. I pulled on the ribbon. The wrapping paper fell away. Iridescent bubbles the size of my fist rose to the ceiling and popped, releasing the scent of fresh flowers.

"I'd hate to see what they do when they really go to the trouble to fancy something up," Aahz said, dryly.

In the center of the shimmering paper stood a carved wooden box. It had been painted the same pale blue as the

Winslovaks themselves. I was almost twitching with anticipation. I couldn't wait to see what was inside. I lifted the lid and pushed aside nests of feather-soft tissue paper to reveal the object it concealed, and gasped. I saw a heavy two-handled cup of chased metal on a twisted gold stem. It had magik. I could feel it before I touched it.

"The Loving Cup," I breathed.

I raised it so the others could see it, too. My hands almost burned with the power flowing from the bowl.

"It's not really what I expected," Markie said.

"Mmmph mmmph mmm," Chumley said. He had his hand held firmly over his mouth. Tears began to leak from his eyes. Tananda started tittering, then burst into raucous laughter.

"HA HA HA HA HA HA!"

Brother and sister hooted until they could hardly breathe. Chumley teetered and fell over onto Tananda's shoulder. She held him up while both of them gasped for air, then broke into gales of fresh hilarity. She poked Aahz in the ribs. He leaned in close for a look at the cup in my hands, and exploded with mirth.

"WHA HAH HAH HAH!" He leaned against the wall until his legs gave out from under him. Then he slid to the floor, still laughing. I looked at Bunny. She was giggling, too.

"What's so funny?" I asked, in bemusement. "Isn't this the Loving Cup?"

They all shook their heads, unable to speak.

I examined our prize.

I had seen my share of magik items that looked like the ugly bric-a-brac my aunt kept on her mantelpiece. This one fit into that category, although it was more likely to be the kind of piece she kept in a cupboard unless the person who had given it to her came to visit. The surface of the golden metal had been hammered expertly into the images of people. Trolls and Trollops, to be exact. The physical differences between the genders were more extreme than I had seen in almost any dimension I had ever visited—though I admit my experience was limited. What was certain, and I had proof right there in my hands, was that the dimorphism didn't interfere with their ability to procreate children. Or even practice at procreating. The closer I looked at the cup, the more I realized that the images that had been lovingly hammered into the metal were decidedly explicit. In fact, it could almost have been used as a three-dimensional how-to manual. I felt my face grow hot with embarrassment.

"But it's magikal," I said.

"So is everything in Achael's Joke Shop," Bunny reminded me. "That doesn't make it an important object. This thing is really tacky. It looks like a bachelor-party door prize."

"Then if it's not the Loving Cup, what is it?" I asked.

"It is *a* loving cup," Tananda said. "From Trollia. It's a present for couples about to go on their honeymoons. Some of these cups actually move, so you can see what goes where."

Hastily, I put our prize down, which provoked fresh outbursts from my friends.

"It's not so bad, kid," Aahz reassured me, wiping tears of laughter from his eyes. "You should see the ones from Perv. They're only sold in the Bazaar in private tents because even the Deveels find them too hot to handle."

"Well, it may not look like much, but if Turista said it's the one, then maybe it is. Does it promote accord between two people?"

Tananda picked up the cup by both handles. "Well, I'm no expert, but it feels friendly to me." She smiled and wiggled her shoulders in a manner that made a thrill go through my whole body. "Very friendly. Should we try it out, tiger?" She held one handle out to me. I raised my hands.

"Better not. Looie warned us not to invoke it, or it'll disappear. I need to ask him if this is it. I just thought it would look different."

"How different?" Tananda asked, with one eyebrow raised.

"Well, maybe decorated with people in elegant dress?" I said. "I bet most diplomats negotiate fully clothed."

Tananda ran a finger around the tip of my ear.

"You'd be surprised, big guy," she whispered.

"It doesn't hurt to ask Looie," Aahz said. "I once saw a magik ring that was so ugly it hurt to look at, but it produced a blast that could knock down a wall."

"Ring-knockers?" Tananda asked.

"Yeah. It was one of a set of two."

I put the cup back in the box so I didn't have to look at it, and went in search of Looie.

I found our client in Bunny's former bedroom, sitting over a huge silver mug from which steam was rising. One sniff was enough to tell me the beaker contained a powerful magikal hangover remedy I had had to resort to more than once back in the days when I drank too much. It tasted awful, but it worked. You just had to keep it down long enough for the spell to take effect. Looie clearly had not yet worked up the courage to drink it.

The headache and nausea didn't make him any more pleasant to deal with. He looked at me out of one bleary eye. His greasy hair hung down over the other eye.

"Well?"

"I have your cup," I said, setting the box on the table. Looie immediately hoisted the goblet and drained it. He tossed it over his shoulder. It clanged as it hit, but it disappeared on the second bounce—the Winslow invisible service. Looie looked revived, even enthusiastic.

"Let's see it," he said, beckoning.

Carefully, I lifted the goblet and set it down before him. His eyes went wide. Then his complexion darkened and his jowls shook with anger. He threw the cup at me. I caught it with a dab of magik before it hit me in the chest, but it made me angry.

"What's the matter?" I asked.

"That's not the Loving Cup, you idiot!" Looie exclaimed. "This is pornography molded in brass. The one I want is plain gold, just a goblet with jewels on the handles!" He held his head and moaned. "My head feels as if it's going to explode. I'm going home. The contingents from our neighboring nations have gone back to their homes to bring our proposed terms to their rulers. You have five days. The next time I see you, you had better have the cup for me, or I'll have you hounded to the far end of the dimensions!"

He pressed a gem on one of his outrageously ornamental bracelets and vanished with a loud BAMF, not letting me get in a retort.

I stomped back to my friends and told them what had happened. I shook the cup angrily. I didn't throw it as Looie had done, but I felt like it.

"I just made a complete fool of myself!" I said.

"I hate to tell you I told you so, partner . . ." Aahz began.

"Then don't!" I thundered.

"If you're so smart, why did you go?" he bellowed at me.

"Because I thought I might be wrong!" I said. "This is the cup they sent us! I believed them when they said they'd get it for us!"

"Did the service desk lie to us?" Bunny asked, taking the cup out of my hands and setting it down out of my reach. "I thought Winslow always gave you what you asked for."

"That is what we thought," Chumley said. "This calls for further investigation."

CHAPTER THIRTEEN

"Be very specific what you ask for."

—ALADDIN

I set the goblet down on the Central Help Desk. Turista looked apologetic.

"I am so terribly sorry that this doesn't fulfill your request," Turista said, hastily offering it to the air, which swallowed it up without a trace. "I thought you wanted a loving cup. And since this lady"—she nodded to Tanda—"was with you, it seemed only right that we offer you one that depicted Trollops. Did you have a specific Loving Cup in mind?"

"We do. Did." Trying hard to resist the calming spell that pervaded the Central Help Desk's building, I gave her Looie's description of the cup he wanted. "And it's very magikal," I added. "A very powerful item. One of a kind."

Turista raised her pale eyebrows.

"Then let me see what we can find," Turista said. She set an enormous crystal ball between us on the counter and gripped my hands in hers. "Concentrate, please."

I peered into the ball from the other side. The clear crystal instantly filled with fog. I kept the description in mind and thought hard about diplomats and negotiators holding on to each handle of the cup. Thousands of tiny images spun past my wondering eyes. All kinds of drinking vessels appeared inside the ball, from a beaker carved from solid diamond, to a lowly paper receptacle from the Yellow Crescent Inn. The obviously wrong items popped and disappeared. That left hundreds more, but as Turista squeezed my fingers, those dropped away until only one was left.

From within the clouded depths of the crystal ball, a beautiful goblet arose. The gleaming golden bowl was a perfect inverted parabola, smooth and unornamented. The sapphire-encrusted handles invited hands of any size or shape to take hold. On the pedestal were inscribed runes too small and intricate for me to read.

"I think that must be the one," I said.

"Yes, I see," Turista replied, studying it very closely. She let go of my hands and reached into the air. An enormous silver-bound book appeared on her outstretched palms. She paged through it. "I don't know if the item you want exists in Winslow, sir. It isn't in our inventory list. But we will try to locate it for you. The request has been sent to our Fulfillment Department. Er . . ." Her voice trailed off, as if she were embarrassed at what she had to say next. "Mr. Skeeve, such an item of major importance and historicity is not generally covered in our all-inclusive fee. An extra charge might be levied, depending on how difficult the item is to obtain."

"I understand," I said. "If it's hard for us to find, then it's worth paying extra. But we would only pay a reasonable amount. And I want it as soon as possible."

"We'll inform you as to the cost. It will be your choice whether to accept it." She waved a hand over the surface of the crystal ball, and the picture dissolved into the swirling whiteness. She beamed up at me. "In the meantime, why don't you and your friends take advantage of our wide range of entertainment? We will deliver the cup to you as soon as we can."

"Can I check back with you?" I asked.

"Any time, Mr. Skeeve!" she said, with a smile.

"What now?" I asked, when I had related to my friends what Turista told me.

Aahz shrugged. "I don't know about you, but I've got a massage scheduled on the beach. Why don't you just enjoy yourself? I bet my masseuse Sveda has a partner who could give you a great back rub."

"No, thanks," I said, feeling impatient. "What about the rest of you?"

"Bunny, Markie, and I are getting our nails done," Tanda said, rubbing her fingertips against her brief leather jerkin. "Chumley's got a book he wants to finish. Come and talk to us."

"Gleep!" said my dragon, eagerly. Tananda pulled his head close and scratched vigorously between his ears. His eyelids drooped with bliss.

"Gleep's coming. How about you?" she asked me.

I didn't want to snap at them, even though I thought they were wasting time that could be better used looking for the cup. I no longer really trusted the staff to find it on their own. But I didn't know where to start.

"I think I'll just walk around," I said at last.

"Mind if I join you?" Haroon asked, cocking one ear.

I would have preferred to be alone. I opened my mouth to say so, but he fixed those big brown eyes on me and let out a low, sorrowful whine, the kind of noise Gleep made when I wouldn't let him eat the upholstery. I relented.

"Sure," I said.

Haroon and I set out walking along the wide thoroughfare that led toward low hills in the distance. I saw no vehicles whatsoever, not even a flying carpet. Everyone walked in this dimension.

In the short stretch from the Central Help Desk to the first intersection, I had to turn away blue-skinned Winslovaks offering me drinks, souvenir items, and maps of the resort. Evidently, word got back to the hospitality hub, because the friendly staff stopped bothering us. If I caught their eyes, they smiled. Other than that, they left us alone.

"Some reason you don't want to go relax, Mr. Skeeve?" Haroon asked, after we had walked for a while in companionable silence.

I thought hard for a moment. The tension I felt wasn't normal. I was a pretty easygoing fellow as a rule. I simply couldn't sit still.

"Gee, I just don't feel as if I can," I said. "It's not just waiting for the cup to show up."

"A guy who just saw his whole life pass before his eyes might have a different perspective than someone who spent the night on the beach," Haroon said, with a wise look.

"Uh, yes," I said. I hammered my fist into my palm. "That's it, exactly! I feel like I don't have any more time to waste."

"You're young to get perspective like that, but it's not a bad thing. In time, you'll learn to relax again."

"Never," I said, firmly. "I won't be able to rest until we find the Loving Cup. Then we can go back to Deva, where . . ."

My voice trailed off. I didn't have an extended plan for the time when our mission had been completed. In fact, I felt lost. Something had been taken out of me. I hadn't realized it at first when we returned from Maire. We had been in terrible situations before, but that was the first time I had ever felt utterly trapped with no means of escape. M.Y.T.H., Inc.'s mission was to solve problems for people. To that end, we had walked into plenty of places that were probably just as dangerous. I just had never been so aware before that I might not be able to walk out again.

"How about we just stroll around for a while?" Haroon asked. "Turista and the others will turn themselves absolutely inside out to find you that cup, now that they know exactly what you want. Can't do anything until you have it."

"I suppose not," I said. I glanced around, and my eyes lit on the sign swinging above a pair of wooden doors. It read *The Noisy Toddler.* Tough-looking visitors pushed inside. As the doors swung open, I heard a clanky musical beat. A thirst such as I had not experienced in months overwhelmed me. "I need a drink." I strode toward it.

"Can't stop you, sonny," Haroon said, loping along beside me, "but can an old fellow tell you that I think it's a bad idea?"

"You can try," I said. I threw open the double doors and marched up to the bar.

CHAPTER FOURTEEN

"I believe in drowning your problems."

—THE WHITE WHALE

"May I help you, sir?" asked the motherly Winslovak in the tight dirndl behind the bar.

"A glass of your strongest spirits," I said. "Something to take my mind off my problems."

"Coming right up, sir."

She poured a measure of dark green liquid into a glass, and I knocked it back. The liquor hit the back of my throat like a horde of Trolls taking down a stone wall. I staggered backward and stumbled into an obstruction. I glanced around to apologize and found myself looking down at Haroon. I was abashed at my own rudeness.

"What are you drinking?" I asked, hooking one hip onto the nearest bar stool.

"My usual," the Canidian said to the barmaid.

"Of course, Mr. Haroon," she said, with a smile. "One beef-sheep soup, coming up.

"Don't you want something stronger?" I asked.

"Maybe later, son," the Canidian said. He put his front legs up on the tall seat next to me and hopped up. The server placed a deep crystal bowl before him, partly filled with a savory-smelling, rich brown liquid. He lapped at it. "Mm-mm! This place does pour a tasty potation."

"Same again." I tapped my empty glass. The barmaid refilled it. "And keep it coming for me and my friend."

"Of course, sir," she said, with a saucy wink.

The familiar warmth filled my throat and stomach. It started to radiate outward, stopping the blare of my nerves. They settled down. The next glass relaxed them so much that I felt the muscles in my neck loosen. Then I started to hear tiny voices singing in my head. I glanced around and saw miniature winged creatures hovering next to my ears, playing lyres and singing. I waved an irritable hand at them.

"Get lost!" I snapped. The little fliers looked startled. They buzzed away, muttering irritatedly in their high-pitched voices.

"Sorry, sir," the barmaid said. "I thought you wanted the Green Fairies. They're very good at distracting people."

"That's not what I wanted!" I said. I couldn't tell her exactly what I did want, but like any good bartender she had a lot of experience in translating frustrated hand waves and pent-up expressions.

"Let me pour you something else."

"Uh, yes," I said. "Sorry." It wasn't her fault I had expressed myself badly. "Maybe something a little less, uh, occupied?"

She placed a clean glass in front of me and filled it with a dark brown liquid from a square bottle. It smelled like grease from a cart axle mixed with a handful of cooking herbs. I sipped it. It tasted worse than it smelled and hit me like a dire portent. I gulped down the rest. It had a vile aftertaste, too.

"Perfect," I said, once I caught my breath. "Another, please." I downed the next draught before the flavor could catch up with me. My eyes watered, but I beckoned, and she refilled the glass. Haroon waited patiently for her to ladle more soup into his bowl and took a meditative lap. He looked up at me.

"That was one heck of a situation we were in, wasn't it?" the Canidian asked. "That Wince, and all his henchmen? And the band!"

"I've been in tougher places," I said, turning the glass in my hand. It wasn't bravado to say so. It was true. But why did it sound so defensive when I said it? "Lots of times. Many."

"So, what's botherin' ya about this time, son?"

I sighed and put the glass down.

"I don't know." I tried to put my finger on exactly what was bothering me. "It never hit me this hard before. I just got up and kept going. Maybe this was just one time too many. Maybe I should quit."

"Maybe," Haroon said, tasting his soup. His long, pink tongue swept around his chops, cleaning away every drop. "So, what would you do instead?"

"Why would I have to do anything?" I countered. "I have lots of money. I own an inn. I could go back there . . . Again."

My voice trailed away. The thought of sitting out by myself in that lonely hostelry in Klah made a shiver go down my spine. My previous self-imposed exile was meant to let me do some serious thinking and revising of my opinion of myself. I had done all that. I didn't really want to do it again. Haroon gave me a wise look.

"Sounds kinda borin' to me. Seems like it wouldn't be long before you'd be lookin' around for an occupation."

He was right.

What else would I do? My future had been a serious point of argument between my parents. My mother saw a budding scholar in me. My father, a farmer, the latest in probably a thousand generations to work the land. Neither poring over old manuscripts and teaching youngsters as ungrateful as I had been or backbreaking labor from dawn until after dark suited me. Nor, I had to admit, did thievery, which had been my own chosen profession until I came across the magician Garkin. When he convinced me to sign on as his apprentice, I had nothing better on my agenda. For all the complaints I had made, and I had always been complaining, Garkin had been a considerate master, and I liked practicing magik. Being part of M.Y.T.H., Inc., had given me a chance to be the best magician I could, while surrounded by friends who could fill in when I fell short. I wasn't ever going to be a master mage, but I could probably hack out a living as a small-town spell-caster.

Not that magik was the least hazardous career out there. A stint as a court magician, where my duties were largely ceremonial at best, had still been fraught with life-threatening situations. Still, I had had Aahz to advise me, as well as the people we had met, from whom I had learned other lessons. I drummed on the counter with impatient fingertips.

"I really don't know," I said. "My previous choices were made pretty much under pressure. I like working with my friends. I like to think I'm good at what I do."

"Then what's stoppin' ya keepin' on the way you been goin'?"

I shrugged, feeling sheepish, but I let the words come out.

"I'm scared of dying," I said.

"Aren't we all?" Haroon asked. "You're a Klahd, aren't you?"

"Yes." I went on the defensive for a moment. "So what?"

"Well, your friends are worried about you, too. Every one of them comes from longer-lived stock, and that's just a cold fact. They want you around as long as possible. They really care about you. I can smell it." He tapped his nose with one blunt-clawed paw. "And this smeller is never wrong, my friend."

My heart swelled with pride, and shame, since I hadn't been so good a friend to all of them as I could have been. I've made some mistakes. I regretted all of them.

"I never want to feel I let them down. Or you. I did in Maire."

Haroon cocked his head. "And how did you let us down, son?"

The wave of shame rolled over me again. I could hardly meet his honest brown eyes.

"I panicked! I should have kept my head clear and figured a way to get us out of there. I made a fool of myself!"

"But we got out."

I snorted.

"Only because Aahz tricked me."

"Your friend Aahz is a mighty smart fellah, isn't he?"

"Much smarter than I am," I said. Sometimes I resented it, but at that moment, I was proud of it.

"Well, you trust him, like he trusts you. He told you somethin' and you believed it."

"But it wasn't true!"

"'Zat really matter, young'n? It was the thing you needed to hear that minute. Somethin' we all needed to hear that minute. It got you outta yer slump. You rose to the occasion, son, and handsomely, too. He knew you could do it. He trusted you. You came through. You worked together and saved us all. What's still twistin' yer tail?"

I was reassured by his confidence, but that confidence caused the seething resentment in me to boil over.

"How come the others didn't fall apart like I did?" I demanded. "How come they aren't here with me, drinking the inn dry? Why aren't you?"

Haroon shrugged. "When you get to be my age, son, any day where you wake up breathin' is a good day. Any situation you walk away from don't matter the minute you turn your back on it. It's over. You win *because* you get to go home. Way I read yer friends, they see that. You oughta learn to understand that, or you're gonna tear yerself apart." He studied me and shook his floppy ears. "Maybe you just need a vacation. Ye're in the right place for it, y'know. Have the time of your life. These Winslovaks are the nicest people you could ever meet. They'd take good care of ya."

"Maybe after we find the Loving Cup," I said. "We accepted a job. I don't like the client. Looie's a tough guy to warm up to. But Aahz agreed to his terms. The way I see it, we just have to come through for him. And it's the only way we'll get paid. Then I'll relax."

"Y'all need to relax now, son, or you aren't gonna be too good at looking. You're holdin' yerself back, to my way of thinkin'."

I shrugged. "I can't, Haroon. Maybe at the moment, I just don't know how."

"Uh-huh." The Canidian took a long drink of gravy. "You'll learn."

A heavy arm fell across my shoulders. I looked into the silver-gray face of a Titan. He grinned down at me. I gawked up at him. Titans were dangerous. They were so strong they could tear most other beings apart without really trying too hard. He blew a sodden alcoholic gust in my face. I coughed.

"Sing me a drinking song, Klahd!"

"Sorry, but I don't know any," I said, trying to edge away. He grabbed me with one huge hand that encircled my neck and hauled me back.

"Ya don't? Then sing one of mine! Iss real good," he said, his voice slurring. He leaned on me. I had to use a handful of magik to keep my spine from collapsing under his weight. "Hey! How come I can't see the bottom of the bottle? / Because there's too much liquor in the way! / So I think I better drink a lottle! / My drinking will help clear it all away!" He hoisted a clear bottle and held it to my lips. It was full of blue fluid. The sharp, sweet smell went right up my nose and cleared my sinuses all the way to the top of my head. "Thiss iss the chorus. And, glug, glug, glug! Glug, glug, glug! . . . ! Drink, Klahd!" He tipped the jug, flooding my mouth with the azure potion.

I had no choice but to swallow or drown. Rivers of liquor ran out of the corners of my mouth. I gulped down the most I could. The Titan finished the chorus and reclaimed the bottle.

I gasped in a deep breath of air. With the back of my hand, I dashed the side of my mouth to dry it. I missed a couple of times but eventually cleared my face. The blue liquor was hot enough to burn my skin.

"Now you sing it, and I'll drink!" the Titan said.

"Uh, bayme not," I said. My words were starting to mix themselves up. I tried to clarify. "I'm sing much of a notter. I mean, a mucher not of sing." I heard low growling behind me. I turned around. The bar was full of Titans, all of them swaying as much as or more than my new companion. They showed their teeth. While not as fearsome as Aahz's four-inch choppers, these were sufficiently threatening to sober me halfway up. "All right. Sure! Um. Hey! How come I can't see the bottom of the bottle . . . ?"

To my surprise, I found that the Titan's tipple had improved my singing voice. The more I drank, the better I sounded. When I finished caroling the chorus, with the help of all his Titan friends, I grabbed the jug and gulped another mouthful on my own. The liquor didn't burn so much that time. In fact, it tasted pretty good.

"Thass right, Klahd!" the Titan said, slapping me on the back so hard my chest bounced against the edge of the bar. I gasped, but I didn't let go of the bottle. He held it up to my mouth and started pouring. "I'll verse the singond seck. Won't you join me in another joyous skinful? / There's plenty more booze in the jug to share / Leaving this much liquor would be sinful / Come drink with me and wash away your care!"

Haroon sat on his bar stool and grinned at me.

CHAPTER FIFTEEN

"Sometimes the cure is worse than the disease."

—H. JEKYLL

A piercingly shrill sound went through my head. I sat bolt upright and looked around. Water trickled down my face. I wiped it away, but it kept coming. I tilted my head up, and a cascade of water poured down on me. I sputtered. It took me a while to figure out exactly where I was.

I sat astride a gigantic marble frog, which also spat an arc of water from its wide, pursed lips into the twelve-foot-wide stone pool of a massive ornamental fountain. Somewhere in my memory, I recalled seeing it not far from the entrance to the Noisy Toddler. But why was I sitting in it? The thought baffled me. All the noise wasn't helping while I tried to clear my mind.

Barely an arm's length from me were the six Titans, now draped against one another's shoulders and snoring deeply, chest deep in the pool, not at all disturbed by the water raining down on their heads. The first one still had the big bottle clutched to his chest, though it was upside down now. All of them wore wreaths of pink and yellow flowers on their broad foreheads. I ran my hand through my hair and came away with a handful of pink petals. I guess I had one, too.

I didn't remember exactly how we had ended up in the ornamental stone fountain outside the Noisy Toddler, but it must have seemed like a good idea at the time.

Not to my friends, however.

"Skeeve!" The high-pitched noise resolved itself into words. Specifically *a* word. My name.

Bunny stood at the edge of the rimmed pool, alternately glaring at me and Haroon. The Canidian reclined nearby on a park bench. He looked cheerful and well rested.

"What is the matter with you?" Bunny asked him, her voice shrill. "How could you let those Titans take advantage of him?"

"No advantage taken at all, little missy," Haroon said, jovially. "He just needed to have a little downtime. I kept an eye on him all the while, you know. As a friend."

"But he's drunk!"

"No," I said. I staggered to my feet, unsteady because the bottom of the fountain was slippery. I splashed over to her. "I'm not, honest. In fact, I feel pretty good!"

"How much did you have to drink?" Bunny asked, narrowing her eyes at me.

"A lot," I admitted. "I lost control. But whatever that barmaid served me didn't act like Deveelish liquor. I feel as though I didn't drink anything at all."

Bunny looked at the state of my clothes. I probably didn't look too good.

"How is that possible?" she asked.

"Local brew," Haroon said, with a wise nod. "About ninety proof magik. Tole ya Winslow would take care of ya, my friend. You ready to get back to work?"

I grinned because I felt like smiling. I stepped out of the fountain, grabbed up a double dose of magik from the nearest force line, and dried my hair and clothes instantly. In spite of sleeping under a cataract, I didn't have a cold, or a headache, or the bad-tasting dry mouth I used to get when I drank too much wine. I felt as if I had had a month's vacation overnight. No wonder people loved to visit this place.

"You bet I am."

"Your nails look nice," I said. I strode beside Bunny. For all that my legs were much longer than hers, I struggled to keep up. Haroon galloped along behind us, his long ears flapping. "Is that a new outfit? It goes really well with your polish."

"Hmph!" Bunny kept her chin high and her eyes on the graveled path ahead. She didn't look at me. Nor did she look down at her dress, a form-fitting garment of deep sapphire blue that matched the shade of her nails and set her hair off becomingly. She was very angry. I tried again to open a neutral-sounding conversation.

"Did Gleep behave himself?"

"Hah!"

"Did you have a good time?" I asked.

"Mmph!"

"Why are you angry with me?"

Bunny whirled to a stop and grabbed a handful of my shirt collar. She yanked it down hard, bringing me nose to nose with her. I found it hard to face her glare.

"After all the time it took to get you to put yourself back together, you throw it away and try to drown yourself in a bottle!" she said.

My shoulders drooped.

"I'm sorry. I'm not proud of myself. I . . . I just couldn't stop thinking about being back in Maire. I'm better now."

"Are you going to do that again?" she asked.

"No! Honestly!"

"I just want to know," Bunny began, with tears starting in

her wide blue eyes, "if this is going to keep happening. I can't keep caring about you if you are going to do that to yourself. It's too hard!"

I was horrified at how hurt she looked but angry at her lack of trust.

"I'm not! Why would you assume that one slip means I'm going back to the way I was?"

"Because . . . because I've seen it happen! I can't go through that time again!"

I caught her wrists and held them.

"You don't have to! I promise!"

A Deveel woman with a huge blue shoulder bag over her arm passed us at that moment. She glanced at Bunny's hands.

"Hey, love your manicure! Where'd you have it done?"

Bunny, startled, smiled at the stranger.

"Thank you," she said. "I went to Doot's, down near the beach."

"Well, they did a great job," the Deveel said, looking at her claws as though comparing them with Bunny's. "I ought to get an appointment. Who was your stylist?"

"Um, I think her name was Concertina."

"Thanks!" The Deveel hoisted her purse and walked off. Bunny glanced back at me. I faced her with the most sincere expression I possessed.

"I'm not going to drink too much anymore," I said. I drew her over to the nearest bench. She resisted, but I made her sit down and alit beside her. "I promise. This was just one time. It hasn't happened since . . . well, you remember."

She nodded but clearly couldn't trust herself to speak. Her nose grew pink. I felt in my belt pouch for a clean handkerchief, but I didn't have one. A vine growing down from a tree next to the bench twisted to display several overgrown buds. One of them burst open to reveal large white petals of tissue thinness. I plucked one and handed it to Bunny. She buried her face in it. I sat helplessly as she cried. I didn't know what else to do. I never did know what to do when she was unhappy.

"I'm sorry," I said. "It won't happen again. I can handle myself. I will handle myself."

She wiped her eyes with the petal and raised her face to mine. The sorrowful expression she wore tore at my heart.

"I'm sorry, too," she said. "I didn't mean to take it out on you. I feel guilty that all of you got into trouble in Maire. This is all *my* fault."

If I was confused before, I was baffled now.

"No, it isn't. Why do you say that?"

"Because I insisted we stay on the job. We don't have to. I'll figure out a way to . . ."

"To what?" I asked. "Are you in some kind of trouble?"

"No," she sighed. She looked around for a place to put the petal. A blue-winged bird swooped out of the sky and plucked it out of her hand. She rose and began walking again. "Not exactly. I was so worried about you when you didn't come back last evening. And then to see you in that fountain . . ." She giggled. "Actually, you looked silly."

"I felt pretty silly, too," I said. "It's the first time that ever happened to me."

"It's a wonder you didn't drown."

I stood up and extended a hand to her.

"I was safe," I said. "Winslow took good care of me, even when I didn't take good care of myself."

"Where was he?" Aahz asked. He lay in a hammock swinging between two palm trees. The fronds fanned him gently. He had a tall glass in his hand filled with bright pink liquid and topped with skewered fruit and a stick with an eyeball on it.

Bunny pursed her lips and shot a cautionary glance at me.

"In a fountain. Asleep. With six Titans."

"Sounds more like me than you, tiger," Tananda said, coming over to enfold me in a cuddly embrace. To most people, it was a wildly passionate kiss. To a Trollop, it was just a morning peck on the cheek. I enjoyed it even while it overwhelmed me. Gleep came racing over to give me a happy slobbery slurp of his long tongue. I enjoyed that, too, but not as much. The slime he left on my face smelled of rotten meat.

"Gleep?" he asked.

"I'm all right," I assured him. He whacked my leg playfully with his tail and galloped in a circle around me. He jumped away and bounded over to Haroon. The two of them sniffed one another's tail regions.

So we weren't going to mention my failure to keep sober. At least at that moment, if I read Bunny's expression correctly.

"Like my nails?" Tananda asked, brandishing a full set of inch-long claws. They were painted emerald green. Rainbow sparks flew out of them every time she moved.

"Gee, I like the effect," I said.

"Thanks, big guy," she said, running the sharp tips down the side of my face. I quivered. She laughed.

"Has the Loving Cup shown up yet?" I asked, to cover my embarrassment.

Tananda unwound herself from me and sashayed over to a hammock tied at one end to one of Aahz's trees. She swung into it and patted the netting invitingly.

"Not yet. Come and lie down. I'm sure it'll be along in a while."

I shook my head.

"No. I'd rather concentrate on our mission. I'll keep looking."

"Why?" Markie asked. She toasted me with her bright orange beverage, garnished with a cherry, a paper parasol, and long strands of silver tinsel. "They'll come and get us when they find it."

"I'm tired of waiting," I said.
"So go ask again," Aahz said.
I didn't want to sit still, so I went.

"Not yet, sir." Turista was off that morning, so I spoke to a new Help Desk helper, Porta. She checked the crystal ball and several notes that she pulled out of the air, then shook her head. "So sorry, Mr. Skeeve. I don't have a record of it being here in Winslow."

"But it *was* here," I insisted.

"Did you see it?" Porta asked.

"Well, no . . ." And again, I didn't want to go into details of the magician-thief we had found ransacking the room. "But my friend Haroon followed the scent to the last place it had been."

"Oh, yes, Mr. Haroon!" Porta said, and smiled. An enormous gold-trimmed ledger appeared in her hands. "Yes, I see. He investigated a room that subsequently had to have several repairs done to it."

"Uh, I'm sorry about that," I said. "I said we'd pay for the damage."

She waved away my offer, as all her colleagues had done.

"The magik mirror in that room had to go in for counseling, so I can't ask it what became of the room's contents until it comes back. But I promise you, Mr. Skeeve," she said, fixing large, sincere eyes on mine, "we are looking for the right cup, and it will be in your hands just as soon as we can find it."

"Thanks," I said. What else could I say? No news was . . . well, no news. I planned to keep looking, just in case. I returned to my friends.

CHAPTER SIXTEEN

"Everything on this list is important!"

—MOSES

"Owwww!" **Chumley bellowed, as a group of young** Deveels raced away, a tuft of his purple fur clenched in one of their hands. "Crunch punch!" But they were out of reach in an instant. We had just emerged into the sun from the Winslow Museum of Hospitality. My notion that the Loving Cup might be on display there turned out to be a false hope. All of us were caught off guard by the sudden attack.

"I'll get them," I said. With determination, I took to the air. Then I saw a plump, slightly balding but rather distinguished-looking Winslovak male in a white jacket. I thought it would be better if the local authorities handled the matter. I flew over to him and explained what had just happened.

"I'm sorry," he said. His name tag read *Servis.* "They should not have troubled you, Mr., er, Crunch. It's all part of the

Scavenger Hunt we have going on today. Wouldn't you like to play?"

"Scavenger Hunt?" I asked. He turned to me eagerly.

"Yes, sir, Mr. Skeeve the Magnificent! We have several group competitions going on. Everyone loves them."

"Crunch despise. Game not wise," Chumley warned, shaking a gigantic fist under Servis's nose. The Winslovak bowed deeply.

"I'm so sorry about that, sir. The Troll who was supposed to be the source of fur today is in the middle of town. Those Deveels shouldn't have troubled you, sir. I offer you our deepest, most heartfelt apologies!"

Chumley allowed himself to be mollified.

"Deveels lazy, drive me crazy."

"It's all in good fun, sir. Come and play!" Servis looked around at my friends. "You have a large enough team to qualify. Except for you, Mr. Haroon. You have an unfair advantage, since you are a professional investigator who works with our staff now and again."

"That's no problem," the Canidian said, easily. "I won't help look, but I might just hang around with my friends here."

"That's allowed," Servis said, with a smile. "Campfya!"

A cheerful female in white shorts and a bandanna top rushed over to me and handed me a blue-tinted parchment scroll and a large white sack.

"What's all this?" I asked her.

"It's simple. Find all the items on this list by midnight tonight and win a prize!"

"Big deal," Aahz said, holding up his hand and beckoning. A waiter appeared out of thin air and presented him with a bucket-sized goblet sloshing with beer. He glugged down half the brew and let out a sigh of pleasure. "What do we get? A T-shirt? No, thanks."

"No, sir!" Campfya said. "Winslow offers only attractive prizes to our honored guests! One hundred gold pieces!"

Bunny's big blue eyes shone. "A *hundred* gold pieces?"

"Yes, Miss Bunny!"

"We don't have time for a distraction like that," I protested. "It would be better to keep looking for the cup."

Bunny turned to us.

"No! We need to win this. It would be great to earn an extra hundred."

The rest of us looked at one another. I was more determined than ever to get to the bottom of her concerns about money.

"We're overqualified," Aahz said, with a yawn. He handed the empty pail to the server, who promptly vanished. "But it might be entertaining to shellac the competition while we're waiting for the cup to turn up."

"So you will enter?" Servis asked. His face creased in a delighted smile.

"Yeah, why not?" Aahz said. "What are we looking for?"

Campfya tapped the parchment in my hand. I unrolled the scroll and read down the list.

A handful of Troll fur
A Deveel's hoofprint
A Klahdish expression
Two ounces of pink sand
A blank look
Some blue air
A pair of dice
Dragon breath

I skimmed down. I wasn't sure what a few of the items were, but I was sure the others would know. Then I read the final entry:

The Loving Cup

"What?" I demanded. I pointed to the final item. "Why is this on the list? It's one of a kind. That's supposed to be ours! We're waiting for it to be delivered."

Servis looked at the list. His kindly brows drew down.

"Oh, my. That wasn't on the original list. There should be only twenty items. I have it here." He reached into the air and pulled a purple-rimmed scroll out of nothingness. "You see?—Oh, my courteous aunt, it is there! That's not right!"

"How many groups are on this Scavenger Hunt?" I asked.

"About a hundred and fifty," Servis said. He looked worried, but no more worried than I felt. "Someone has tampered with the list!"

"But who?" I asked.

"Your girlfriend," Markie said, in a flat voice.

"She's not my girlfriend!" I exclaimed. But the expressions on my friends' faces told me they didn't believe me. "Look, Servis, we put in a request with the Central Help Desk. They promised to deliver it right away. They can't do that if it's part of a resortwide game."

"I will try to get to the bottom of this, madams and sirs," Servis said. "I will research the matter thoroughly, I promise you!" He and Campfya trotted away.

Bunny took the scroll out of my hands.

"We *have* to win this now," she said.

"But why would she, I mean the other magician," I corrected myself hastily. "Why would she need other people to find the cup for her? She found it before, or at least where it had been."

"Simple," Aahz said. "Because she can't take it from where it is by herself. She has got to be privy to the inner workings of Winslow's operation. So, what's the problem?"

"The problem is," I said, "that if you invoke the cup, it vanishes. Everybody working for Looie knows that. But there's nothing in the instructions to keep anybody from who finds it from testing it out to see if it works."

Tananda clicked her tongue.

"She can't be that stupid," she said. "We know she isn't. So what's her game?"

"I don't know," I said. "But it means we have to get to the cup before anyone else, or we won't know where in the dimensions it went."

All at once, the peaceful mood of Winslow became as wild as a tavern after the tapping of a new keg of Deveelish ale. Instead of lying on the beach, sipping blue umbrella drinks and listening to mediocre musicians plunking away at various forms of stringed instruments, groups of holidaymakers ran from shop to hotel to garden square, looking for the items on their list. They shook sacks already partly filled with finds from the list. My friends and I knew we were starting at a disadvantage.

"Who wants to hold the bag?" Aahz asked.

"I will," Bunny said at once. "We ought to divide up the list."

"In a minute. First, number one," Tananda said. She beckoned to Chumley to hold up his arm. The big Troll cringed.

"But, Little Sis, it hurts when you do that!"

"I'll try to keep it painless," she said. Chumley held still with admirable patience while his sister plucked a sizable pinch of fur from the back of his arm and placed it in the bag. A check mark appeared beside the first entry on the scroll.

"Another easy one," Aahz said. "Dragon breath. I can't believe they want a dose of halitosis. They must mean fire."

"But Gleep's fire will just burn the bag up," I pointed out.

"Gleep!" my dragon agreed.

"Piece of cake," Aahz said, with an expansive sweep of his hand. "Remember when I taught you to levitate? Same thing."

I frowned. "How could it be the same thing?"

"To lift yourself off the ground, you use magik to push against it. The same principle applies here. Take some magik out of the force line. Picture it forming a globe with one arc still open. Like a hollow ball with a hole in it. Imagine all the force pushing inward. Got it?"

"I think so," I said.

It was easy enough to pick up a small quantity of magik from the wavy blue force line that ran beneath our feet. In my mind, I shaped it as Aahz directed. It formed a bubble about the size of my fist, pale green, right in front of my stomach. I nodded.

"Good," Aahz said. "Show me where it is."

I held my hands on either side of the globe.

Aahz turned to Gleep.

"Can you breathe into that?" he asked. "Without causing a massive house fire or giving Skeeve a hotfoot?"

"Gleep!" my dragon protested, hurt in his large blue eyes. But he flared his nostrils and took a deep breath.

I turned my face to one side as Gleep exhaled a narrow stream of bright golden fire directly toward me. The heat was unbelievable, but to my delight and amazement the force bubble absorbed it all.

"Close it, kid!" Aahz bellowed. I turned back to look. The lance of dragon breath bounded around inside the globe, trying to find a way out. A tongue of flame licked out of the one place on the bubble that faced my dragon. Swiftly, I pinched the opening shut. The fire kept ricocheting around, drawing patterns of red light against the magikal surface.

"That's one neat piece of magik!" I said, turning the small orb over and over. "Thanks, Aahz!"

"It's nothing special," Aahz said, with a shrug. "Just doing my job as an instructor. Looks like you still need continuing education, if you never worked out that you can use magik to press against other substances or itself for other purposes on your own."

My face grew as hot as the bubble.

"Maybe if you'd explained that in the *first* place, I would have known it!"

"Some people figure it out without being told! I didn't realize your aptitude was so low you never tried to experiment!"

"You always stressed how dangerous it was!"

"You won't know how to minimize the danger if you don't try!"

"Boys, boys," Tananda said, putting a hand on each of our chests and shoving us away from one another. "Let's get a move on. There are a lot of things to find!"

"What about a Klahdish expression?" I asked. "What does that mean?"

Aahz shrugged. "Same thing as a blank look, is my guess."

"What?" I asked. Suddenly, a pink haze covered my face. It moved outward and shrank to an oval the size of my hand. In it, I could see my own reflection. My mouth was open and my brows were high up. Two check marks appeared on the list.

"Perfect," Markie said, gleefully. "Just don't let anybody else get you to make that face, and we're ahead of the game. And don't let your dragon breathe fire anywhere else, no matter what."

I patted Gleep's head.

"He's pretty smart," I said. "He knows not to give help to the other teams."

"Gleep!" my dragon said.

"What about you?" Aahz asked.

"What *about* me?" I asked.

"Try not to let anyone surprise you. It's too easy."

"Don't worry about it," I said. I couldn't help feeling resentment that he believed I was so gullible. I stuck up my chin. "I'll be on my guard from now until the end of the contest."

Aahz shrugged.

"Let's cut straight to the chase," he said. "None of the other stuff really matters. Putting the Loving Cup on the list means it's somewhere in plain sight somewhere in this resort that Miss Fancy Pants can't get at without help. Split up and search. We'll meet for dinner at the Rusty Hinge and compare notes."

"I say," Chumley exclaimed. "A practical notion, that."

"Sounds good to me," Tananda said.

"What about Skeeve?" Haroon asked. "Seems to me that young lady has targeted our friend here. If she's really behind this, then he's vulnerable on his own."

"I can take care of myself," I insisted.

"Do you want company?" Tananda asked me. I appreciated her concern as much as I resented it. I waved away the suggestion.

"No. Why don't you stay with Chumley? He's in more danger than I am! The rest of the groups will pluck his pelt bald to get item number one!"

"I say!" Chumley protested, looking down protectively at his coat. "Perhaps I should go home to Deva for the duration."

"Not a chance," Tananda said. "I'll look after you, Big Brother."

"Thank you, Little Sis. We shall be a team, what?"

"I'll come with you, Skeeve," Markie said. "She'll think you're running the race with your baby sister."

"Gleep!" my dragon said, leaning his head against my leg.

"Thanks, buddy," I said. "No, thanks, Markie. I'll take Gleep. The rest of you go ahead. We'll be fine."

"Why don't you team up with me, pretty lady?" Haroon asked Bunny. "I can't help you find items, but I can show you around."

"Thanks," Bunny said. "Want to come along, Aahz?"

"No. I'll make better time on my own."

"Me, too," said Markie. "I do better alone."

Tananda rolled the list tightly into a solid rod, then waved a hand over it. When she unrolled it again, it had increased from one sheet of parchment to five, each with just a few of the mysterious items on it, though all the lists included the Loving Cup. Tananda handed one to me with a kiss.

"See you later!" she said. The group split up, following hordes of other teams all running and shouting to one another.

Aahz's assessment made sense. The girl was on the trail of the Loving Cup, the same as we were. I guessed that she must be one of Looie's other agents. If only I could speak to her, I was sure we could come to some kind of equitable arrangement!

"If only she doesn't try to have me killed again," I said, glumly.

"Gleep!" my dragon exclaimed, slurping my face.

CHAPTER SEVENTEEN

"Missed it by that much!"

—SISYPHUS

With the beach just steps away, I had no trouble obtaining two ounces of pink sand. Just to keep in practice, I sealed it into another force bubble like the one Aahz had just taught me to make. A check mark appeared on the list in my hand beside that entry. I read down below it.

"But where do we find blue air?" I wondered aloud, as we threaded through the narrow lanes filled with shops.

My partners never believed me when I told them how smart Gleep was. He lollopped around behind me and put his head in the small of my back.

"Gleep!" he exclaimed happily, and pushed me forward.

"Where are we going, boy?" I asked. Guided by nudges from behind, I walked around the corner and into a side street. Three doors down, my dragon stopped pushing me. He snaked his long neck around and slurped me in the face.

"Ughhh!" I protested. His stinking breath almost distracted me from my errand. But I understood. It meant that we had arrived. I looked up at the sign swinging above us. We were in front of the Rusty Hinge. "Good dragon!" I said, grabbing his head and scratching vigorously between his ears. No one ever believed me when I said how smart he was.

"Gleep!" my dragon said, with a blissful expression. He shook loose from my grasp and bounded forward. He bumped the neatly painted doors open with his head and glanced back at me. I followed. All I had to do was wait for the inevitable: someone having an attack of bad language.

I didn't have long to wait.

Part of a table swooshed past my nose as I entered. It looked for a moment that the person swearing might be me. It crashed into the nearest wall. I threw up a handful of force to protect me and Gleep from flying splinters.

"You cheat, I beat!"

A Troll brandishing a leg of that table faced a couple of Imps and a female Deveel. Scattered cards told me what must have ensued just before my arrival.

"It wasn't us!" the Imps insisted, almost in unison. "It was her!"

The Deveel woman had evidently dealt with Trolls before. She sidled up to him and ran her long claws up and down his hairy arm.

"You're not going to believe Imps over me, are you?" she asked, in a wheedling tone.

"All foul, no fair! I rend and tear!" the Troll bellowed. He flexed his muscles, throwing her halfway across the room.

"Why, you molting rug!" she shrieked, catching herself in midair. She came at him, her fingernails aiming for his eyes. "How dare you accuse me of foul play!"

The Troll batted at her again, knocking her squarely into the two Imps. They had been trying to make a quiet escape.

The Deveel landed on top of them. All of them fell into a Kobold who had just crossed the threshold.

"#%#=?>!" he declared, symbols spewing from his mouth and circling around his bulbous gray head. They were tinted an unmistakable blue!

"Good boy!" I praised my dragon. My newly learned spell at the ready, I jumped forward to capture some of the Kobold's symbols. They dodged me all over the front room of the inn, but I pursued them with determination. At last I trapped a puff of the blue air between my open bubble and a pane of window glass. I felt triumphant as I closed the spell. The symbols danced and shuddered within their magikal prison. The Kobold, still prone on the floor, looked abashed at his attack of invective.

"☹," he said, his gray skin darkening to charcoal.

"It's nothing personal," I assured him, helping him to his feet. "I would have said worse if they'd landed on me."

"Mind your own business, Klahd!" the Deveel screamed, shaking a fist in my direction. Gleep jumped in between us and snarled at her. She backed away. Without a control rod, no Deveel ever challenged a dragon. I noticed that he was careful not to breathe fire in her direction. Who knew if she was a contestant or not?

I hadn't been in the Rusty Hinge since our first day in Winslow. The Loving Cup could not have been there then, or Looie would have spotted it. It had certainly been in that hotel room for a time, but I guessed that it had been removed by the time we caught the girl magician searching for it. So where could it have gone?

Since it had become a clue in the Scavenger Hunt, my guess was that it was hidden in plain sight. An inn was the ideal location. If you wanted to hide a cup, where would you put it? In the midst of hundreds of other cups.

All I had to do was find it.

Admittedly, it wouldn't be easy, or one of the other teams would find it first. It had to be so cleverly concealed that only someone willing to look at things in a different way would spot it.

Still, my friends and I knew more about the cup than anybody else participating in the hunt. We knew what it looked like and had an idea of some of its properties. We also knew that it was very magikal.

All throughout the inn, steins, mugs, cups, and all manner of things to drink from stood on shelves or hung on the walls on pegs, hooks, nails, and dabs of pure magik. Some might have been purely for decoration, but I saw the bartender and his assistants reach up to take cups down to serve their customers. The rest were fully functional. But that didn't mean the Loving Cup might not be used to serve liquor.

"Stay here, boy," I commanded Gleep. He settled down in an empty inglenook beside the massive stone fireplace and put his head on his front paws.

I strolled idly through the public rooms of the inn. If the cup was part of a game, it couldn't be hidden in any of the private rooms upstairs. Most likely, it was right there in front of my eyes. I scanned the drinking vessels being used by the customers, looking for the familiar shape and jeweled handles.

The usual bar brawl was under way. The temperamental Troll had resumed his seat at a new poker table and pounded his fist on its top. The Imps and Deveel that he had been fighting with had left. Instead, a fast-talking Landshark, a Werewolf, two Djinn, and a Gnome took their places, and the broken furniture disappeared as if it had never existed. The Gnome shuffled the cards, letting the Werewolf cut.

The Troll was a sore loser, though. He started a fight with the Werewolf almost immediately over the way he stacked the cards. Like the rest of his kind, the Werewolf was impatient and took offense easily. Both of them reached for cups and trenchers to throw at each other. I ducked a flying jug.

It shattered on the wall over my head. I sputtered angrily as beer splattered me and everybody in a four-table radius.

"Hey!" yelped a tall, muscular Whelf in a tight yellow tunic sitting on a nearby bar stool. His conversation with a fetching Fairy in a low-cut pink gown had been interrupted by the rain of ale. He stood up, towering over me, and leveled a fist at my nose. "What do you think you're doing? My coat is soaked!"

I shoved his hand out of the way.

"I didn't splash you. Look at me! I got wet, too!"

"Who did it?" he demanded.

I pointed. The Whelf's eyes followed my finger. The combatants were grabbing bottles off nearby shelves and heaving them at each other. The Troll flexed his enormous muscles and let out a bellow that shook the rafters.

"They did."

"*They* did?" The Whelf's voice rose to a squeak. "Well, I'm sure they didn't mean to do it." He turned back to the Fairy, who rolled her big green eyes.

"You're kidding me, right?" she said, scornfully. "You're afraid of a drunken Troll?"

"You bet I am, sister," the Whelf exclaimed.

"He's smart," said an Imp female in a low-cut blouse. She sidled up to the Whelf and wound her arms around his elbow. "Anybody with any sense wouldn't get near a wrecking ball like that!" The Whelf looked down at the bright-pink girl in bemusement but beamed at his stroke of luck. The Fairy gaped in outrage.

"You get your hands off him! I saw him first!"

The Imp turned up her nose.

"Looks like you were about to abandon your claim, honey. Better luck next time."

"You won't have a next time! You're going to have to find your nose in some other dimension!" The Fairy leaped into the air, her wings buzzing. She brought up her feet and kicked the Imp backward. The Whelf, having more sense than to get in the middle of their brawl, ducked behind me. This time, I rolled my eyes. Then I, too, edged away.

I walked around the Rusty Hinge several times. Although a few of the drinkers had two-handled cups in front of them, none of them was the one I was looking for. But would the magician who placed it here have left its appearance unchanged? I wouldn't have, and I was by no means the most devious person I knew.

So it was likely disguised. All I had to do was look for a cup giving off a magik aura and dispel the glamour concealing it. I was pretty good at that simple cantrip. I glanced around for groups carrying the list and bag that declared them my opponents in the Scavenger Hunt. I didn't want to give them any ideas.

It was better to go through the bar in a methodical fashion. At the very back of the inn were several small tables divided by low walls. A few of them were occupied by couples holding hands and looking at one another intently. All along the top of the low walls were lines of steins and tankards. A blue-enameled stein with an ornamental pewter lid gave off a visible glow of magik. I pointed a fingertip at it, sending a filament of magik into it. If the stein was disguised, that would remove the concealment.

Nothing happened. It remained a stein. I guessed that the spell it possessed had nothing to do with shape-shifting. Deva, the dimension in which M.Y.T.H., Inc., did business, had lots of cups bespelled to keep the beer from poisoning the drinker. Considering the underhanded behavior that was typical of Deveels, that was just a simple precaution. I tipped up the tankard to see the bottom. Yes, as I guessed, it bore the mark of a Deveelish potter.

I went down the wall, checking each magikal beaker in turn. A few of them were disguised. One particularly gaudy figured goblet with gold leaf rim and foot, and a handle in the shape of a curvaceous Trollop, turned out to be a plain wooden tankard, although there was a naughty picture of the same Trollop in the base.

I glanced at the nearest sconce. The candle in it had been at least an inch higher when I started looking around. I was wasting time. I couldn't look at just one mug at a time. I needed to do several at once.

The irregular yellow force line that ran above the inn yielded enough magik for me to fill up my inner reservoir. In order not to attract attention, I focused my aim on just the twenty or so cups balanced on the next section of wall. Three mugs changed shape. I paid attention only long enough to realize none of them was the Loving Cup. I gathered more magik and threw another dispel charm at the next row of cups. Nothing.

"Hey!" an outraged male voice bellowed. "You told me you were a college girl!"

"But I am!" a female voice replied. "I'm just nineteen!"

"Nineteen hundred, more likely!"

I peeped around the corner of the booth. A Pervect stood glaring at a twisted, wizened, wrinkled creature. It was a Hag. She had on a trim white blouse and a flared plaid skirt with a big, perky bow that stood upright in her stringy, orange hair. I gulped. She spotted me as I tried to duck behind a nearby chair.

"You!" the Hag shrieked, pointing a wrinkled finger at me. "You did that! You ruined my date!"

"It was an accident!" I said. She crossed her forefingers. A ball of red-hot energy gathered in their junction. With a roaring crackle, it hurtled toward me. I dodged just in time. It just singed my ear before blasting a shelf full of knick-knacks into shards. She threw another one that exploded the chair I had ducked behind for cover.

"Hey, baby," the Pervect said, his eyes lighting up. "I didn't know you could do *that*!"

Surprised, the Hag stopped throwing fire at me. She wound her way into the Pervect's arms and looked up into his yellow eyes.

"I can do a lot of things, even better than that."

"Oh, yeah?" the Pervect asked, with avid interest.

"Oh, yeah. Come on back to my room, and I'll show you."

I was completely forgotten. I wiped my forehead with relief as they disappeared.

With disappointment, I surveyed the debris on the floor. Among the broken pieces were many that shimmered with magik. Not knowing whether the Loving Cup could be destroyed, I removed any glamour I could. No luck. All the pieces belonged to very ordinary drinking vessels.

The same held true for the next hundred or so I examined. I was running out of magik and time.

I moved up into the gallery that looked down on the main bar area. Over my head, a thousand more tankards hung on hooks. Dozens of them radiated with magik. No one was nearby to catch an accidental backsplash of my spell, so I gathered up as much power as I could and threw it at the ceiling. Several of them dropped their original appearance, but one in particular twinkled with light. To my delight, a dusty old tankard changed from gray to golden and sprouted a second handle across from the single one holding it on its hook. The bowl of the cup even seemed to be the right shape. Could it be the Loving Cup? Could I really have found it this time?

I kicked off from the railing and flew up to look at it.

Before I could reach my goal, something closed around my ankle and pulled downward. Helplessly, I fought to regain some magik, any magik, to save me. I swam upward against the air. I almost got free, when my captor yanked hard on my foot. I plummeted to the floor and landed with an audible thud. As I lay moaning, I looked up at two moon-shaped eyes and a purple-furred face.

CHAPTER EIGHTEEN

"I've been thrown out of better places than this."

—ADAM

"Klahd play nice! Cards, not dice."

It was the gambling Troll. He showed all his teeth in a fierce scowl. I scuttled backward on all fours.

"No, I can't play cards right now," I said. "I'm on the Scavenger Hunt." I retrieved my copy of the list and my bag from the floor. "See? I can't stay."

"Never mind what you find," the Troll said. "Play with me. Later see."

"But, I . . ." I almost pointed upward, and then I realized that other teams might be among the patrons crowding the bar counter. I didn't dare look up in case anyone followed my eyes. I could almost see the golden cup beckoning to me. It was just overhead. If I could just distract the Troll for a moment . . .

He picked me up by one arm and slammed me down into an empty chair at his table.

"You play or I slay!"

I glanced at the other players. A resentful-looking Deveel with a scrawny beard sat to my left with his arms folded. To my right, a Vampire woman in a low-cut black dress, dark sunglasses, and high-heeled shoes filed her black-painted nails. On her other side a miserable little wormlike being in a tasteless flowered shirt hunched nervously. The Troll wasn't going to let any of us go without playing at least one hand.

"All right," I said. I exchanged a few silver coins for a small stack of blue chips. I could afford to lose that much. Then I hoped the Troll would let me go back to my quarry. I hoped no one would notice the cup in the meantime. It took every bit of self-control I had not to look up toward the ceiling. Out of the corner of my eye, I saw people walking up into the gallery. Were they carrying white sacks with them? My fingers twitched nervously.

The Troll slammed a deck of green-backed cards down in front of me. I shuffled it. I had had plenty of experience playing Dragon Poker with my friends in the Even Odds casino in Deva.[6] I had picked up a few tricks over time, none of which had to do with accumulating winning hands. The rules were too complicated for me to follow, especially the daily, even hourly rule changes, not to mention the specific regulations depending on which seat you occupied or the color of the deck. I enjoyed the game, but to me the greatest pleasure was the camaraderie with my fellow players. If I wasn't good at winning, I could at least amuse the other players.

I flipped half of the deck, cascading the cards down in a showy stream. Once it had rejoined the other half, I ruffled the two together, pulling my hands higher and higher until

6. See how Skeeve came to acquire a share in a gambling establishment in the stirring adventure tale of *Little Myth Marker*, a must-have addition to your library.

the cards were bouncing off the table. The Deveel grinned, showing his sharpened teeth, and the wormlike fellow applauded openly. Even the Troll was amused. He laughed and slapped the Deveel on the back.

"Five cards, odd Elves wild," I said, flicking cards out to each of the other players. They gathered and sorted their hands.

The Vampire pushed a chip forward with one sharp nail.

"One silver," she said.

The wormlike fellow clutched his cards nervously. He plunged forward as though he were going to fall into the table and shoved all his chips into the pot.

"Nine silver," he declared.

"No way! Bad play!" the Troll bellowed. The little male recoiled, but he kept his cards clutched against his chest.

"Don't yell at him," I said. "Call him."

The Troll slammed a handful of chips into the center of the table, making everything else on it jump.

"Ten blue, call you."

The wormlike fellow quivered nervously, then shoved his cards into the center. He folded.

I read my cards again. I couldn't believe my eyes. I had the ace, three, five, and nine of Elves, with a dragon joker. Four wild cards meant I had five jokers. It was the highest hand possible for the day and time. I kept my face straight until the betting came to me.

"Eleven blue," I said.

The Troll threw chips into the center. They bounced and danced, but landed in the pot.

"Bad call! Show all!"

"You're betting out of turn," I said.

The moonlike eyes widened until I thought they would pop out. The Troll rose to his feet.

"You dare! No fair!"

"I dare because you're not being fair!" I said, rising in my turn. If I started an argument with him, it was my best chance to get away from the table and examine that cup.

"Aaarrrrggghhhh!" The Troll didn't like being questioned. He grabbed the front of my shirt and hauled me across the table. He raised his fist, the cards still clutched in it.

"Look," I whispered to him, as he shook me. "I have a friend who is a Troll, Big Crunch. Will you take it easy on me?"

The Troll's left eyelid lowered a fraction. Then he twisted his grip and flung me across the room.

I scrambled to capture some of the magik in the line below the inn, but I came up almost empty. With only a fraction of the power I needed, I used my magik to soften my fall, but I couldn't change my trajectory. I crashed into a table of Deveels. They had just been served drinks by the barmaid. Their steins of beer went flying. Heads of white foam splattered their red skins, not to mention my clothes and hair. I sprang to my feet.

"Sorry!" I said, brushing off the nearest Deveel with a cloth napkin.

"Klahd!" one of the Deveels exclaimed. He rose to his feet, dripping beer. He put his fists together. A ball of energy hit me under the jaw. I flew up in the air, my ears singing from the blow. I grabbed for one of the rails that surrounded the gallery but missed. I pushed down against the ground with what little magik I had left, but it wasn't enough. I plummeted down toward the Deveels.

"Oh, no," said a female Deveel. With one finger, she arrested my fall. "You want him, you take him!" She tossed him back toward the Deveel who had hit me.

That Deveel snarled and ducked. I slammed into the wall behind him and slid to the floor.

"You owe us a round of beers, Klahd!" he bellowed, as I climbed uneasily to my feet.

"I'll order it!" I promised.

"I mean *this* order!"

I frowned at him.

"You want me to clean this up and serve it to you again?" I asked, unbelievingly.

"No! Just clean it up!"

And with that, I found myself being swiped back and forth like a rag across their table and chairs and over the floor underneath. One of the Deveels even used me as a towel to dry off. My clothes became saturated with ale. I fought to free myself from their influence, but they had much more magik than I did. All I could do was think myself out of the situation. I let my head go limp as they passed me around the table.

"Oooh," I said, clutching my stomach and putting a hand over my mouth. "I'm getting dizzy! I think I'm going to . . ."

"No!" one of the females shrieked. "You're not going to get sick on me!"

She grabbed me by the foot and heaved me over her shoulder. I flailed at the air, unable to catch myself. One of my arms struck an obstruction. I looked up from the floor when I landed. A Titan with a faceful of foam glared down at me. I had hit him just as he was taking a drink.

"Clumsy Klahd!"

He threw a punch at me. By this time I had regained my feet. I ducked to avoid his blow. By chance, the biggest of the wet Deveels was right behind me. The Titan's fist hit him square in the chin. The Deveel staggered backward, a circle of little red birds twittering around his head. His eyes rolled back in his head. He sagged to the floor. The Deveel's friends rushed to confront the Titan.

"You owe him for damages!" the first female screamed. "He just got his chin fixed!"

"I don't owe him or any Deveel a single copper piece!" the Titan shouted, towering over them. His voice echoed in the enclosed room.

"And interest!" the injured Deveel yelped, picking himself up painfully from the floor. "Look at these bruises! I shall have to go back for more quackery, I just know it!" He pointed to his jaw. It was dark purple on one side.

"Then I'll even it out!" the Titan said. He raised his fist and smashed the Deveel in the other side of his jaw.

"He did it!" the second Deveel female shrilled, pointing at me. "That Klahd! First he spilled our beer, then he hit you!"

I was already backing away, but the room was so crowded that I didn't have much room to maneuver. Instead, I took what small measure of magik I could glean and disguised myself as an elderly Imp in pants pulled up to my chest and a loud yellow shirt that clashed with my bright pink skin.

"What Klahd?" I asked, in a quavering voice.

"You're hiding him!" the Titan boomed. He grabbed for my belt but got only a handful of my tunic instead. I could change my appearance, but not the reality beneath it. The Titan's eyebrows went up, then down. He swept his hand past my face. I could feel the disguise spell lift. He raised his fist.

"Now, wait a minute," I said, holding my hands up to forestall the punch I knew was coming. "There's no need for violence!"

"Klahd cheat! *Me* beat!"

The Troll thundered over. He showed his tusks in a fearsome snarl and loomed over the Titan.

"You give, you live!"

"Are you threatening *me*?" the Titan demanded, leaning close to the purple-furred face. They were almost as strong as Trolls.

"Now, fellows," I said, trying to extract myself from the Titan's grip. "There's no need to fight. I'll just be on my way . . ."

The Troll took hold of my right arm. "No way! Klahd play!"

"You want half?" the Titan said. "No problem!"

The Titan seized my left arm. He pulled. I yelped as my arms were extended almost to the point of popping out of their sockets. The Troll picked up the nearest chair and battered the Titan on the head with it. The Titan fought back, grabbing cups and platters off the tables and throwing them at the Troll. I danced, trying to avoid getting hit by the missiles. I couldn't soak up enough magik to protect myself or pull free from my captors.

"Gleep!" I shouted, looking around for my dragon. "Help me!"

"Hey!" said the big Deveel, with bruises evident on both sides of his face now. "Are you ignoring me? You'd better make good on these injuries. Look at me!"

Without letting go of me, the Titan shot out with his free fist. The Deveel took the punch full on the jaw and measured his length on the sticky wooden floor. The rest of the Deveels mobbed the Titan, scratching and kicking and employing every dirty move I'd ever seen in a bar fight. He pointed a finger at each in turn, knocking them several feet away. A few of them retreated, but the others closed in again, screaming threats.

"Hey, let go, let play!" the Troll demanded, shaking me like a rag doll.

"Shut up!" the Titan bellowed. The Deveels threw spell after spell at him, covering him in red-hot Scorpion Flies and raining down Blue Slime. The Deveel who had been punched in the face climbed unsteadily to his feet and fell on top of me. Under his bulk I could see legs of red, gray, or purple scuffle around. I danced to avoid getting kicked. Suddenly, a loud voice interrupted the argument.

"All right! Enough! Break!"

The bruised Deveel staggered back. I hauled in a huge gasp of air and looked over to see a Winslovak no taller than

I was regarding the combatants with his hands on his hips. He wore a plaid shirt and heavy blue-Djinn trousers under a white apron.

"Who started this?" he asked.

The Titan and the Troll looked at one another sheepishly. Then, as one, they pointed at me.

"He did," the Titan said.

"I did not!" I yelped.

"Who spilled our beer?" the Deveels demanded.

"Who hit me in the back?" snarled the Titan.

"Well, I . . ." I began.

"Sorry, sir," the Winslovak said, in a calm but implacable voice. "You'll have to leave now."

I glanced up toward the ceiling. "But I . . . it's not my fault! No. I'm not going . . . !" I sat down in the nearest chair and attempted to look casual.

The Winslovak waved a hand. Suddenly, I felt myself dangling by magik by the back of my collar and the seat of my pants. He marched toward the swinging double doors with me floating helplessly behind him. The doors parted. I protested, but the invisible hands tossed me easily out into the street. The Winslovak surveyed me with deep regret as I lay on the blue flagstones in front of the Rusty Hinge.

"It probably would be a good idea not to come back in here until you've learned some manners, sir," he said. The Winslovak dusted his hands together and turned away, and the doors closed behind him.

My bag was still inside! I picked myself up and pushed with both hands at the double doors. They wouldn't budge. I summoned up all the magik I could muster from the yellow line overhead, though I admit it wasn't much, pictured the doors swinging open, and flung it and myself at them.

The doors opened, all right, but outward, not inward. I went tumbling backward. Suddenly, my bag and scroll came hurtling out of the door. They skidded several yards into the public footpath. I scrambled to retrieve them before it was trampled by a horde of children led by two cheerful employees wearing whistles around their necks. I brushed myself off, trying to regain some of the dignity I had just lost.

I was annoyed but at the same time oddly proud. In all the time I had been in Deva, I'd never been thrown out of an inn. I had passed a milestone. Too bad none of my friends had been here to see it.

Speaking of my friends, where was Gleep?

As if he could hear my thoughts, the doors of the inn parted. My dragon came galloping out. In his mouth was an object that twinkled in the sunlight. Gleep dropped it on the ground with a clang and slurped me with his long pink tongue.

"Gaaaah," I protested, scrambling to my feet. "Stop that!"

Gleep looked hurt.

"I'm sorry, fellow," I said, scratching him between the ears. "But why didn't you come and help me?"

"Gleep!" he said, with a wise look in his eyes. He bent his long neck and nudged the object on the ground toward me with his nose. It was the golden cup. I dove for it. My dragon was so smart! When I couldn't retrieve it, he had! I grabbed Gleep's head and massaged between his ears, admiring the prize he had brought me.

"Good boy!" I exclaimed. "So you spotted it when I took the disguise off?"

"Gleep!"

"It did kind of stand out, didn't it? I hope no one else saw it."

". . . Gleep . . ."

Gleep made a noncommittal noise. I guessed what he was thinking. I shrugged.

"So someone else spotted it, too. But you got to it first."

"Gleep!" my dragon said, his blue eyes wide with innocence.

Something in his voice worried me. I crouched down and took his muzzle in my hands so he couldn't look away.

"You *did* get to it first, didn't you?" I asked him, staring him straight in the eyes. "You took it fair and square, right?"

Instead of answering, he slurped me with his long pink tongue. When I let go of him to wipe the noxious slime off my face, he pulled away and raced off down the street. I glanced at the door of the Rusty Hinge. I hoped that no one had gotten badly hurt, especially not by my dragon. I would probably never know. Gleep only spoke when he wanted to. I felt a trifle guilty.

But I had the cup! I tucked it into the bag and sat down to wait for my friends.

"So this is the Loving Cup," Aahz said, turning my prize over in his hands. Since I was temporarily banned from entering the Rusty Hinge, we had taken the recommendation of a friendly young male Winslovak at the Central Help Desk to try the Skewer and Corkscrew, a popular restaurant several blocks further inland. I had asked for a private room where we could talk without being disturbed. Except for the waiters in knee-length trousers sashaying in and out of the room with a dozen kinds of roast meat on long metal pikes who were completely immune to my warding spell, it was pretty quiet. "Doesn't look like much."

I had to agree with him. The bowl, although beautifully wrought, was plain gold. The jewels inlaid on both handles were plain precious and semiprecious stones. On the whole, I doubted whether it would bring more than four gold pieces in any curio shop in Deva.

Tananda took hold of one of the ear-shaped handles. "Should we try it out to make sure it's the right one?"

Chumley adjusted the pair of gold-rimmed pince-nez he

had balanced on his rather large nose and peered down at the cup.

"Better not, Little Sis. I say, I believe we have confirmation," he said.

"Where?" I asked, eagerly. "Does it say so? Is it etched in the metal?"

Chumley chuckled. "Not at all, old fellow. I refer your attention to the scroll that you were careful enough to bring back with you, along with your, er, sack of swag. Peruse the final item on the list."

I unrolled the sheet of parchment. All five items that I had searched for had big blue check marks beside them, including the final one: The Loving Cup.

"That just seemed too easy," Bunny said. She examined the cup as if she were afraid it was going to change shape in front of her. "I can't believe that Skeeve just spotted it hanging on the ceiling."

"Why?" Aahz said. "I told you we were overqualified for the game. We've got experience unmatched across the dimensions, and this contest was set up for bored accountants on vacation who want to burn off a few of the calories they've been eating at the buffet. The important thing is Skeeve found the cup."

"Gleep!" my dragon protested.

"I found it, but Gleep got it," I corrected Aahz.

"Whatever," Aahz said, impatiently. "When we're finished eating, we can pop over to Looie's dimension and get rid of it."

"No!" Bunny protested. She set the cup down in the center of the table. "Let's collect the prize first. A hundred gold pieces is a substantial sum."

We couldn't argue with that.

"Why not?" Markie said. "We got all twenty-one things on the list, probably broke a few records doing it. I don't mind rubbing the other teams' noses in our victory. Then we can blow this pop stand."

"Well, cheers to ya, friends!" Haroon said, raising his face from his bowl full of soup. "Y'all done right well gettin' done so quick. Winslow contests always have a little bit of a twist in 'em."

"Well, we saw through their disguise spell," I said, toasting the Loving Cup with my wineglass. "That wasn't much of a twist."

"I told you, partner," Aahz said, pouring himself another huge mug of ale. "Bored accountants and vacationers."

"Gleep!" exclaimed my dragon.

CHAPTER NINETEEN

"Good staff is hard to find."

—DR. F. N. FURTER

According to a little scroll delivered to us with dessert, contestants in the Scavenger Hunt were invited to a party at Winslow Center at the stroke of midnight. In no kind of hurry, we finished our meal and complimented the restaurant staff on their skill.

As we departed, the servers lined up and created an arch with their swords between us and the door. I proceeded down it, feeling a bit like a successful general after a hard-won campaign. And since I knew a successful general, Big Julie, now retired, of Possiltum, I understood why he regarded the end of a battle with regret, exhaustion, a little annoyance, some embarrassment for the praise he received, and relief that it was all over. I couldn't wait to get back to Deva. Who knew how many assignments we had missed while we were in Winslow? And I hadn't checked on Buttercup since we had left. I was sure the war unicorn was fine in his pasture behind our auxiliary office. I had a standing agreement with the little curly-nosed girl who lived next door in the dimension into which that building extended to feed and curry him daily. She was as thrilled to have a unicorn to care for as I was to find someone so devoted to looking after him. But I liked to sit in the field and watch him graze, play with Gleep, or pretend to charge and skewer invisible enemies.

The way to Winslow Center was well marked with torches that burned with blue flame. Hundreds, if not thousands, of holidaymakers crowded the path with us, not all carrying the official collection sacks denoting them as Scavenger Hunt teams. I suppose that the rest just wanted to watch the prize-giving and celebrate a little. I preened as I went along, listening to them speculate among themselves. They didn't know yet that my friends and I were the grand-prize winners.

I was struck by an uncomfortable sense of familiarity as we passed under a squared-off arch into the crowded torchlit arena. Although it was almost as bright as day, I half expected a big, wooden stage hung with black velvet curtains and Wince stalking back and forth with a sword in his hand. I ran a finger around the inside of my collar. Gleep bumped against my leg and snaked his head up to look me right in the eye.

"Gleep!" he said, warningly.

I shook my head, as if to dislodge the memory.

"You're right, fellow," I said. "It's not the same. We're here as winners!"

I gagged at the putrid smell of his breath as he licked the side of my face.

"Gleep!"

As each team entered, a young resort employee joined us and took us to an individual small table behind a braided blue rope barrier. Our guide identified herself as Fayva. Her white hair was tied up with blue ribbons in little ponytails that stuck out over her ears. She had a clipboard and a feather pen in one hand. She shook our hands vigorously with the other.

"Congratulations on finishing the hunt!" she said, beaming. "Now, let me see your items. We have to verify them to see how you did!"

With a satisfied smile, Bunny opened the white sack and began to take our finds from it. Fayva ticked off the items on her clipboard. I thought our collection looked snazzier than the others, with the dragon breath rocketing around inside the little force globe.

". . . Pink sand—everyone found that one," Fayva said. ". . . Dragon breath. Much rarer! Oh, but you have your own dragon," she added, as Gleep came to lean against her side. "Aren't you cute?" He licked her cheek. She didn't seem to mind. "Troll fur . . ."

I glanced around while she counted.

Not all the groups had managed to locate even the twenty non-unique items on the list. A quintet of Kobolds stood with shoulders drooping while the young male Winslovak checked off the twelve that they had brought in.

"-@%=?" their leader asked.

"Most people have more than you," the Winslovak admitted, with a sympathetic smile. "But, hey! It was a fun day, wasn't it?"

The Kobolds conferred among themselves.

"½ ☺. ½ ☹," their leader said, at last.

"Don't worry! We have new games every day. You'll win one of them, I'm sure. The day after tomorrow is a mathematics competition! I am sure you'll beat all of the participants in that one."

The Kobolds brightened up. I turned back to my friends.

"And the last item," Bunny said, presenting the golden goblet with a little flourish, "the Loving Cup!"

"Well done!" Fayva said, checking off the final entry on her clipboard. "That makes six of you."

"Six?" I asked, puzzled. "There's seven of us."

"Oh, not your team," Fayva said, laughing. "You found all twenty-one items! Five other teams did, too."

"That's impossible," Tananda said, pointing to the cup. "There's only one of those."

"Not at all, Miss Tananda," Fayva corrected her. She pointed to a nearby table. Six Deveels were jumping up and down and hugging one another. To my shock, a standing cup with two handles was among their collection. "They have one, too. There were only a limited number out there, so you were lucky."

"Wait a minute," Aahz said. The ochre veins in his eyes started to protrude with anger. "That's one of a kind! The others must be fakes! You can't count them."

"Not according to my instructions," Fayva said, patiently. "But congratulations! You're one of the finalists for the grand prize!"

"We should be the only ones to win," Bunny argued.

"I'm sorry. You'll have to wait for confirmation from the judges!" Fayva reached above our heads and pulled on an invisible rope. A blue halo appeared above us. From the stands, a cheer went up.

"Hang on a minute! Come on, kid!" Aahz said. He grabbed my arm and pulled me over to the Deveel team. They, too, had a halo above them. He pointed to the cup on their table. It looked exactly like the one I had found, jeweled handles and all. "Can we take a look at that?"

A hefty Deveel woman with dark cosmetic outlining her eyes pushed in between us and the cup.

"For how much?"

Aahz snarled.

"What do you mean, for how much? All we want to do is look at it!"

"If you want it that badly, it must be worth something to you." She put out her palm. "One gold piece."

"Not a chance!" Aahz bellowed.

"All right, two!"

"Two! My offer is zero!"

"Then you don't get to look!"

"Never mind, Aahz," I said, tapping him on the shoulder. "I'm sure that one's a fake anyhow."

The female rounded on me. "A fake! We found it fair and square, you Klahd! Here! See for yourself!" She snatched up the gold cup and shoved it into my hands.

Trying not to smile, I closed my eyes and tried to picture the aura around the cup. In my mind's eye it glowed with a golden light, just like the one that we had.

"Congratulations!" I said. I was reluctant to give it back to the Deveel, but she snatched it out of my hands. "Looks like you found the right one! C'mon, Aahz, let's go back."

"Well?" Aahz demanded as soon as we were out of earshot.

"It's magikal," I said. "But I can't tell what its spell is."

He frowned. "This whole setup is fishy. We'd better take a look at the other so-called winners."

We had ample opportunity to size up the competition. Soon, six haloes hovered above the crowd of contestants. Aahz and I pushed through the mob toward the hovering symbols and had a look at their collections. As Fayva had said, there were six groups who had finished the whole list. All of them had a gold cup in their possession identical to ours. All of them gave off the same aura as the one we had. We reported back to Bunny.

"That's impossible!" she said, looking worried. "Are you sure we have the real Loving Cup?"

"I don't know," I said. "There's no way to make sure."

"How can there be six of them?" Bunny asked.

"Maybe the wizard who crafted them made several," I said. "Diplomacy is a necessary art in all the dimensions. I mean, if there can be thousands of novelty Genuine Fake Doggie Doodle with Real Fake Smell That Really Sticks to Your Hands, why not six useful cups that can help forge accord between warring parties?"

"Novelties are one thing," Aahz said. "Complicated magik items are different. That cup's the work of years of crafting. You're not going to see a single magician devoting the rest of his life to making identical copies of one piece, and I've never heard of a sweatshop that made major artifacts in bulk, not even in Deva."

"But which one does Looie want?" I asked.

"Does it matter?" Aahz asked. "We'll collect them all and hand them to Looie. Let him figure it out. He'll get six for the price of one."

"Well, well, congratulations!"

A balding and distinguished Winslovak appeared at our side. He favored us with a jovial smile.

"How nice to see you all again!" Servis said. "Congratulations on being one of our finalist teams!"

"There's been some kind of mistake," I said.

"Oh?"

I pointed to the cup. "We thought there was only one Loving Cup. It looks as if there are six. Some of them might be fake."

"Well, there was only one real one," Servis said. "I did check with the Central Help Desk. You do have first claim on it. But we have all these people we have to make happy! Our panel of independent judges has to verify all of the finds to determine who is the winner of the contest. Then you can take it wherever you wish."

"I guess that will be all right," Bunny said.

"Good! I'll be back just as soon as I can," Servis said. He vanished.

"Hey!" Aahz bellowed. I turned. The table where our collection of scavenged items had been was empty. A general outcry arose around us. All the artifacts had disappeared.

CHAPTER TWENTY

"If at first you don't succeed, try, try again."

—HENRY VIII

I turned to Fayva. "We can't let that cup out of our sight!"

"It'll be back soon, sir," she said, patting my hand reassuringly. "The judges rarely take more than a few minutes to make their decisions. In the meantime, why don't you enjoy the dance?"

"What?"

A band struck up and began to play lively dance music. Fayva swayed to the beat. She held her arms out to me. The other resort employees encouraged the contestants and the audience to join them. I backed away.

"I'm not much of a dancer," I said.

"Oh, come on, Mr. Skeeve," she encouraged me. "Anyone can dance to this music!"

Chumley came to my rescue. He moved in and swept the dainty Winslovak off her feet.

"Crunch prance, great dance!" he exclaimed. They whirled

away in step to the music. I suppose I shouldn't have been surprised that the enormous Troll was light on his feet. After all, he had worked in covert security. But he showed skill that impressed some of the people near us into applauding. I was grateful for his intervention.

Servers plied their way through the enormous gathering with trays full of drinks and bite-sized canapés. Three eager waiters crowded around me, each enjoining me to try the treats on their platters.

"You cannot go wrong with donk eggs filled with caviar!" the first one said.

"Skewered gingerfish!" the second said, waving bits of bronze-colored meat on a small metal spike in front of my nose. The savory aroma interrupted my worries over the cup. I started to reach for one.

"Oh, Mr. Skeeve, these are the ones for you!" insisted the third, elbowing his companions aside. "Lizard-bird dressed with woodland berries! A taste of your own home dimension!"

I looked at the last-named with bemusement. The components of that dish would have described pretty accurately the results of woodland foraging I used to bring back to Garkin's hovel in the woods. I took one, to the delight of its purveyor, and chewed it thoughtfully. The lizard-bird had been barbecued over a charcoal fire. The flavor brought back memories of my life before Aahz had appeared in Garkin's magik circle. No one could possibly have known what that time was like for me. How things had changed! Instead of starvation fare, those foods were being presented to me here as gourmet delicacies. It just proved I didn't understand fine cooking.

"Take more!" the waiter said.

"No, try mine!" said the first server.

"You will really love gingerfish," the second said. "It's like nothing you've ever tried before."

My stomach rumbled. I didn't realize that I was so hungry. How long had it been since I had breakfast? Platter after platter revolved before my eyes, each offering me morsels so delicious that I couldn't wait to try the next one. Gleep sat next to me, his eyes shining, as I tossed him samples from the plates. He chomped each out of the air and licked his chops.

"It's been long enough!" Aahz said, breaking into my thoughts. I put the last tiny skewer back on the nearest tray. He tapped Fayva on the shoulder. She turned away from Chumley and began to dance with him. "Cut that out! Where's our stuff?"

She beamed. "I will go and check how the judges are doing," she said. Just then, a shrill noise sounded over the arena. "Wait! It's happening now, Mr. Aahz!"

The dance music died away. A high platform appeared in the middle of the roped-off area. Several Winslovaks appeared on the stage. A handsome male of mature years whose white hair was combed straight back over his head, giving him the look of a Klahdish noble, held up his hands for silence. He wore a waist-length white tunic, short trousers that revealed muscular legs, and a golden whistle around his neck on a ribbon, the source of the blast that I had just heard.

"I hope you are all having a good time!" he said. His hearty voice carried to the far edges of the gigantic enclosure. "Many of you lovely people already know me. I am Discus, the head of the Activities Center here in Winslow!"

A cheer went up from the crowd, probably from past visitors.

Discus acknowledged the applause.

"Thank you all for making today's Scavenger Hunt such a success! Our panel of judges"—here he nodded to the others with him on the platform—"have made their decisions! Let me get the formalities over with, and you can get back to the dance! We have six teams who all brought back every one of the twenty-one items on the list. Let's give a big hand to them now!"

Although no one near me was clapping, I heard the sound of wild acclaim.

"Canned applause," Aahz said out of the corner of his mouth.

I wondered how noise could be preserved in a tin. It was probably a spell like the one I had used to seal up a sample of Gleep's breath.

". . . Our sixth-place winners earn a purse with fifteen gold pieces! Will the team from Caf come on up here? Yes!" Discus and his fellow judges clapped enthusiastically.

Four Caffiends, beings with Klahdish torsos atop long, sinuous snakelike tails, slithered up the blue-painted staircase. A lovely young Winslovak female met them at the top and escorted them to the judges. Discus handed them a certificate and a dark blue purse tied with a golden cord. The lead Caffiend, a male whose pupils were smaller than the tip of my knife, waved jubilantly to the crowd. The wild cheering erupted again.

One by one, the teams that had sported blue haloes were escorted up onto the judges' platform and given their awards.

The third-place winner was a mixed group like ours, with one very insistent Imp who held their purse of twenty gold pieces up over his head and shook it in triumph. He was so excited that he slid all the way down the steps to the ground. He picked himself up, still grinning.

". . . And in second place, Team Deva! Let's get all those Deveels up here!"

"I protest!" the female wearing heavy eye makeup complained as soon as she reached the top of the steps. "Why are we the runners-up? We got everything you asked for, and we clocked the fastest time of all!"

Discus put a chummy arm over her shoulders and turned her to face the crowd.

"All of the items for which you searched today were locally sourced, madam. Now, since there was nothing about that in the rules given to you by our wonderful staff—let's hear it for the activities staff!—but that dragon breath you brought us had just a *tiny* scent of Deva about it, didn't it? As well as a few of the others? So, please, accept this fine purse containing fifty shining gold pieces!"

The Deveel woman snatched it out of his hand. Ignoring her Winslovak escort, she stomped down the wooden steps, her hooves raising sparks out of sheer fury. Her group followed sheepishly behind her.

"I bet they popped back to Deva and collected everything on the list from the Bazaar," Markie said, with a wicked grin. "I've hired some of their personal shoppers. They do all the bargaining for you for a fee. It wouldn't cost more than a fraction of the prize money."

"We should have done that," Aahz said.

"No," Bunny said. "It would have been an extra expense!"

"And in first place," Discus said, holding out his hand to us, "also from Deva, Team M.Y.T.H., Inc.!"

In almost indecent haste, Bunny ran up the steps. I ran to catch up with her. Chumley put on his most fearsome grimace and snarled at the audience. The rest of us just smiled as Bunny collected our dark blue purse; the certificate, which had all our names on it in beautiful gold letters; and the congratulations of the judges.

All the other teams were awarded ornately lettered certificates of participation and a box of blue candies as a consolation prize.

"One hundred gold pieces," Bunny said, as we descended into a crowd of well-wishers with a comely young female showing us the way. The band music rose and the canapé servers moved in with fresh trays. The podium, with the panel of judges, vanished silently. Bunny shook the bag. It jingled impressively.

"That's a lot of cash," I said.

"Gleep!" my dragon said, looking at the bag avidly. I held him back. He liked to eat gold.

"They can afford it, I dare say," Chumley said, admiring it through his eyeglasses. "What? Our resort fee rather adds up. Three gold pieces a day per person? It would take very little time for them to recoup even the large prize we have just won."

"This is going to look *so* good on our bottom line!" Bunny exclaimed.

"It sure is," I agreed. "Haroon, you earned a share."

"You certainly did," Bunny said.

The Canidian shook his head until his long ears flapped. "That's right nice of you fellows, but I can't accept it. Didn't really help much. Just showed Miss Bunny around the place. She did all the lookin'. Just keep the money. I got plenty buried around."

"So, how long until we get our stuff back?" Aahz asked our perky escort. Her name was Grays.

The girl looked blankly at us. "Sorry, sir?"

"Servis just took our stuff away with him. We want our items back."

Grays smiled and shook her head.

"Oh, you don't need them back, Mr. Aahz! None of them are worth anything."

"That's not true," I said. "One of them was unique. The gold cup? The Loving Cup?"

"That was an ordinary cup, sir. It wasn't magikal at all."

"Yes, it was," I said. "I know how to detect if an item has magik or not. I'm a magician."

"Yes, I know," she said, with a wide smile. "You are Skeeve the Magnificent. We are so pleased to have you at our resort!"

We all looked at one another.

"I told you this smelled fishy," Aahz said. "Didn't Servis

tell us that the cup got onto the list by accident? And suddenly there are five other cups just like it floating around for just anyone to find?"

"Yeah," Markie said, her eyes narrowing. "He must be working with that girl."

"Not necessarily," I said, automatically. I realized what I had said, and clamped my mouth shut for a moment to think. "Yes, you're probably right. It makes sense that they are working together. Unless . . ."

"Unless what?" Bunny asked.

"Unless both of them are working separately for Looie. She might have more magik at her command, but he can get the whole population of the resort to work for him just by making a game out of it."

"And we fell for it," Tananda said. "Good thinking, tiger!"

Bunny moaned.

"The cup was here all the time," I pointed out. "Why couldn't he take it out of the Rusty Hinge by himself?"

"Perhaps he didn't know where it was," Chumley suggested.

"With their magik and resources?" Aahz scoffed. "That seems a stretch."

"What about it?" I asked Grays and Fayva. "If one of you wanted to, er, borrow something that was on display in an inn, wouldn't you just go get it?"

Both females looked at me aghast.

"No, sir! Employees are not permitted to take any items from one venue to another," Fayva explained.

"It gets too confusing when we have to sort it all out," added Grays.

"What about guests?" I asked.

"Oh, they can move anything they wish," Fayva assured us. "Winslow is a place to enjoy yourself! If you really want to take all the mugs out of the Rusty Hinge, please go ahead!"

"So he was waiting for us to bring it here so he could steal it," Aahz said. "I like the way this guy thinks."

"That still doesn't give us a cup to bring to Looie," Bunny pointed out. "How do we get it back?"

The two girls looked at one another.

"We don't know where he went," they said. "You should put in a special request at the Central Help Desk."

"We already did that!" I yelped.

"Come on, kid," Aahz said, hooking me by the collar. "Let's go rattle some cages."

CHAPTER TWENTY-ONE

"It's all about motivation."

—D. CARNEGIE

"**I can't believe we had the Loving Cup in our hands and** let it get away!" Bunny exclaimed.

I kept my gaze fixed on the path in front of me. I didn't want to say out loud that it was Bunny's determination to win the extra hundred gold pieces that had given Servis the opportunity to take it from us. I knew she was thinking that anyhow. All of us were.

Turista was on night duty when we reached the round building in the middle of town. No one was in line, so we went right up to the desk. She put her task aside and waited for us with a pleased smile.

"How nice to see you and congratulations on your win, Mr. Skeeve, Miss Bunny, Mr. . . . !"

"Can the roll call," Aahz said, sharply. Turista nodded. "What can I do for you?"

"You already know we won the Scavenger Hunt," I said. "So you probably also know that the Loving Cup was part of the hunt. We found it, but it vanished along with the other items. We want it back now."

"Of course, sir!" she said. "I will send a request to the Activities Department right away." She pulled a blank scroll from the air and wrote on it with her blue pen. It vanished out of her hands. A moment later, a parchment appeared above the desk. It dropped into her waiting palms. She unrolled it and read. A tiny wrinkle appeared between her brows. "Oh, dear. This is most unprecedented."

"What is?" Bunny asked.

Turista turned a woeful face to us.

"All of the items have disappeared! The judges looked them over, as they always do, but when they returned from giving the prizes, the collections were gone!"

"Servis stole them," I said. Turista looked shocked.

"Servis? That's not possible! He's one of our most reliable and willing employees. Everyone trusts him!"

Aahz looked grim.

"Sounds like the perfect setup for an inside job," he said. "So what are you going to do about it?"

Turista pulled her shoulders back.

"We will do our utmost for you, sir," she said. "We will search night and day! We will find the cup and get it to you as soon as we possibly can!"

"Where's Servis now?" I asked. "Can you find him for us?"

She reached into the air for a small golden crystal ball.

"He's not on duty at the moment."

Aahz was quick to jump on her phrase.

"Was he on duty during the award ceremony?"

"Well, no . . ."

"Where is he?"

Turista gave him a bland but pleasant smile.

"I'm not at liberty to give you that information, Mr. Aahz. But I promise you inquiries will be made."

We left the round building. As soon as we were out of range of its satisfaction spell, my mood fell.

"We can't do anything else tonight," I said. "Let's go back to the suite."

Bunny protested. "Maybe we ought to check out and pop back to the tent in Deva," she said. "Is there any sense in running up the bill by staying extra nights here?"

"If we leave they might stop looking for the cup," Aahz said. "At least one of us has to stay here. Customer service only holds good as long as we're customers."

Bunny's eyes flew wide.

"Oh! I didn't think of that. One of you stay. I'll go back to Deva. Or should I be the one to remain here?"

"Skeeve made the request, so he's probably the one the management will monitor. But I don't like having him stay here alone. Miss Fast-Wand might decide to toss him a dozen dimensions away if she spots him. We don't know what form the next attack will take. We've all got a stake in keeping Skeeve safe. So we might as well all stay."

I could see Bunny making calculations in her head.

"Come on," I said, taking her hand. "I bet your new room is a dozen times nicer than the one you had before. Let's go see." I started to walk. Bunny followed me reluctantly.

"Well, all right," she said.

Her hand felt tense in mine. Her preoccupation with money had been preying on my mind for some time. I could tell most of the others felt the same way. A series of glances went back and forth between us as we walked along the torchlit path. At the end of the corridor in the round building, Bunny put her hand on the knob of her new room.

"We'll get a fresh start in the morning," she said. "I am so tired. Good night!"

"Not just yet," Tananda said, smoothly moving in and putting an arm around her. "Come and have a drink with us. There are plenty of seats in our room, and a fully stocked liquor shelf."

"But . . ." Bunny protested.

Gleep interposed himself between her and the door.

"Gleep!" he exclaimed. He licked her on the cheek, making her close her eyes. While she was wiping her face, Tananda towed her up the hallway and into the rooms she shared with her brother.

Open doors led to the two opulent bedrooms to either side of a luxurious common area. I could tell that this suite had been especially designed for visitors from Trollia. The lighting was soft, almost seductive. All the surfaces were comfortably padded, including the floor. The green carpet, beneath thick, velvety pile, was like walking on spongy forest moss. Most of the heavily upholstered furniture was in a mix of purple and green shades. Tananda all but pushed Bunny into a deep violet chair. The padding exhaled as she sank into it. Bunny struggled for a moment to get free of its enveloping embrace, then collapsed, defeated. I perched on a soft-topped footstool next to her. The others sat down close to us.

"Do you want to talk about it?" I asked.

"Talk about what?" Bunny asked, her tone so bright it was brittle. "There's nothing to talk about."

I raised my hands and let them fall.

"All right, then. If you won't, I will. The rest of us have been worried about you. We've been losing out on little jobs to other businesses who've been undercutting us. That's no big deal. I haven't been around that long, but long enough to know that the pendulum eventually swings back. Once customers see that you really do get what you pay for, we'll get all the work we can handle, and more, just like we always did. We may even end up outsourcing to some of the people who underbid us. But not for the important stuff. Those, no one can do as well as we can. Looie's job looked pretty easy from the outset, and it should have been. It was a straightforward task to locate one magikal cup and bring it back to him. He was paying outrageous coin to get it. If I'd made the deal instead of Aahz, I might have charged him less."

"Up until you met him, what?" Chumley asked. "Unpleasant little wart."

Aahz smiled. So did I.

"Aahz was right, of course. But we took the job, which meant we had an obligation to complete it."

"We still will," Bunny said. She looked as if she wanted to run away, but she couldn't get out of that chair without help or magik.

"And we could have, this afternoon, even before dinner, if we hadn't gotten sidetracked by the Scavenger Hunt. We would never have fallen for a simple trick like that if your eyes weren't fixed on the bottom line instead of the outcome. You've been grabbing for big income instead of jobs that no one else could do. This one has been a waste of our talents. It would have been great to visit this place on a real vacation instead of all of us hanging out here waiting for someone else to do the work."

"That's not true!" Bunny said. "If all it took to get the cup was to ask the Central Help Desk for it, then Looie wouldn't have hired a plethora of treasure hunters."

"Looie didn't know about that service or he would have used it himself," I pointed out. "He's cheap, but he's busy with the negotiations at home. He doesn't have time to get into the small details, or stay pending a thorough search. That's why he hired us."

"But we failed!" Bunny cried.

"So far," Haroon said.

"Not really," Aahz said. "Not until you decided we had to get the prize money on top of our fee. Two hundred gold pieces would set up a Klahdish family for more than a year. Yeah, we deal in big numbers. We have a lot of overhead. We live well, better than some kings I've known. But you sacrificed the catch. Once Skeeve came back with the cup, why didn't we just go back to Mishpaka and cash in?"

Bunny looked at her knees. Tananda rose like a butterfly and glided to the polished maroon wood cabinet against the wall. She returned with a glass and a bottle of clear liquor and poured a generous tot for Bunny.

"Drink it," she said. "I insist. We've all had a hard day."

We waited until Bunny took several sips. She began to relax.

"You going to tell us, or let Skeeve keep speculating about it?" Aahz asked.

"About what, Aahz?" Bunny asked, wearing her sweetest smile.

"About why you let us keep working for Looie. He's a small-timer. It'd be a good paycheck, sure, but we've had better. We also like taking on missions for good people, but I doubt that he ought to keep his job, when he's relying on one piece of hardware to do all the work for him. He proved he's no diplomat. He ran through a good hunk of the treasury to get back an item that if he was good at negotiation he might have gotten for a fraction of what we charged him—and if he was good at negotiation, he wouldn't need a powerful item like the Loving Cup. So, what's really on your mind?"

"Nothing," Bunny said. "I don't know why you keep asking me."

"I don't buy that," I said. "We're your friends. We know you pretty well after all this time, I think. You've been worried about money for a while. If I had a hundredth as much money back on Klah as we sit on casually, *I'd* be a king. Even Hemlock doesn't have the kind of disposable income we've got at our fingertips. Something else is bothering you, too. When your cousin Sylvia comes in, you get defensive and nervous. That's not like you. You've handled worse situations."

"It's because she's family," Bunny said. "She's always been a little difficult. But Uncle Bruce trusts her, so I have to put up with her little surprise visits. She reports back to him."

"But you're his favorite," I said. Her expression changed just a little, and I felt enlightenment hit me like a bucket of cold water. "Oh, I see."

"See what?" Tanda asked.

"Don Bruce," I said. "Am I right, Bunny?"

She didn't look at me.

"Yes."

I turned to the others. "Don Bruce wants to groom Bunny to take over the Mob if he, well, retires. He's been checking up on her a lot lately. He must be thinking about having her come home to stay."

"But that would mean she would leave M.Y.T.H., Inc.!" Tananda said. Bunny nodded. "I thought he liked us. If you were doing a great job for us, he wouldn't make you come home."

"He does like us," Aahz said. "And we'll always come a distant sixteenth to his own interests."

"That's why she's been pushing to up our income," I said. I turned back to her. "You want the bottom line to look as big as possible. If you're indispensable to our business, you can stay."

"If I don't, then he'll recall me," Bunny said, big tears standing in her blue eyes. "I didn't really know what to expect when he sent me to you as a gift. I thought being your moll would be just like any other part of the Family, but it's been different. You didn't impose any expectations on me. With all of you I don't have to fit a mold. I don't have to wear tight clothes. I don't have to pretend to be stupid. I can be . . ."

". . . You," I finished for her.

Tananda sat down on the arm of the chair and put her hand on Bunny's shoulder.

"I don't see what the problem is. You're an adult. You're free to do whatever you want to do."

"I say, no, Little Sis, she's not," Chumley put in. "It's a matter of culture. Don Bruce is a powerful man in many ways. He even made life a bit hot for us, what? We deal with him on a basis of mutual respect. It is not up to us to decide on whom he picks as an heir, or interfere directly in the workings of the Mob, any more than we would welcome his input on our way of doing business. The Family's structure is as important to its survival as are its rapacious greed and disregard for the lives of others. Bunny is an impressive organizer. She has kept our disparate personalities functioning together like the proverbial well-oiled machine. She would be a truly great Don."

"But I don't want to be the Don!" Bunny said. "It doesn't have to be me! Sylvia would love to take over from Uncle Bruce."

I shuddered. "I would be afraid to work for her."

"I bet most of the Mob feel the same way," Aahz said. "And Don Bruce probably knows it. That's why he wants you."

"Can't you tell him to choose someone else?" Tananda asked.

"Not really," Bunny said. "Questioning his word makes him vulnerable in the eyes of his subordinates. I can't do that to him. All I can do is look too valuable where I am. That's why I wanted to show him substantial growth from quarter to quarter." She looked down into her cup. "I nudged the entries a little to make our income look higher last quarter, but there wasn't enough wiggle room this time. We might even show a slight loss. That's why when Aahz came to us with this job, I jumped at it. I had no idea that a simple retrieving job would throw everyone into danger. And I shouldn't have gotten distracted. Easy money never is easy. I won't make that mistake again."

"All right," I said, dashing my fist into my palm. "Then we'll finish the job for Looie and collect. There's no way I'm going to let Don Bruce take Bunny away from us."

"Hear, hear!" Chumley said, bustling over to the liquor cabinet. "Drinks for the house! A toast to keeping our happy company together."

I accepted a glass with alacrity.

"I will drink to that," I said. I toasted Bunny. "You're our president. I know we can keep it that way."

Bunny beamed at us and raised her glass in turn. "I wouldn't want Uncle Bruce to hear me say it, but you're the Family I always wished I had."

CHAPTER TWENTY-TWO

"What could possibly go wrong . . . go wrong . . . go wrong . . . ?"

—THAT CRUISE LINE

The next day had me feeling more optimistic than I had the night before. We had had the cup in our hands once. We could find it again. I broached my plan over breakfast under the shade of a circle of palm trees near our suite building.

"Haroon can help us locate the Loving Cup," I said. "We all touched it. He'd know the scent if he came across it again."

"Sure would, young fellah," the Canidian said. "Let me give you all a good ol' smellin' 'fore we set out, and I'll have it fixed in my mind. Y'all come with me, and we'll track that fancy goblet down before too long."

"We need to find Servis before Looie comes back," Bunny said. "I'll look for him. If he still has the cup, I'm going to take it away from him."

"We'll help," Tananda said, with a glance at her brother.

"If you do find him, you don't want him to give you the slip again. He must know we're onto him."

"Why wouldn't Servis just go to Looie?" I asked.

Chumley shrugged, his fur fluttering on his massive shoulders.

"He may not have experience traveling across the dimensions on his own. As you know, it's a dangerous feat."

"Servis is on the run," Aahz said. "Locating him has become an internal matter. Chances are the management will find him before we do. The best thing we can do is wait."

"All right," Bunny said, all business once again. "I'll find a manager and make sure they don't just sweep the incident under the rug. Tananda and Chumley will come with me. Haroon's the only one of us who might be able to locate the cup other than by chance. We might get lucky. Now that there are six cups, the chances are better that the Help Desk might find one of them."

"I'd be happy to lean on them," Aahz said. "In a purely diplomatic way, of course."

He showed all his teeth.

Haroon, Gleep, and I spent the morning painstakingly walking up and down the manicured footpaths of Winslow. The flawless weather beamed kindly on us, not too hot or too cold, with a fragrant breeze that wafted the scent of the gardens everywhere. After the cup had disappeared right out of our grasp the night before, I found myself resenting the happy holidaymakers who lay in the sun or played carefree sports or games. In a way, we were trapped in Winslow until we finished our task.

I couldn't be angry at Bunny. She was only doing what she thought she needed to do to avoid having to go home to Klah and the Mob. I only wished that she had confided in us before. We would have worked out a scheme, as we had with Guido and Nunzio, to make certain Don Bruce would never pull her back. But I was frustrated.

"Whoa, young'un," Haroon said, pulling up suddenly in front of a shop. I glanced in the window. The display was full of novelty toothpick holders, hip flasks, and parasols, all pale blue with *A Souvenir from Winslow!* printed on them. "I'm gettin' a strong scent in there. C'mon!" He put his nose to the ground and wove between the legs of the tourists. "'Scuse me, ma'am, sir. Hi, there, kiddies. Hey, there! Nice t' see you folks!"

"Stay out here, boy," I said to Gleep. He whimpered at me, but I didn't want to risk the accidental devastation of a hyperactive dragon romping past shelves packed with little ceramic knickknacks. But a puffy little cloud overhead suddenly rolled off, letting a sunbeam hit the pavement just where Gleep was sitting. He curled up with a happy sigh. I went into the shop.

"Greetings, sirs!" said the chartreuse-haired man behind the counter. "Is there anything I can help you find?"

"Uh, we're just looking," I said.

A tall stand of five or six glass shelves stood next to the clerk's table. On it stood petite footed mugs that looked like coffee cups but were too small for practical use. Haroon walked around and around it, sniffing energetically.

"What have you found?" I asked.

"Cup was here," he said. "I'm sure of it."

"Not ours," I said.

"Nope. Looks as if all o' them had the same smell. I mean, *exactly* the same smell. Strangest thing I ever heard of."

"Me, too," I said. "Do you know who picked it up?"

"Too many darned scents on this here stand, son," Haroon said. "Can't tell you where it went, but let's see if we can figger out where it came from. Follow me!"

He headed for the back of the shop. I hurried after him. On the way there, I passed a shelf filled with dirty dishes.

Cups stained with coffee and lipstick lay on their sides on top of plates caked with bits of food. A tangle of sticky silverware was scattered across the whole display.

"Look at that!" I said.

Haroon glanced back and did a double take. He circled around to take a better look.

"That ain't right," he said, shaking his long floppy ears until they rattled. "No one is gonna buy those!"

Somewhere, someone else had the same thought. Suddenly, the dishes disappeared. In their place was a collection of soft-soled shoes adorned with seashells.

"That's a whole lot better," Haroon said. "C'mon!"

He went toward a closed door in the rear wall.

A clerk who had just finished with his last customer ran to head us off. Instead of stopping us and telling us we couldn't go in there, he hurried to open the door for us. Behind it was an open-fronted cabinet filled with embroidered shirts and a few of each of the knickknacks in the shop.

"Can I help you find anything?" he asked, as Haroon had a good sniff up and down the shelves.

"Sure, young man," Haroon said. "Gold cup. Gems all over the handles. Probably sold it sometime yesterday afternoon."

"Yes, sir!" the blue-skinned youth said. "Only we didn't sell it. It's not part of our usual merchandise. We gave it away. It was part of the great Scavenger Hunt, one of the most successful contests we have ever had here!"

"Who did you give it to?" I asked.

"A really lovely lady," he said. "A Caffiend! She came in here about twilight."

The sixth-place team!

"And where did you get it from?" I asked. "Who brought it in here?"

"No one brought it. It just appeared on the shelf."

"Got any more?"

"No, sir! It was one of a kind."

The same answer came from everywhere else Haroon found the scent. The good-natured clerk with a whistle around his neck at the front desk of the Activities Department didn't know how the Loving Cup had been placed on the list for the Scavenger Hunt.

"I'm so sorry, sir!" he said. "We almost always use the same list. The master copy is in our air safe until it's needed. No one can take it out until we need it."

"But someone did," I said. "Do you know Servis?"

The young man beamed.

"Everybody knows Servis! He's the best."

"Was he in here the other day?"

"Yes! He was part of the recruitment group to find teams to play."

"Did he have access to the safe?"

The young man thought about it for a moment.

"No. He and his assistant took the pile of scrolls that were copied from it."

"How many?" I asked.

"All of them, sir! He's so good at getting people involved in our games."

"That answers that," Haroon said. "He changed it and made it look like an accident. Awful good at lyin', I gotta say."

"Knowing that doesn't help us find him," I said. "Thank you."

"Always a pleasure, Mr. Skeeve, Mr. Haroon!" the young man said.

We emerged from the office into the street.

"Wal, that didn't help none," Haroon said. "I'm a mite dry. How 'bout you, Skeeve?"

I nodded. I had run out of ideas, and my feet were beginning to ache. One of the refreshing cocktails would cut the dust in my throat.

"That would be great," I said.

"Hey, how 'bout some cold drinks here!" Haroon said to the

air. He waited. "Y'know, that's downright strange. I never waited more than a breath or two before someone showed up with . . ."

Out of the air a few feet away, a pretty young Winslovak with light blue hair appeared, holding a tray in her hands. Her name tag read *Refila*.

"Here you are, gentlemen!" she said. She handed me a silver beaker that was topped off with a cone of whipped cream.

"Ow!" I exclaimed. It was hot! The cup fell out of my hand and splashed me all the way down my tunic and trousers. The server's free hand flew to her mouth in horror.

"Oh, Mr. Skeeve, I am so sorry!" she exclaimed. She turned away and disappeared. Two other employees appeared with towels. They mopped me up and down.

"We apologize deeply, sir," the first said. He was tall and thin, with charcoal-gray hair. "She should have offered you a cocktail, not hot coffee."

Under their ministrations, the pain disappeared along with the stains.

"It's all right," I said. "Anyone could make a mistake."

The two employees exchanged a worried glance.

"We don't," the second one said. He was short and stocky, with a square head between his little round ears. He reached into the air and brought forth a tray with clinking crystal glasses and bowls filled with pink liquid on it. He offered one to each of us. "Please enjoy these. And if there is any problem, please let us know."

"I'm sure it'll be fine," Haroon said, lowering his face to take a slurp of his drink. "Just perfect. No problem." He lapped the bowl empty.

The two Winslovaks sighed with relief.

"Thank you for saying so, sir," said the second.

I finished my drink and handed my glass back. I noticed that Gleep hadn't touched his.

"What's the matter, boy?" I asked, putting my arm around his neck. "Doesn't it taste good?"

He snaked his head up and looked directly at me.

"Gleep!" he exclaimed. His glance was full of meaning.

What could make him so uneasy? Now that he mentioned it, I could feel a malign gaze.

I looked around.

"Haroon, is that girl anywhere near us?"

Haroon lifted his nose to the air and sniffed mightily.

"Harooooon!" he howled. A few families walking by turned to see if his cry heralded anything interesting, then kept going. "No, sir. I'd know her scent anyplace, and she ain't within sniffin' range."

I shook my head. Someone was watching us.

"Let's go back to the others," I said.

CHAPTER TWENTY-THREE

"Blood in the Nile? At least nothing else bad can happen."

—RAMESES II

Bunny, Markie, Tananda, and Chumley were already under the trees when we returned. As soon as I sat down, a charming young Winslovak appeared with a tray of drinks and nibbles and served them.

"No luck, huh?" Markie asked.

"No," I said. "Any signs of Servis?"

"Everything but the actual guy," she said. "I found his room, in the senior employee district, back behind the arena. Bed's made. The place is spotless. No sign of him. His neighbors haven't seen him since yesterday morning."

"He can't hide forever. Where's Aahz?" I asked.

"Hark," Chumley said, raising a finger to the air. "I believe I hear his dulcet tones."

Aahz stomped into view. He looked furious. If he could have breathed fire, he would have scorched the path ahead of him.

"What's wrong?" I asked. "Bad news?"

"I don't want to talk about it. What's this?" he snarled at the young lady who proffered him a green cocktail. "I don't need an eye-cup!"

She promptly vanished.

"All right, Aahz," Tananda said, a slow smile curving her lips. "What happened?"

Aahz threw himself into a hammock and clenched his fists on his thighs.

"They threw me out of the Central Help Desk!"

"Why?"

"No reason!"

"No reason?" she asked, with a little smile. "You managed to provoke *Winslovaks* into making you leave the courtesy desk instead of letting you do what you want? Jeopardizing their dimension-wide reputation for never saying no to any request?"

Aahz pursed his lips until he managed to squirt the words out.

"I was just trying to push them a little. The sooner we get that cup back, the sooner we can get out of here."

"And by push you meant bully, cajole, and harass the staff and probably everyone who was waiting in line. Maybe even random passersby who were minding their own business?"

". . . Maybe."

Tananda put her hands on her hips.

"Aahz!"

Bunny looked crestfallen.

"Look, Aahz, I'm sorry. If you want to go back to the Bazaar, go ahead. It's my mess. I'll stay here until I finish cleaning it up."

"NO!" he bellowed. His voice rang off the nearby buildings, startling a flock of birds into flight. "I'm going to get a beer. Anyone else want to come along?"

"Sounds like a tip-top idea," Chumley said.

"Buy a girl a drink, big guy?" Tananda asked, twining her arm through mine.

"Or two?" Bunny asked. She took my other arm. Feeling like the wealthiest man in Winslow, I escorted them both up the main street of the resort. Aahz turned inland and stomped up the street toward the Rusty Hinge. When I realized where we were headed, I halted.

"I can't go in there," I said. "I got thrown out yesterday and told not to come back!"

"If anyone stops you, we'll talk to them," Tananda said. "And by talk, I mean negotiate." She took her dagger from her belt and flipped it nonchalantly in the air. When the hilt slapped into her palm, she holstered it. It would take a braver man than me to turn her down.

To my enormous relief, nothing stopped me from passing through the doors. Chumley pushed them open without any trouble. The bartender, a sturdy female Winslovak with ample blue cleavage peeking out from the top of her drawstring-necked blouse, nodded curtly to us as we came in.

The eternal poker game was going on at the front table. Nervously, I peeked around Chumley to see if the crazed Troll was still there. I sighed with relief. He was gone, probably home to Trollia. Instead, a slim, pale-skinned male who resembled a Klahd sat shuffling the cards.

"How about a friendly game?" he asked, turning to us. He had red eyes, and when he smiled, his canines were as pointed as Aahz's teeth. He beckoned with his long fingers. I noticed he had very sharp nails painted black.

Aahz halted in his tracks. "No, thanks, pal."

He started to back out of the inn. Gleep and I edged behind him and pushed him forward.

"Let me go!" he hissed. "That's a Vampire!"

"He's not going to come after you," Markie said. "He has a whole tableful of players he could bite. Why would he want you?"

"Pervects are known to be delicious to Vampires," Aahz said. "I take no chances."

Keeping the maximum distance between them that he could, Aahz edged toward the rear of the inn to a table in one of the wooden enclosures. Aahz took the seat in the corner of the booth with his back to the wall. Nothing was going to get behind him if he could help it.

I pulled a tall stool close to the small round table. Chumley stalked over to the bar and pounded a fist on the polished top.

"Service haste! Don't time waste."

The bartender, polishing a glass in her apron, came over and listened intently to his murmured order. He stomped back to our booth. Once he was concealed behind the wall, he dropped his Big Crunch persona.

"It is a shame that our search today bore no fruit," he said.

"Nothin' yet, son, but there's always tomorrow," the Canidian said. "I figger that I'm gonna run into someone who smells like those cups who shouldn't oughter. Then we'll have 'em. Mr. Skeeve here'll nab 'em with his magik, and Bob's yer uncle."

"Derreck, actually," Chumley said. "Our mumsy's brother is a big fellow, but I take your point."

"Find Servis, and we'll find the cup," Tananda said. "He can't hide forever."

"We don't have forever," Bunny said. "Looie comes back for the cup the day after tomorrow. In the meantime, we're spending twenty-one gold pieces a day in resort fees. I don't want to have Uncle Bruce think I can't handle this business!"

"Showing a loss for one quarter isn't the end of the world," I said. "Plenty of businesses have temporary downturns."

"You don't understand," Bunny said. "He's not looking at the long run. He's waiting for an excuse."

I exchanged a quick glance with Aahz.

"We'll renegotiate our terms with him," I said. "Make

him think we might ally ourselves even closer with him, as he hoped from the beginning."

"Make him think you're going to marry me?" Bunny asked. Her cheeks turned pink.

"He can think whatever he wants," I said, offhandedly, though I felt far from casual about it. "We'll just go on the way we have so far."

"That won't work. He'll just want to make wedding plans. He loves big, fancy events!"

That would just cause another round of problems. I put my chin in my hand to think. I had been trying not to think of Bunny in that way. She had followed me loyally back to Klah when I had my crisis of confidence. Now that she was our president it would have been a definite conflict. Bunny and I had never really discussed such deeply important things since then. It was a subject I didn't really want to revisit while we were in the midst of a crisis. But it would have torn my heart out to have her leave. What could we do to keep Don Bruce from taking her away? I would do anything for her.

"I won't use that as an excuse to him," I said.

"Fine," Bunny said. "I wouldn't want him to think I'd marry you like that."

I opened my mouth and closed it again. I didn't know what to think then. Maybe she had already decided I wasn't worthy of her. And that was definitely something I didn't want to discuss while we were working on a difficult assignment.

"Mr. Skeeve!"

One of the endlessly cheerful employees appeared at my side. She had a large cloth bag with her. I pulled myself upright.

"Is that the Loving Cup?" I asked eagerly.

"No, sir," she said. "I'm from the Customer Appreciation Department! This is an award for all of you for being such good guests of the resort! You've passed two days here in

Winslow, and we just want to let you know how much we love having you with us." She reached into the bag and came out with a handful of necklaces strung with sparkling blue stars. She draped one around each of our necks. "There! Now, all of you have a really great day!"

She disappeared.

"Well, that and a dime will get you a cup of coffee," Aahz said. He wrenched off the necklace and put it on the table. "Piece of junk."

"What's a dime?" I asked.

"A coin worth a cup of coffee," Aahz said. "Mostly in metaphors."

That was a dimension that I had never visited, so I took Aahz's word for it.

I noticed a couple of young male Winslovaks in short but formal-looking white jackets and black bow ties going from table to table with a leather-bound book and a pad of paper. I watched with growing curiosity. Some of the patrons they spoke to just returned to their drinks, but others vanished into thin air.

"Now what?" Aahz asked, impatiently.

"Good afternoon!" the first employee said. "Have you made plans for dinner tonight?"

"No," I said. "It's too early. We were just going to have some lunch."

"Even better!" the second one said, opening the leather-bound book and displaying its parchment pages to us. "We're from Le Snoot, the very finest restaurant in all of Winslow! We have a table by the window that you would just love. There's an excellent view of the manicured grounds of one of our golf courses, and a magik show in the foyer!"

"Not to mention the quartet of singing troubadours who will delight you with their dexterity on the strings," the second one put in.

"So, which one of them uses the fourth . . . lute?" Aahz

asked. He paused, as if waiting for applause. The two males looked at him blankly. "Forget it. Not interested. All I want is a sandwich and a beer."

"I sense that you are a trifle discontented," the first one said, with deep sympathy. "What can we do to make you fully content?"

"And happy?" the second added.

"You can shove off," Markie said. Her tone did not discomfit the two males one bit.

"Of course! Please enjoy your lunch. And remember that you can make a reservation with Le Snoot just by shouting for your nearest attendant." They went on to the next group.

Aahz rolled his eyes. A surly-looking barman came by with a tin bucket. He hoisted it onto our table. Some of the contents slopped over. The heady smell of hops slapped me in the face like an offended maiden. Aahz picked it up in both hands and glugged down half of it.

"Ahhh! That's better," he said, wiping his mouth with the back of his hand. "What's on the menu?" he asked the man.

"Usual," the man said, curtly. "Yesterday's leftovers."

"Sounds good."

The hefty woman behind the bar delivered the rest of our drinks with a scowl. I felt a wave of nostalgia, as if I were home again in Deva. She took her time returning with a huge tray containing trenchers of barely edible meat pies and unrecognizable vegetables, which she shoved in front of each of us. Bad attitude, terrible food, messy tables, with the noise of an ongoing brawl with breaking crockery in the background. I sighed with pleasure. Much better than the fancy food they had given us the night before, or the perfect breakfast with pastries that all looked like works of art. I felt myself relaxing.

A little. A pang of doubt kept interrupting my reverie.

"What's on your mind, Skeeve?" Markie asked, picking a gray chunk of carrot out of her bowl. She flung it to Gleep, who snapped it up as if it tasted good.

"I can't get away from the feeling that I'm missing something important," I said.

"The part where they know everything going on everywhere in this dimension, or the weird part when they don't?" Markie asked. "I'm used to the first one. It's the second that throws me."

"I agree," Tananda said. "The perfection isn't consistent. That's not like them."

"That's it!" I said, dashing my fist into my palm. "They know what we're doing. They always know. They're letting us waste time looking all over the place. Maybe they're even leaving clues for us to follow, although they never go anywhere. They're keeping us distracted. Deliberately. They either can't get the cup or won't get it. They're *stalling*. But we never notice it."

"How do you know?" Bunny asked.

I turned to her, all the ideas in my mind rushing to my lips at once.

"Haven't you noticed that whenever something starts to get serious, it's defused almost immediately? This is how Winslow does what it does. Markie told me that from the moment we got here, but I forgot about it. Yesterday, I was feeling terrible about our experiences in Maire. I went into an inn deliberately to drown my sorrows." The others kept their faces neutral, but I could tell they were dismayed at my admission, Bunny more so because she hadn't been going to tell them. But in a way they looked relieved that I had told them the truth. "Suddenly, a bunch of Titans, who would have used me for a punching bag almost anywhere else, turn up and drag me into a drinking game. They fed me doctored liquor that made me feel good without making me drunk."

Aahz slammed his fist down on the table, making our trenchers jump. "I'm going to find those Titans and take them all down," he said.

"Gee, Aahz, don't!" I said. "They *helped* me. When I woke up in the morning, the bad mood was gone. I'm all right now. Better than all right. And afterward, when you and I were starting to have an argument, Bunny . . ."

Far from being upset that that truth, too, was being aired, Bunny beamed with enlightenment.

". . . A complete stranger came by to tell me how much she liked my manicure! Very clever."

"They know what we're going to do, or they have a pretty good idea. They manage our emotions. They find a way to make us feel better when we're unhappy. When the direct approach doesn't work, they use an indirect one."

"I suppose I knew that all the time," Tananda said. "Is that a bad thing?"

"No, not really," I said. "It's fine if you're here for pleasure. But for us, it's only wasting time. And money. Every day we spend here costs us a sack of gold pieces." I knew that would appeal to Aahz's sense of economy. In other words, his pernicious cheapness. He never let go of a coin without exhausting all the options of obtaining goods or services without spending one. "I'll bet that they're counting on us running out of time or money so we have to go home."

His brows drew down.

"Are you trying to say they're in collusion with Servis?" he demanded.

"Just the opposite. I think he's in hiding. They're unable to come up with the cup we requested, and they're stalling us, hoping we will eventually go away. The satisfaction spell on this place keeps us calm and happy. Maybe you've noticed how hard it is to stay in a bad mood. You have to really concentrate to keep it going. It's too nice here. Except when it isn't."

"I noticed that," Bunny said. "I thought it was because we've been here too long. Something is going wrong with their system. We shouldn't be feeling impatient."

"They're used to relying on that to keep troublemakers like us from overreacting," Markie said. "It isn't working. I wonder why?"

"I say, do you think it has something to do with the cup?" Chumley asked.

I shook my head. "The Loving Cup promotes accord, or so Looie says, but only between two people."

"Could it be a side effect that no one talks about?" Tananda asked. "The cup might make those two people come to an agreement, but it causes general discord among everyone else? A lot of magik items work that way."

"Then you'd think they can't wait to get it out of this dimension," Bunny said, reasonably.

"It doesn't add up," Aahz said. "Something else is going on, and it's distracting the management. Take those two waiters from the snobby eatery. They're out of place in here. This is a dive. If we were home in Deva, they'd become part of the wall décor. And the cheap Mardi Gras beads?"

"I thought they were kind of nice," Bunny said.

"Out of character," Markie said.

"We're being manipulated," I said. "I'm tired of it." I raised my eyes to the ceiling, where I imagined Earwigs or some other spies that reported to the management were concealed. "Stop trying to make me have fun!"

An enormous furry hand landed on my arm.

"Ware there!" bellowed the Troll.

CHAPTER TWENTY-FOUR

"Appearances can be deceiving."

—D. GRAY

I **scrabbled for a handful of magik, but I came up nearly** empty. The repulsion spell I tried did absolutely nothing. The Troll advanced upon me, his huge yellow eyes almost glowing. His big furry body blocked out the lamplight. I prepared myself to fight. But what could my puny strength do against him without magik?

"Stop!" I cried, jumping off my stool and holding it up as a barrier between us. "I was just leaving. Don't throw me again!"

The Troll did stop. He reached out and patted me gently on the shoulder.

"Don't have to, old chap. I'm off duty."

"You're what?" I asked.

He reached into the fur over his heart and came out with a pair of golden spectacles, which he fixed over his eyes.

"Off duty, my dear fellow. My shift is over, but I heard your outcry." His eyes twinkled. "You saw through my subterfuge the other day. I knew you knew what most everyone else does not about Trolls." He laid a finger alongside his large purple nose. "But I thought that I would ask if there was anything I could do to help."

"Uh, thanks, I think," I said.

By this time, Chumley was on his feet. He moved to embrace the other Troll. I jumped hastily out of the way as the two massive bodies collided.

"Benjy!"

Benjy's face creased with delight.

"Chumley, you old lint wad! Haven't seen you for ages! What have you been doing?"

"Oh, this and that," Chumley said modestly. "I believe that you've run into my partner and colleague, Skeeve?"

Benjy nodded. "Threw him into a table of Deveels, what?"

"You . . . you did that on purpose?" I asked. I slapped my own forehead. "Of course you did!" Like a fool, I had fallen into the trap that most people outside Trollia did. I had been brought up believing that Trolls were large, dangerous, and stupid. Only the first two characteristics were accurate. And I *knew* that; had known it for years. "Wait a moment, you said you're off shift. You *work* here?"

"I do," Benjy said. "Jolly good job, too. Seasonal, you know, but most rewarding."

"Sit down and have a drink with us," Chumley said. He picked up a heavy-duty stool and plunked it down near our table. "I would love to hear about it."

Benjy glanced over his shoulder toward the counter, where the bartender was pulling a pitcher of beer.

"Can't do it here, old thing. This is my station. Not permitted to break character in public. Come with me back to the employee's canteen. We'll have a good old chin-wag."

Benjy led us to a blank section of wooden wall beyond the booths. He ran a finger down a flaw in the grain, and a section of wall opened up. I was astonished. I had no idea that a door was there. It was sealed by magik so subtle I hadn't detected it on my last visit. I admit, though, that I had been focused on finding a cup, not a door.

Behind the door was a cupboard whose shelves were full of disreputable-looking rags that nevertheless had been washed, pressed, and folded. To the right, a flight of steps stretched upward in a narrow passage. The Troll mounted them, gesturing us to follow.

"Watch yourselves here," Benjy said, his voice echoing dully. "The last step always takes one by surpri—"

His voice was cut off suddenly as he vanished. When his bulk no longer obstructed my view, I saw a ring of crackling blue fire at the top.

"Oh, I say!" Chumley exclaimed. "Come along, then."

"I'm not going through that," Aahz said.

"Nonsense," Chumley said. "Benjy would never lead us awry. He was the captain of our cricket team at school."

He pushed upward past us and disappeared through the flames. They roared up and danced at his passage.

"Ooh, fun!" Tananda said. "I love tunnel spells!" She ran up the steps and plunged in. The flames wiggled sensuously. It was my turn next.

"Is it dangerous?" I asked Haroon.

"Heck, no, son. Just means his room's on the far edge of the resort. Saves a bunch o' time reporting for his shift. C'mon." The Canidian walked up and backed into the roaring flames. Instead of disappearing completely, he paused, his hindquarters now invisible. "See? Nothin' to it!"

Aahz grumbled.

"I'm not going to be shown up by a hound dog," he said. He took a running start and jumped over Haroon's head. The flames engulfed him. I waited for a cry of pain, but none came. Bunny, Gleep, and I followed at a more cautious pace.

The flames tickled. My laugh echoed hollowly in the corridor.

CHAPTER TWENTY-FIVE

"Nothing wrong with a little inside information."

—G. GEKKO

When I stopped laughing, I had emerged into a brightly lit chamber. It was almost a perfect cube of white that rose higher than the gallery of the Rusty Hinge. Dozens of beings sat at long tables made of blue glass, eating, drinking, talking to one another or into palm-sized crystal balls, or reading scrolls and books. Few of them were actually Winslovaks. I recognized Titans, Trolls, Landsharks, Trollops, and the occasional Deveel, Imp, and Wyvern. Aahz must have been relieved that no Vampires were there. At the sight of so many strangers, Gleep snaked his neck in front of my legs, waving his head back and forth threateningly.

"It's okay, boy," I said, patting him on the head. He turned a wary glance up to me. "Are you feeling those eyes on you again?"

"Gleep!" he said in assent.

I leaned close.

"Keep an eye out, and let me know if you figure out where it's coming from."

"Gleep!"

Benjy gestured to me from a table with several empty seats. I slid onto the blue glass bench across from him. The seat was actually pretty comfortable. A magik carpet swooped over and lowered itself to my eye level. It was loaded with potables of every kind and trays of food.

"Do have anything you wish," Benjy said, helping himself to a tray of dainty sandwiches and a teapot with a cup upside down over its spout. "We eat and drink well here."

"So I see," Chumley said, serving his sister before himself. With little finger cocked, he nibbled at a small finger sandwich.

"What's this place?" I asked, taking a lizard-bird leg and a strawberry milk shake. Gleep snaked his head up to survey the carpet's contents and seized a whole roast. He vanished under the table to eat it. I heard disgusting sounds of chomping and slurping near my feet. "Who are all of these people?"

"Guest workers," Benjy explained, pouring tea for himself and Bunny. "Most of us are local color, imported for a season or two. We fulfill roles in many of the locales. The inns such as the Rusty Hinge are prime postings. We have a great deal of fun while we earn a rather tasty crust."

"Wait, you mean that all of the card players in the inn were phony?" I asked.

Benjy smiled.

"Not at all. Usually there's just one of us, possibly two there to get the action under way. The table serves as an introduction among guests. When one isn't at home, sometimes one is reticent about asking to join a game in progress. It's our responsibility to involve as many would-be players as we can. That is what I did when I invited you in."

"Uh, you didn't exactly give me a choice," I said.

Benjy clicked his tongue.

"You were hovering near the ceiling among thousands of breakable drinking vessels, Mr. Skeeve, and you had already had a few potentially dangerous encounters with other guests. Management is passionate about making sure that our guests don't hurt themselves."

"So instead you threw him at a bunch of Deveels?" Tananda asked, grinning.

"They're rotten cowards, Deveels are," Benjy said, folding his hands complacently across his furry midsection. "Chances were slight that they would actually attack him. Sorry about that Titan, though. I failed to factor him into the reverse trajectory. He was a genuine guest, but he would not have been drinking in the Rusty Hinge if he did not enjoy the occasional random encounter. I must make certain assumptions about those who enter my ambit. My being the inept, bad-tempered player does allow our visitors to feel smug about outsmarting the big, furry fool. When I do explode in a tantrum, they experience a frisson from their brush with danger. All very safe, of course. No one is ever badly injured."

"What a lot goes into your day!" Chumley said. "Sounds most enjoyable."

"Oh, you have no idea," Benjy said, waving a hand. "What a relief it is to finish grading undergraduate term papers, then come here over the summer and throw people about! Stress-relieving, what?"

"Indeed," Chumley said.

"Who's this, Benjy?" asked a Landshark a few seats away, putting down a news scroll. "One of your fellow Trolls here for employee orientation?" He showed rows of sharp teeth not as impressive as Aahz's but several times more numerous.

"Oh, Swush, old man! Swush, this is a schoolmate of mine, Chumley, his sister Tananda, and his companions." He introduced each of us. "I say, Swush, what a brilliant idea! They're always looking for more local color, Chumley. You ought to sign on. You have always had a reputation as a marvelous play-actor. The wages are rather good."

"It's a terrific stress reliever, too," Swush said. "I'm an economist, but I spend my vacations scaring tourists. It makes me a lot more productive when I go home."

Benjy nodded agreement. "Once I retire from the university, I plan to keep my position here for the busy season. The hours are long but rewarding. You'd recognize a number of our old friends. Tim-Tim takes nights and weekends in the Hinge. Harrowby Minor has a lovely gig sitting under a wooden bridge upriver, scaring passersby. He's been working on a book of poetry in his spare time."

I admit I goggled at the thought of a Troll writing poetry.

"Harrowby's here?" Chumley said. "My goodness, if that old fussbudget is happy in Winslow's employ, I should think about it very seriously, though I have been equally stimulated by working as part of M.Y.T.H., Inc. It accords me rather more freedom than it seems you have."

Benjy smiled. "I envy you. It's not all garlands and champagne, or rather, cards and beer. The oversight can be a bit onerous. All of us have the rules hammered into us from the moment we come to work here, but it becomes ingrained in our very souls: The customer must always be happy, all of the time, and some of them are very hard to please."

"Well, *we're* not happy," I put in.

"I did notice, my friend. Why are you not happy?" Benjy asked, with sympathy. "I hate to sound like the brochures, but Winslow is here to fulfill every yen, regardless of complexity. Is there anything we can do?"

I explained our mission as briefly as possible.

"We had the Loving Cup in our hands, but we had to surrender it briefly to get credit for the find in the Scavenger

Hunt," I concluded, careful not to embarrass Bunny. "We should have gotten it back right away."

"Sounds like a simple request," said Swush, flicking his finned tail.

"It is," Benjy said, lowering his brows. "There is no good reason why the cup shouldn't have been brought back at once. You say *Servis* took it?"

"Yes. He insisted on taking it. He stole it right from under our noses!"

"Not Servis!" exclaimed Swush, appalled. "He is one of the workers who is always being held up to the rest of us as a sterling example. He mentored me during my first season. There must be some mistake!"

"I'm sorry, but there's no mistake," I said. "We've been waiting ever since. We have to get it back before our client returns here the day after tomorrow. If we don't get it, we're on the hook for the expenses we've already laid out."

"Are the stakes that insurmountable?" Benjy asked.

"Two hundred gold pieces," Bunny said, grimly. Swush's lower jaw dropped, showing all his teeth.

"My goodness, that is a virtual fortune!" Benjy said.

Aahz shrugged, polishing his nails nonchalantly on his tunic front, though I know the thought of surrendering that much money irked him.

"You gamble big, there's always a chance you lose big," he said.

"Well, you must have ice water for blood, my good sir," Benjy said, with a respectful glance for Aahz. "I couldn't afford such a loss."

"It's not just the money," I said. "We have a reputation as the best in the business. We took on this job and we don't want to fail. I'd find it hard to look at myself in the mirror if I let Looie down."

"Is there anything we can do to help you?" Swush asked.

"You work behind the scenes here. Can you help find Servis, or see if there's a lost-and-found where the cups might have ended up?" I asked.

The Landshark and Benjy exchanged glances.

"No can do, I am afraid," Benjy said. "We're not permitted to take official notice of requests that have been submitted through the Central Help Desk. As you may have seen in other walks of life, the customer's wish is the only one taken into account by the great powers-that-be. You have no idea how I tire of the off-key rustic music that is piped through the inn—it is part of the ambience! But if a customer complains, the matter is resolved as swiftly as possible."

"Why don't you complain until they change it?" I asked.

Benjy and Swush exchanged nervous glances.

"It's not really a good idea, you know. Chronic complainers don't prosper here."

"What can they do?" Aahz asked. "I wouldn't put up with a situation that drove me crazy."

"Sometimes people just . . . disappear," Swush said. "There one day, and *Help Wanted* the next."

Haroon nodded.

"Seen it happen myself. Werewolf gal in Gift Demo, great at her job, but she had issues about how the management wanted the goods displayed. Not arranged to her likin', and said so a lot. I walked in to see her once, and *fft!* Gone. No idea she was on her way out."

I was puzzled.

"Were they fired?"

Swush raised his lateral fins.

"We have no idea. All I know is I tried to get in touch with a fellow Landshark who worked here when I was home two seasons ago, but no one had seen him for months. So, we don't push too hard. Anyone can quit if he's unhappy." Benjy looked up toward the ceiling. "Mind if we drop this subject? We have a measure of privacy here, but . . . you never know."

I felt those eyes on my back again, so I was happy to drop the subject.

"Well, look," I said, "what if I asked specifically for you to help us?"

"Ah, would that we could. If you were to see me on the street and ask for my assistance, I would be able to aid you, but"—Benjy held up a finger to forestall my outburst—"you will never see me on the street because that is not my assignment. I am terribly sorry not to be helpful. The onus toward excellent service does become ingrained after a few seasons."

"You make it sound hopeless," I said.

"I wish we could be of more direct aid," Benjy said. "But it is not hopeless. If you are certain that the item is still here, you have power."

"What power?" Bunny asked, eagerly.

"The power to insist," Swush said. "They're stalling you."

"We know," I said grimly.

Benjy bent close to us and dropped his voice to a murmur, scarcely audible over the hum of conversation in the room.

"It's worse than you realize. I don't want to be heard saying this, but it seems that you have been the victims of a massive kerfuffle, not to mention a bit of bollixing," Benjy said, "but I suggest you insist. Insistently. Your Pervert friend here . . ."

"Per-VECT!" Aahz snarled. A few of the employees looked up from their conversations. Benjy peered at him over his glasses.

"So sorry, old man. My job in the Rusty Hinge is to offend. My apologies for letting my *anima de guerre* slip over into my off-hours. This good Per*vect*, then, nearly made them fold, but he let them give him the boot, so to speak, before they reached the breaking point."

Aahz glared at him, the veins standing out in his eyes.

"I *let* them kick me out? *Me?* Are you out of your mind?"

"You left of your own volition, didn't you, sir?" Benjy asked. "They never used magik or force to make you go forth from the Central Help Desk? Just gentle persuasion, insistence on fulfillment of your request, and a deeply hurt expression?"

The words worked themselves reluctantly out of Aahz's mouth.

"Well, yes."

"They are really good at that," Swush said. Benjy nodded agreement.

"I must tell you that to have you give in, or go away, or both, is a success for the management. Most visitors feel that *they* must have been the unreasonable ones if they do not accomplish perfect relaxation or obtain that one experience that they yearn for. And, as you mentioned, the delay when a request is particularly difficult does mean most people run out of time. Their vacation is over, or the fees are straining the pocketbook too greatly to remain. Winslow never has to do anything really hard. When one is told one can have *everything* here, one really runs out of requests long before reaching that point where a wish would be difficult for the management to accomplish. Thus the perception of perfection is maintained."

"That is some deeply diabolical psychology," Markie said. "Mind if I make notes?"

"Not at all," Benjy said. "Let me send you a copy of the treatise I am writing about it."

"But everything has not been perfect," I said. "Things have fallen between the cracks that shouldn't have. Servis *seemed* surprised that the Loving Cup had gotten onto the Scavenger Hunt list, but Campfya, his assistant, really was."

"Insufficient briefing," Swush said. "That's not like the

management. That never happens. We always get thorough documentation before events. Some of these games are planned a year in advance. To slip one over on the Activities Department takes some serious chutzpah."

"And the magik," I continued. "If you're not magicians you may not read the force lines like we do, but if they're the source of all that powers Winslow's hospitality industry, something is going to break down, and soon. The force lines are stretched to their limit. I've never seen anything like it."

"How so?"

I explained the difficulty I had had in pulling magik out of them when I needed it.

"I've been running short at some pretty inconvenient moments," I added. "And it's happened in other places." I told them about the dirty dishes and the mixup with the drinks. "Haven't you noticed any discontinuities?"

Swush flipped a fin.

"Sure we have. I nearly drowned the other day when riptides started erupting off the coast. I got yanked down sixty feet before the magik came back on."

"How could you drown?" I asked, looking at his fins and tail in surprise.

"Landshark, Klahd," Swush said, with a pained expression. "Land. Shark. I'm an air breather. I'm just a natural-born swimmer."

"It has been a bit worrying," Benjy said. "Central management seems to have its mind elsewhere these last few weeks. The problem has been growing ever more obvious to the staff. Customers, with the very notable exception of you, have not yet noticed, but I fear for Winslow if it continues. But you think it is connected to the disappearance of the Loving Cup?"

"We don't believe in coincidences," Aahz said.

"So what's your advice?" I asked. "How do we get the Loving Cup back?"

"No other choice, old man. Make a fuss," Benjy said. "Refuse to take no for an answer. It will be an effort on your part, because it is difficult for a nice chap like you to maintain an obdurate attitude. Once the management notices that you are unhappy, they will try various subterfuges to balk you. Escalate when necessary. But do not give up. Otherwise, you won't succeed. They can help you, but they need to be made to focus."

"No problem," Aahz said. "I might even enjoy it."

"No, Aahz," Bunny said. "They know how to push your buttons now. Let me try."

"You think you can be pushier than me?" Aahz asked, clearly incredulous. Bunny put her chin up.

"I know how high the stakes are. I can do it."

"I'll do it," Markie said. "In my other job I test the stress point of systems to the breaking point."

That was one way to look at Markie's main profession. But I shook my head.

"I'm the one who seems to have been the most immune to Winslow's effect from the beginning. It had better be me."

"Gleep!" said my dragon. We stood up, as did our hosts.

"Good luck, old fellow," Benjy said. "Dearly as I would like to see your efforts, I had better not be nearby when you begin. Otherwise, I would be contractually obligated to try to make you stop, and one of us could get hurt. For really obvious troublemakers, my instructions are to throw one through a wall. After a spell in our infirmary, they wake up in their own dimension, completely uninjured but with little to no memory of the last moments they spent in Winslow. All a regrettable accident, you know—the conflict seemed so real, we thought one was enjoying oneself. Many come back for a second visit, invariably better behaved. But you must be focused."

"I will."

"Good to see you, old man," Chumley said, shaking Benjy's hand.

The Troll took my hand in a solid grip, but it was only a friendly clasp, not a bone-crushing squeeze.

"I wish you good luck, Mr. Skeeve. By Marmel's candy kitchen, I wish I could watch."

"It will undoubtedly be a show," Chumley said.

Benjy guided us to one pristine, white wall of the canteen. "Let me see, which door would be best to drop you into the action?"

"Wherever we will get maximum exposure," Aahz suggested.

"Right you are." Benjy walked about a third of the way along the wall and opened a hidden door. On the other side was a ring of green flame. He waved us through. "Good luck, chaps."

Tananda stood on tiptoes to kiss him.

I stepped through first. It was hard to steel myself not to enjoy the tickling sensation. I had to be hard. Resolute. Implacable.

I shoved open the plain door that appeared before me.

"Ayiee!" a female server said, as I nearly walked into her. "Oh, I am so sorry to be surprised! May I offer you a drink, Mr. Skeeve?"

I had emerged into twilight in the middle of the main street. All around me, shoppers strolled in and out of the stores, while dozens of others sat lazing in lawn chairs or in hammocks, glistening cocktails and other beverages in hand. She had obviously just come out of the same door. I almost bumped her.

"Hold that thought," I said. I picked her up by the elbows, tray and all, and stepped to one side. We moved just in time before the rest of my friends came tumbling through the glittering portal. I put her down.

She looked past us. The door had closed invisibly behind us.

"How did you get in there?" she asked me.

"Got lost trying to find the . . . you know," I said, trying to look embarrassed.

"Oh! Please do ask next time," she said. "Any of us would be delighted to help you!"

"I know you would," I said. I took a couple of glasses off her tray and offered one to Bunny.

"So that's how they do it," Bunny said, admiringly. She clinked her glass with mine.

CHAPTER TWENTY-SIX

"Who says tantrums don't work?"

—TSAR I. THE TERRIBLE

I felt eyes on my back again from the moment we appeared in the square. Not only that, I was more aware than ever of a cloying sense that there was something wrong with me. I ought to let myself relax and be happy. I couldn't do that, not if we were to get the cup back. I had to be the biggest pest that Winslow had ever seen.

It wasn't going to be easy. It was a beautiful evening. Everything conspired to make me feel happy and content. I had to concentrate. This couldn't be harder than trying to light a candle with Garkin looking over my shoulder. I took a few deep breaths.

"Can you pull this out, partner?" Aahz asked.

"I think so. Whatever is in the air doesn't seem to agree with me. I like it here, but I can feel the magik. I know what's real and what isn't. I'm tired of the unreality. I want to get what we came for and go home."

"Who says you're not much of a magician?" Aahz said, with a sideways glance at me. "What the heck. Hey, waiter!" He raised an arm and beckoned broadly.

A blue-skinned attendant appeared out of nowhere at our side. This muscular and mustachioed gent had a tray full of beers on his arm, which he distributed among us. For Aahz and Gleep, another server walked into existence with a couple of buckets in hand. Gleep put his face in his and started gulping it noisily.

"Thanks," Aahz said, accepting his refreshment. "But that's not what we were going to ask for."

The attendant beamed. "A request? It would be my great pleasure. What can I bring you?"

"The Loving Cup," I said. "I really want it. I don't think I can go on being happy without it."

His pale white eyebrows rose high on his round forehead. He looked deeply troubled.

"Not be . . . not be happy? I . . . I will see what I can do, sir." He turned, and in two steps vanished from sight.

"That rattled their cages," Markie said.

In a moment, the waiter was back. With him was a young, pretty woman with her white hair scraped up on top of her head in a bun. Her name tag said *Soona.*

"Sir, I am from the Central Help Desk. Why don't you come with me and we'll work on your request?"

I wasn't faking the resentment I evinced when I replied to her.

"You've *been* working on my request for days!" I said. "You kept promising me I could have the Loving Cup. I believed you. Then you sent me a really embarrassing substitute. Then I only found the real thing because you accidentally put it on the list for a scavenger hunt. That meant anybody could have picked it up!"

"But you did have the cup for a while, Mr. Skeeve," she said, trying to placate me. "Surely that fulfilled your expectations."

"And it was stolen from me. Stolen!" I shouted, making sure all the other tourists within earshot could hear me. They could. Their mouths rounded with horror. A few surreptitiously touched their purses and belt pouches. "I thought Winslow did everything it could for its visitors. So far, you have made big mistakes on every request that I have made. And I still don't have what I came for!"

The two Winslovaks looked at me with pleading eyes.

"Mr. Skeeve, we always do our best. Please give us another chance!"

"I've given you a lot of chances!"

A call for emergency measures must have gone out. From the hidden doors all around us poured employees with handfuls of balloons, trays of dolls and model cars, drinks, sweets, and meat on a stick. So many people in colorful costumes hemmed us in that I could no longer see the ordinary tourists. Calliopes on rolling platforms and hordes of musicians began to play, drowning out my voice. The sight and sound of a disagreeable customer had been banished from sight. I was being isolated. Winslow was closing ranks against its greatest enemy: displeasure.

I had been steadily amassing magik from the tiny sparks that the force lines released. There was plenty in my internal supply for what I had to do. I levitated over the heads of the crowd and flew toward the Central Help Desk. Below me, Aahz started throwing people out of his way, making room for the rest of my friends to follow.

I touched down just out of reach of the serenity spell that the round building cast, threw my arms to the skies, and shouted.

"I'm unhappy," I said, bellowing it to the wide blue skies. "Do you hear me? I'm not happy! Winslow is making me miserable! I'm grim! I'm discontented! They promised to fix it, and they aren't doing anything!"

A queue of visitors stretched out the door from the round

lavender building. The longer I shouted, the more of them turned to look at me. One or two waved a hand in dismissal, but the rest started to shift uncomfortably from foot to foot. A couple even left the line and walked away. I smiled to myself as horrified staff poured out of the building and hurried to reassure the rest.

"He is only experiencing a temporary lull in enjoyment," announced a Winslovak with a cone that magnified his voice. "Please stand by. We are handling this matter. Please go on having fun. Winslow cares about you! Pay no attention. Please, pay no attention!"

"They're ignoring me!" I shouted, waving my arms. "Stop! Look at me!"

"Ha," said a small Deveel child being towed past me by his worried parents. He sneered. "You don't know how to throw a good tantrum."

That gave me a great idea. I threw myself on the ground and began kicking and beating my fists against the paving stones. Then I flipped over and punched the air with both hands, wailing.

Aahz and the others had reached me by then, but so had the musicians. The trumpeters and trombone players began to play in the same tempo as my kicks, but diminishing. I noticed that as the music started to slow down, so did my movements. Deliberately I tried to shake my hands at a different pace. It was hard to ignore the music. They were making it hard for me to keep doing what I wanted to do. I grew angrier.

"Stop trying to influence me!" I yelled to the powers-that-be that I knew must be listening. "Stop! You can't make me feel better unless you give me what I want!"

Their response took longer to arrive that time, as if they, too, had to scramble to gather up enough power to make it happen.

"See, everybody?" said a cheerful voice. "We are bringing him what he asked for!"

Dozens of Winslovaks with name tags appeared and crowded around me. Every one of them had double-handled gold cups in their arms. They offered them to me. Some were magikal, but most were just decorative.

"Would you like this one?" a tall male asked.

"No, take mine!" a shorter, skinnier male said. "It's what you really want!"

But none of them were the Loving Cup. I snatched each of them out of the hands of the Winslovaks offering them and threw them aside. The cups vanished either in midair or after the first clanging bounce.

"No. Nope. No. Not right. No." The next was made of paper-thin metal. I grabbed it and mashed it between my palms and tossed it over my shoulder. "Do you think I can't see what you're trying to do? You can't distract me! I am Skeeve the Magnificent, and I know a real magikal cup when I see it! Bring me the Loving Cup!"

By then, I was surrounded by Winslovaks, all looking worried. Not just brows wrinkled with friendly concern, but fearful and nervous.

"Mr. Skeeve, you are getting all worked up," Soona said. "It's not necessary."

"Yes, it is." I did my best impersonation of one of Aahz's snarls. "Nothing else seems to work!"

"All you ever have to do is ask."

I crossed my arms.

"I have been asking! I have been waiting too long!"

"Miss Bunny, Mr. Aahz . . ." Soona began, appealing to my friends.

"Just Aahz," my partner said.

"Aahz, please! Can't you reason with him? Everything takes time. We need time!"

I felt sorry about the desperation on her face, but I hardened my will. I would keep on being difficult for as long as it took. I recrossed my arms and, for good measure, crossed my feet as well.

Aahz snarled at them. "Excuses don't impress me. Action impresses me. My partner asked you to find him the Loving Cup. You said you'd get it. Now, get it!"

Soona turned to Bunny.

"Miss Bunny, please! You are his employer and his good friend. Won't you calm him? We will keep up our efforts, but please ask him to be patient!"

Bunny put on the expression she used for bill collectors and would-be clients who were wasting our time and theirs.

"Do you know what really burns my socks?" Bunny asked. "I've been to Winslow before. I loved it! I told everybody I knew how nice it was to come here. In spite of the nosebleed fees, I always thought it was worth it. Now my friend wants *one tiny little* magik cup, and you have strung him along for so long that he's about to blow his top. I am just going to have to get on the Crystal Ethernet and tell everybody I know just what happened here. And you know what will happen after that? They'll tell everybody they know, too!" She brandished Bytina. Her PDA radiated a fantastic glow of light from its tiny crystal screen that seemed more powerful than the little device was capable of producing. "And they will all be so disappointed!"

"That's what I think, too," Tananda said.

"Miss Markie, how can we make this better?"

"Don't even ask me," Markie said, with her tiny brows lowered. "Ask Skeeve."

"Then what can we do, sir?" Soona asked plaintively, turning back to me.

I put out my lower lip.

"I want the Loving Cup. I want the real one. I'm tired of waiting. If I don't get it I'll have to tell everyone how I feel. I want it now. If I don't get it, then I will have to make all your other visitors as unhappy as I am."

It was a bluff. I was pretty sure they could neutralize any action I took, even bouncing me out of Winslow completely or sending the free-ranging equivalent of Benjy to throw me into a wall, but I thought it was worth a try. I kept the sorrowful expression on my face. The Winslovaks went into a quick huddle in the lantern-lit twilight.

When they broke, their faces were woeful.

"We *can't* help you, Mr. Skeeve," Soona said.

Inwardly, I felt triumphant. I had gotten more of a response than I ever did playing Dragon Poker. I had forced them to make an admission that hurt them more than anything else could have.

"Then I want to talk to somebody who can."

The employees huddled again. I could tell that passing me up the chain of command was the very last thing they wanted to do, and I had forced them to that extremity. Or at least I thought I had. I waited, defensive magik at the ready. I had to be prepared to fight for my life.

At last, Soona turned back to me.

"Please come with us, sir," she said. I refused to move.

"Where are we going?"

"We are taking you to the Disconsulate."

I couldn't help it. I held my chin up proudly as I followed them.

CHAPTER TWENTY-SEVEN

"Just another story, and we're through."

—SCHEHERAZADE

"What's the Disconsulate?" **Markie asked, her** voice echoing off the tiled walls. Soona had taken us to one of the uncountable invisible doors that were peppered around the resort, and through not one, but two glittering rings of blue fire. The doorway at the end led into a brightly lit hall whose end was too far away for me to see. The brightly lit passage was as colorful as a garden, lined with intricate mosaics in colors of ruby, emerald, sapphire, gold, and silver. In fact, I thought, glancing at a depiction of yellow flowers floating on a stream under a bridge, the stones were probably real gems and precious metals.

Soona sighed miserably, a noise that I never thought I'd hear from the happiest place in all the dimensions.

"It is where unhappy people apply for what they want so they won't be miserable any longer."

"Who runs it?" Aahz asked. "We're not talking to just any minion."

"No, sir," Soona said. "The executives in the Disconsulate have the ultimate authority in this dimension."

"Good," Bunny said.

I strutted down the passageway, excitement growing in my belly. At last, we were going to talk with somebody who might have the power to locate Servis and get the Loving Cup back for us. We would be able to hand it over to Looie and fulfill our contract. I could almost feel the smooth surface of the cup's bowl in my hands.

"You're cheering up," Aahz growled at me under his breath. "Knock it off!"

"I'm not!" I protested, but I slowed my pace and let my shoulders droop a little.

"That's better. Don't break character."

I couldn't even begin to figure out that sentence.

"What does that mean?" I asked.

"It's a term actors use. This isn't over. It's just another test. You're still supposed to be disgruntled. I realize you're only a Klahd, but try to keep your mind on your job."

That was a low blow! A retort sprang to my lips, but the steady look in his eye told me the problem was me, not him. He wanted me to stay angry. I should be. If I was the discontented customer I appeared to be, I had to keep my ire at the forefront of my mind. I would not break character. I lowered my brow and kept it there.

I fervently hoped Benjy was right about making sure I got to the people at the top. The corridor seemed to stretch on into infinity. With what I knew about architects such as those in the Bazaar who could make buildings that had a back door into other dimensions to extend their square footage, Winslow could be making me walk until I dropped or turned back, so they wouldn't, in his words, have to do anything hard.

Cheerful scene succeeded pretty picture, and was in turn followed by images of joyful Winslovaks giving one another gifts, animals frolicking and fish leaping out of sunlit waters with diamond sprays scattering. Music with a catchy refrain provided a subtle undertone. Before I realized what I was doing, I was walking in rhythm, then bouncing to the tune. It's hard to stay in a bad mood when you're dancing. The music was so infectious that no matter how I tried to walk between the beats, it caught me again and again.

Finally, I sat down on the floor.

"That's it. I'm not going any farther. We've been walking for over an hour."

"But you have to, sir," Soona pleaded. She took my arm to help me up. "We're almost there, I promise!"

"There you are, Mr. Skeeve!"

We finally reached the end of the hallway. A couple of beautiful women emerged from the door at the end and came to take me by the arms. They pulled me with them. Beyond the portal was a room so beautiful that I found myself gasping wherever I looked. A tent of cobalt blue silk enveloped the ceiling and hung to the floor in shimmering folds and swags. Standing lamps of black wood with gilded tips provided a warm golden glow. The heady air was filled with a smooth, exotic perfume that seemed to caress my face.

"Please, sit down," the first girl said. They guided me to a deep armchair like the one my grandfather had had, with a high back and broad, curving arms. I had always thought of it as a throne. I settled into it. It was more comfortable than Granddad's. In fact, I had never enjoyed a piece of furniture so much. The women sat on the arms. "You must be hungry and tired."

"I am, a little," I said.

The second one poured wine from a tall golden jug into a silver cup.

"Drink," she said, holding it to my lips. I took a sip. The

smooth, sweet wine made me feel warm all over. I swallowed hastily. She kept it tilted up until I had consumed at least half.

"My friends, where are my friends?" I asked. I tried to look around, but all I could see was the two of them and more of the cascading blue silk.

"We are taking good care of them, too," the first one said, leaning close to me. She wore a spicy perfume that tickled all of my senses. Her lush hips protruded from the chair arm just over my lap but never touched me. "Now, how can we help you?"

She toyed with a lock of my hair. The other stroked my hand. It felt so good I started to relax against the cushions.

"Yes, that's it," the second one said, leaning in close. "All we want is for you to enjoy yourself. Be calm. You can tell us anything you want."

I was tired from days of fruitless searching. It seemed like hours since I had started my necessary tantrum. It was so nice just to sit there, being quiet and content. The wine warmed my belly. The girls didn't push me. They just spoke to me in their soft voices. I could stay there for days.

"That's right," the first girl said, stroking my forehead. "Later on, if you want, we can . . ."

"Gleep!"

A scaly green head shoved in between the girls and pushed them off their perches. My dragon slurped my face. His stinking breath, reminiscent of a long-dead skunk-weasel that had had cabbage for its last meal, brought me back to my senses. I sputtered and wiped slime off my cheeks. I started to scold him, but his unhappy eyes reminded me that none of this was what I really wanted.

"Good boy, Gleep!" I cried.

With his help, I struggled out of the chair. All of this, the women, the wine, the comfy chair, was another ploy. We were being watched and measured by some unseen force. My will had to be stronger than theirs. I had to resist. The moment I said yes, we were stuck. I would not fail.

My friends had been lured into similar honey-traps. On a chaise longue, Aahz was surrounded by beautiful women from several dimensions. One fed him grapes while another filed his nails. Two of them massaged his shoulders and cooed into his ears.

"Aahz! Come on!"

Aahz grinned at me lazily.

"Are you through being seduced?" he asked.

"Yes! Let's go!"

It took slightly more effort to extract the rest of our friends from their distractions.

"I was having the most stimulating philosophical discussion on architecture with a young lady from Caf," Chumley said, straightening his glasses as he left the bevy of beauties who had surrounded him.

"Yes," Aahz said. "I could tell by the way she was coiled around you."

Bunny's face was red with embarrassment.

"They got us again," she said.

"They're good," Markie agreed. "They really know how to push our buttons. I could take lessons from them."

I went to confront Soona, who stood almost hidden among the swags of hanging silk.

"No more," I said. "You can keep this up until I'm so tired that I collapse, but when I wake up I'll still want the same thing."

Her shoulders drooped.

"All right," she said. "Please come this way."

She pushed aside a tapestry and pushed on the deep red wooden panel behind it. I blinked at the stark light of yet another passageway, this one plain and bare. Gleep bounded out into it and swished his tail eagerly, bounding up and down until I went to join him.

"Love the décor," Markie said, looking around. "Sensory-deprivation gray is in this season."

"Pretty weird," Haroon said. "There ain't no scents here a-tall. Never smelled nothin' like it."

He kept his nose to the floor, letting out puzzled yips and croons until we reached our next destination. Soona pushed open a section of wall and stood aside for us to enter.

Whereas the previous room had been the ultimate in sybaritic luxury, this one was utilitarian in the extreme. Chairs had been bent out of a single piece of gray metal, indistinguishable in color from the walls. A half wall separated us from the only source of sound, a faint scratching noise. I went to peer over it. A Winslovak woman with short white hair in a baggy gray suit went over a single gray document with a gray pencil.

"Ahem!" I cleared my throat. "Excuse me. I need to see whoever is in charge."

She never looked up.

"Please wait. I will let you know when they are available."

I went to sit in one of the chairs. They weren't made for comfort. I kept springing up to pace back and forth. Haroon sniffed all around the room and came back to us.

"Who's the 'they' we're waiting for?" I asked him. His large brown eyes were puzzled.

"Don't know, son. Still no smells. 'Fact, she don't smell of nothin', either! A fellah could get bored to death tryin' to follow a scent here."

We sat for a while in silence. I drummed my fingers on my knee.

"Did I tell you about the little task I took in Karnstel last month?" Tananda began. "I told you that my old friend Takkit had, uh, an interest in some of the pieces that weren't on display at the Art Museum there?"

"Tanda!" Bunny exclaimed. "A second-story job?"

Tananda grinned.

"I know. But they're so much fun! Besides, Takkit had been the one who, uh, provided the pieces to the museum in the first place. And the thieves never paid him, so what else could he do? He swore to me we'd only remove what he was owed, so I went with it."

"How did you get in?"

"Well . . ."

Tananda's words seemed to be absorbed by the plain gray walls. I could almost hear her, but her voice faded in and out like an echo. She tried again. She still sounded as if she were far away. I lost interest in listening and found my attention wandering.

Chumley removed a small book from amid the thick fur on his chest and adjusted his glasses on his nose. He opened to the page and peered down at it.

"I say, the light in here isn't strong enough for reading."

That was something I could help with. I took a small quantity of the magik I had been saving and made a small globe of light. I sent it floating toward Chumley.

"Thanks, old fellow," he said. He prodded it so it would sit over his shoulder. With a contented sigh, he settled back to read.

The light faded out. Chumley glanced up at me. I restored the light, but it faded again. And again.

I renewed the spell, but each time it took more magik and deeper concentration. Eventually, Chumley shook his head and put the book away.

"Thanks anyhow, old fellow."

"You know what? This place needs some livening up," Bunny said, forcing her voice to sound perky. "It needs decorating!"

"You're right," I agreed. I started throwing illusions on the walls, big, colorful images of things I had seen in my travels with Aahz. In my mind, I knew what they looked like, though I couldn't see them with my eyes.

"That's so pretty," Bunny said, looking around. "Look at those red birds! They're the most beautiful creatures!"

"I wish I could see them, too," I said, "but illusions are invisible to the caster."

"Allow me," said Markie. She spread out her small hands. Between them, exotic animals emerged, parading around the room like a circus come to town. Vines crawled up the walls. Snakes and lizards peered out at me from between the leaves. She was much better at lifelike illusions than I was.

"What's that?" I asked, pointing to a tall beast with stripes and a long, treelike neck. "Wait a minute, it's fading!"

"Hey!" Markie said. "My illusions!"

The receptionist rose to her feet and peered at us sternly.

"Please don't deface the walls and floor," said the receptionist. "It's not allowed."

"Why not? I'm bored!"

"At least give us some magazines," Aahz said.

"That's not possible, sir," the receptionist said. "You're just going to have to wait. In this room. Here." She turned to me with a sharp look that reminded me of one of my teachers. "As it is."

Aahz sprang up and paced.

"This is another attempt to get us to give up," he snarled. "Stuck in a waiting room, waiting for what? Another delaying tactic?" He stormed over to the receptionist. "Get someone out here, now!" he bellowed. In spite of the deadening quality of the walls, his voice rang in our ears. "I'm not paying three gold pieces a day to sit in a blank room with no windows!"

"I'm sorry, sir," the receptionist said. She still had no expression, either in her voice or face. "Please continue to wait. You will be admitted in due course."

"When?"

Aahz wasn't the only one who was losing his temper. I hammered on the top of the half wall.

"Let us in! We have to talk to the authorities! We don't have much time!"

"Please wait. It won't be long."

She went back to her paperwork.

I went back to pacing.

After a while, I realized that my stomach was rumbling. After days of feasting on first-class cuisine anytime we wanted it, I started to feel the lack of food. I went back to the receptionist.

"Is there anything to eat or drink around here?"

"No, sir."

I threw up my hands.

"When can we see the people in charge?"

"When they are ready, sir. Please be patient."

I sat down and shifted. There was no way to sit on those chairs that would let me remain comfortable for more than a few minutes. I pulled two together side by side and sat in the space between them. It wasn't good, but it wasn't bad, either.

"Try this, fellows," I said. My friends took my suggestion. We ended up sitting closely side by side on each other's half chairs. I felt a little silly. The authorities had a lot to answer for, when I finally got to speak to them.

Time ticked away.

None of us had had any sleep in hours. I drifted off with my head on Chumley's shoulder.

When I woke up, there was no way to tell how long we had been there. The room had no clocks and no windows, so I couldn't see the sky. The others awakened a few at a time. They looked around at the plain gray walls, torn between disappointment and frustration.

After the lush hospitality we had enjoyed so far, this was an insult. They wanted us to give up and go. I couldn't let

Bunny and the others down that way. I marched up to the desk. The receptionist glanced up at me without interest.

"I want to see someone!" I said. "You can't just make me wait here forever."

"You can always leave, sir," she said.

I smacked my hand on the counter. I used magik to make my voice boom, fighting against the deadening spell that tried to eat my words.

"No! There is no chance I will leave. *Ever.* Tell whoever it is back there that the longer I have to wait here"—I raised my voice so it would be audible on the other side of the wall behind her—"the bigger the story I will spread to the rest of the world about how things really are here, starting with Deva! I'll go on a tour. I'll write a book! I know an author, Zol Icty. He'll help me get started. I'll tell everyone I know what happened! Winslow will go to pieces!"

For the first time, the receptionist wore an expression. It was dejection mixed with a tiny hint of admiration.

"It already is."

She beckoned to us.

"The council will see you now."

I stayed at her heels as she walked to the wall and opened yet another of Winslow's invisible doors. I pushed into the room beyond before she could change her mind.

Eight Winslovaks looked up at me. The four males and four females wore long blue robes that pooled on the floor like waterfalls and necklaces of round white beads, each with a silver whistle on the end. They sat at an oval table made of blue glass spread with what looked like a complex but translucent tapestry of tiny, colorful threads. Each of the Winslovaks had the dignity of a king, the bearing of statesmen and powerful leaders, magicians and world-beaters.

Each of them looked absolutely exhausted.

"Another ploy," Bunny said, grimly.

"More tests," Aahz said.

"No," I said. My heart went out to the people at the table. They were bent and worn with weariness and desperation. "This is real."

The eldest and most august of the Winslovaks looked up at me.

"How can we help you, Mr. Skeeve?"

I pulled an empty chair from beside the wall and sat down beside him.

"I think I'd better ask how we can help *you*."

CHAPTER TWENTY-EIGHT

"Come on back behind the curtain."

—THE WIZARD OF OZ

"How did you know?" asked the first Winslovak, once introductions had been made and the rest of my friends found seats around the table.

"Stood to reason," Aahz said, his chair tilted back and his feet up. "The merry-go-round is winding down. Last time I was here, I didn't even know there was a Central Help Desk. When we got here a few days ago, you could just walk in and talk to one of your reps without waiting. When Skeeve threw his fit out on the pavement a while ago, the line stretched out the door. People aren't getting the *Fantasy Island* dream they expected. Ours is an unusual situation. We're not here to enjoy ourselves. We need just one thing, then we go. We had to escalate on purpose to get to see you. But the ordinary tourist shouldn't be affected."

"You're right," the first Winslovak said. His name was Olk. "We want everybody to have a good time here! We do our best to make certain that the days you spend with us are unparalleled! This should be the vacation of a lifetime! Enjoyment is our product and we want everyone to have all they need."

"But *you're* not having a good time, are you?" Tananda asked, shrewdly. "You do all this for other people, and you don't get anything for yourself."

"One needs to be pleased with one's own accomplishments," said Kurtsie primly. The number six councilor had a long face and a long nose under a firmly controlled crown of braided white hair.

Markie let out a derisive snort.

"Aren't we past the brochure ad copy?"

"Truthfully?" said Relags. The third councilor was an older Winslovak with thinning hair and a paunch. "No. We're not enjoying ourselves anymore! No matter how much you give someone, they always want another thing more outrageous than the last!"

"The requests that people come up with," said Helfa in the fourth chair, throwing her hands up. "You cannot believe what some of them want! We have to work day and night to find enough magik to make their dreams come true. That's our original mission statement, sir. What if you could have anything you ever wished for? It means that Winslow has become a transdimensional wonder! People spend all they have to come here and enjoy themselves. They tell all their friends! Our dimension has become wealthy beyond our most distant imaginings. We have as much business as we can handle! Far more than we can handle, in fact. It has become a millstone around our necks."

"That's easy. Say no," I said.

"We can't!"

"Our reputation rests on keeping everybody happy," Olk said. "Saying no is out of the question."

"But you're miserable," Bunny said.

"And the force lines are being depleted," Aahz said. "How is that even possible?"

The councilors looked at one another.

"Do I have to have my friend Chumley there shake it out of you?" Aahz asked. "What could drain force lines like that?"

"We're overextended," Olk said. "All that we do to maintain the climate and the protective spells . . ."

". . . And the portals, and the food service . . ." added Relags.

". . . Not to mention moving equipment and furniture hither and yon . . ."

". . . And manufacturing treats and treasures to satisfy every whim our customers have . . ."

". . . The amusement rides, the casinos, the lights . . ."

". . . Is why I could hardly glean a decent supply of magik from what looked like powerful sources," I finished. I looked from one pinched face to another. "I got the impression that this shortage of power is recent. Do you have any idea what's going on?"

Olk sighed deeply.

"A dark force is trying to destroy our beautiful Winslow."

"Who? Does it have something to do with the Loving Cup?"

"Oh, no," said Savva. "The Loving Cup has been here in Winslow for some time. We bless its presence. It helps us. Its very aura helps promote agreement. You must have noticed that yourselves."

"So you did make Servis take it!" Bunny exclaimed.

"No, no, *you* had requested it," the fifth councilor, Dure, insisted. "Your happiness takes priority over our concerns. We would never keep it longer than to assure you that it was the real thing. All six of them."

"We have no idea how it multiplied like that," Mannurs said. He occupied the seventh seat. "Most bewildering."

"Nor why Servis has taken it and not returned it," Savva said. "He has always been more than trustworthy."

"You should have received it back within moments of confirmation," Nurgin said, from the last chair on Olk's other side. He was the most elderly of the council.

"Where did he go?" I asked.

"We don't know that," Helfa said. "He wasn't even involved in the judging phase."

"And by the way, congratulations on winning the contest," Savva said, kindly. "You did really well. You finished more swiftly than we expected."

"Thank you," Bunny said, with a sweet smile. "But we are experts. Get back to the point! What happened? Why is Winslow falling apart?"

The council shifted uncomfortably in their blue glass chairs.

"Come on," I said. "You're used to being infallible. It's understandable, but it's not working anymore. We can't help you if we don't know what's going on."

Helfa took a deep breath.

"The problem," she said, "is the Nix Pyx. The Cup of Discord!"

"Seriously?" Aahz asked, disgusted. "There's a magik cup called the *Nix Pyx*? Is there a rhyming wizard who comes up with these stupid names? Every magik sword I've ever seen has a name that would make those trendy parents who give their children weird monikers envious because they didn't go far enough."

"I promise you, it's real," Olk said. "It's dangerous, very powerful, and very negative. The diametrical opposite to Winslow!"

Savva added, "It is causing us to have to redouble our efforts and solve problems that come up where there shouldn't be any problems!"

"If it's just an ordinary magik cup, why don't you just hunt it down and destroy it?" Bunny asked. "You have powerful enough force lines here to do almost anything you want."

"But this Nix Pyx is pouring out discord wherever it lands and causing us the greatest havoc. It forces us to use magik we don't have to keep up with its damage!"

"How?" I asked. "Why don't you just find it and stop it?"

"It's not in our control," Savva said.

"It's an inanimate object," Aahz said. "All you have to do is get your hands on it and either turn it off or move it to another dimension."

"We can't!" said Helfa.

"It's in the hands of another . . . concern," said Relags. "A concern that does not have the best interests of Winslow in mind."

"But why would anyone do such a thing?" Bunny asked.

The council hesitated. I cleared my throat impatiently.

"They want something," Dure spat out at last.

"That's Winslow's big deal, isn't it?" Aahz asked. "Give it to them. Then they'll be happy and go away. Isn't that what you want?"

"It's not so simple, sir." Olk let out a deep sigh, and he seemed even more blue than his garment. "They're blackmailing us."

"Who is?" I asked.

"We don't know. And we are used to knowing everything about everybody who visits our dimension." His eyes were huge with worry. "You have no idea how distressing that is to us!"

"How do you know *they* are there, then?" Bunny asked.

"We received scrolls from them. Requests, in the usual way." I knew what he meant, having watched Turista and the other clerks at the Central Help Desk tuck rolled-up papers into the air. "But these were threats. And if we ignored the demands . . ."

". . . Things would happen," said Kurtsie. They all looked unhappy. "We didn't believe it. But they did happen."

"Why didn't you try to deal with the blackmailer then?" I asked.

"We had everything under control," said Mannurs.

"How?"

He beckoned me to look closer at the table. I realized the tapestry spread over its top was magikal. The images within it weren't static. They moved and changed like a living thing. With thumb and forefinger, he pulled up a thread and spread it along his fingers for me to see.

"Normally, we manage events by using these threads. Most of the time, Winslow's magik keeps everything moving along by itself. When it needs a hand, we intervene."

I peered closely. In the midst of a cheering crowd, a group of Kobolds was scribbling mathematical formulae on a big board with a bright blue pen. When they completed a line of incomprehensible figures and numbers, a massive check mark appeared beside it. The math contest that I had heard about on the night of the Scavenger Hunt was under way. The Kobold team filled the air with cheerful symbols.

"What's wrong with this one?" I asked. Helfa grimaced.

"Nothing! It's this one that is going wrong."

She plucked another one up and held it toward me. It looked oddly dark against the rest of the woven picture. I had a brief look at an Imp toddler sitting in the middle of the street, holding a handful of strings. At the end of each was a blob of color. "All her balloons burst at once. That never happens. It never should have happened!" Helfa closed her eyes and concentrated. As I watched, the blobs grew into translucent spheres. The child stopped crying and laughed happily.

"And this!" said Olk.

He showed me a roomful of teenaged Whelf girls sitting at an elaborate party table. They sat with their arms folded, looking grimly at a clown with a round red nose and a painted smile dancing around with a wooden hoop. "This is a sweet sixteen party. There should have been three of our finest aestheticians giving them manicures." He pointed as the clown vanished, and three Winslovak women appeared. "There they are at last! But this poor fellow had a bad ten minutes. And so did our guests!"

"It doesn't look so bad," Aahz said. "So they suffered a momentary disappointment. They'll live."

"But it all adds up!" Olk cried. "It makes us take our attention from elsewhere. When things are going well, we can manage everything by ourselves. When it goes bad in several small ways at once, we have to turn our attention to it, and our enemies are there, waiting for our inattention."

"We are being pushed too far," Helfa said. "We're afraid that we'll miss something important, and our enemy will take advantage of it."

"We are afraid that they will escalate to"—Savva could hardly choke out the word—"violence."

"Winslow will fail!" wailed Kurtsie.

"That would be terrible!" Tananda said. "I love it here."

"Oh, thank you," Nurgin said, taking her hand gratefully. "To hear that means everything to us!"

"So everything is starting to circle the drain," Aahz said. "Winslow's hit the skids. Just no one knows it yet."

"That's not true," Dure said.

"Don't try to kid a kidder. None of you has had a decent night's sleep. Who's your backup?"

"We don't have any," Olk admitted.

Savva grimaced. "I should be at home with my children. I've been here for days."

Relags nodded. "Our employees are helping to keep everything moving, but eventually, they won't be able to cope. We'll stand behind them as long as we can!"

Kurtsie raised a quavering finger. "I should have retired

a month ago, but I couldn't leave my colleagues in the soup. We won't give in to blackmail."

I was horrified.

"What are they blackmailing you for?" I asked. "Gold? Power? A piece of your business?"

"Why, for all your preferences," Olk said, surprised. "We keep track of what you like and what you don't like, from your first visit onward. We know almost everything about our visitors, and what we don't know, we research. We store that knowledge and make use of it as need arises. These other . . . concerns . . . would like to have that information."

"For blackmail purposes?" I asked, drawing my eyebrows downward over my nose.

"No! *Marketing.* That information is worth thousands of gold pieces to the right people. Blackmail is temporary, and creates lasting resentment. But if you know exactly the person to present your wares to, who you know will buy based on past experience, you will save time and earn much more money than you would otherwise, and for an extended period."

"Years!" added Savva.

"Possibly for the rest of your lives!" added Relags.

I mused on that, but Aahz was expansive in his approval.

"That's brilliant!" he said, clapping Olk on the back. "With thinking like that you could almost be Pervects!"

"Er, thank you," Olk said, not looking as grateful for the compliment as Aahz thought he should be. "But that isn't why we collect that information. We use it to give you the very best service possible and make your visit here as enjoyable as we can make it. Not to exploit you."

"Never!" exclaimed Savva. "What a terrible idea!"

"Looks like those 'concerns' you're talking about agreed with Aahz about your files," Bunny said. "What are you doing about it?"

"Well," Olk said, a sheepish expression on his face, "we

hired one concern like yours to deal with those, er, not-so-nice people, but they don't seem to be getting anywhere."

"But why didn't you come to us?" I asked.

"We considered going to M.Y.T.H., Inc., but well, frankly"—Olk looked embarrassed—"we were talked out of it."

"By whom?" I asked.

"By the, er, concern we hired to find the Nix Pyx and stop the blackmailers."

"Can we get a little more specific?" Aahz said, impatiently drumming his fingers on the tapestry. "I'm getting ticked off by all your *concerns*."

Olk lifted his shoulders, conceding the point.

"A young lady. A magician. Her credentials were excellent. She is the royal magician in . . . er, well, that's none of your business. While we had your record of successes in front of us, she persuaded us that the makeup of your, er, group, may not be suitable to work on our behalf."

"You're kidding!" I exclaimed. "What's wrong with us?"

"Well, it goes without saying!" Olk said. "A runaway apprentice—"

"My master was assassinated in front of me," I yelped.

He went on to my partner.

"A magikless Pervert."

"That's Per-vect." Aahz growled. The ochre veins in his eyes swelled, and he tightened his hands into fists. The councilor didn't seem all that impressed.

"Yes, well, as you please. Pervect. An enforcer for hire." Chumley looked at his feet. "An assassin," he said, looking at Tananda.

"Retired," I pointed out. Tanda caught my eye and shook her head almost imperceptibly. I gulped.

"A discontented Mob moll who is deceiving her uncle with falsified account books . . ."

"They are not falsified!" Bunny exclaimed, her cheeks pink. "The results are skewed, maybe, but every entry is legitimate!"

"And this young lady here . . ." he began, indicating Markie.

The Cupy doll looked up at him with the sweetest expression I had ever seen. She fluttered the long golden lashes framing her large blue eyes.

"If you complete that sentence, I will see to it that you will be more sorry than you can possibly imagine. For the rest of your lives."

Olk swallowed hard. Apparently he had a rather vivid imagination, and he really did know Markie's reputation.

"Er, well. And your dragon here, who has, well, natural dragonish propensities."

"Gleep!" my dragon protested. He looked hurt.

"I admit that you have information on all of us," I said, feeling stung, as he no doubt intended I should. "What we are is not what we do. I think if your files are really complete, you can see our rate of success is higher than anyone else's, and that we treat our clients with the utmost respect. Our experience allows us to think in ways that other groups can't. Has the 'concern' you hired succeeded at getting rid of your problem?"

He squirmed uncomfortably.

"Well, no. She hasn't." He looked right and left as if afraid of being overheard, then leaned toward us, dropping his voice to a whisper. "She might be just the smallest part out of her depth. In my rather uninformed opinion."

"Well, she's preventing us from fulfilling our contract with our client, and it sounds like she's leaving you in the lurch, too."

The council didn't like it, but they were too desperate to ignore it. Olk toyed with the whistle around his neck.

"Er, that is true, sir. What do you propose?"

"We need to find your snobby magician and stop her," said Bunny. "Then we find this Nix Pyx and destroy it. I have a feeling once we get rid of that, the Loving Cup will turn up again. But we don't have much time! Looie returns the day after tomorrow—tomorrow, now. If we don't have it, he's through with us. Uncle Bruce will be so disappointed!"

"We have no idea what this young lady magician looks like," I said.

"Sure we do," Aahz said. "Your girlfriend. The one who tried to get us killed in Maire. The one we caught ransacking a room."

I frowned. "I think you're right. She seemed like she didn't want to be here. She was as out of place as we were."

"Exactly, partner," Aahz said. "We have to find her and stop her, one way or the other."

Helfa pulled a parchment scroll out of the air and unrolled it.

"Is this the young lady that you met?"

A wistful image with beautiful blue eyes peered back at me from the paper. It took only one glance for me to confirm what I feared.

"Yes," I said. "That's her."

"Dorinda of Zaf," Bunny read from the paragraph beneath the drawing. "Never heard of it."

"Small-time dimension," Aahz said. "Agrarian, same level as most of Klah. About as interesting as leftovers on a Thursday."

"Good," said Markie. "Now we have a name to put on her tombstone."

"Wait a minute!" I said. "Who said anything about killing her?"

Markie regarded me with astonishment.

"Why defend her? I bet she's the one who has been stealing jobs from M.Y.T.H., Inc. She's knocking your reputation to get the work away from you, so don't feel sorry for her."

"I wasn't!" I protested. I could tell none of them believed me. I didn't really believe me, either. I was torn. She seemed too nice.

"I presume," Savva said, with a heavy sigh, "that M.Y.T.H.,

Inc., will also demand a fee for the services you are now offering?"

"We can talk about that later," Bunny said, coldly. "We've wasted enough time sitting in your waiting room."

"Where is this Dorinda right now?" Aahz asked the council. Helfa shook her head.

"We don't know. Neither she nor any of our enemies appear in our tapestry. There are, er, numerous blank spots. Natural magik-repelling elements in the soil, plus privacy spells."

"That's inconvenient," Aahz said. "When this is all over, you ought to hire us to check over your security arrangements."

"Find Dorinda, find the cup," Tananda said. "She might be the one who forced Servis to steal it."

"But she's a magician, too," Bunny pointed out. "Isn't she likely to change her appearance?"

I shook my head.

"With the constraints on the force lines here, she might run out of power, so I doubt she can keep a disguise spell going forever. We just keep looking. She can't hide forever." He patted Haroon on the head. "And we have a secret weapon."

"Well, you're right, young pup," the Canidian said, with a wry smile peeking out between his floppy jowls. "Chances are pretty darned good I can sniff her out in no time."

"Good," I said. "Because no time is what we have left."

CHAPTER TWENTY-NINE

"Let's just talk."

—M. CORLEONE

The council promised us full access to all parts of Winslow, both public and private. They put out a notice with the image of Dorinda to several trusted, longtime employees to keep an eye out for her.

It turned out the greatest concentration of blank places in the tapestry map was in the private residences in the resort. After a conference the next morning on the most likely unseeable places this Dorinda could use as a bolthole between her attempts to search out Winslow's blackmailers, we split up. I took Gleep with me.

The most likely way to get in the door of all those rooms was to disguise myself as a waiter. The council agreed that I could deliver breakfast to guests, as long as I didn't make any mistakes or offend anyone. They sent one of the real waiters, Picnick, with me. Watching closely to make certain the lack wouldn't drain a necessary process, they let me, Markie, and Tananda fill up as much as we could from the force lines they were jealously guarding. Keeping back only as much power as I needed to protect myself and Gleep in case the female magician attacked us, I put on the appearance of one of the blue-skinned, white-haired Winslovaks. I donned a uniform and set out to work.

"But I didn't order a dragon!" bellowed the Deveel wearing a damp bath towel as he opened the door to my knock.

"But it's a chance to pet a dragon," I said, cheerfully, as I helped Picnick float the room service table into the room. "Specialty of the house. He's very tame. Safe even for small children to play with."

The Deveel was not alone. A very beautiful, gold-skinned female with four arms, tusks protruding from her lower jaw, and clad in a filmy white gown waved at me from the small dinner table against the wall.

"I'll pet him!" she said. "Oooh, what beautiful green scales! Can I have one?"

I glanced at Gleep. He shed scales all the time, but I had never tried to pluck one from his skin. But my dragon was game for anything that would get him some attention. He bounded over to the woman and shoved his head up under her lower right hand. She ran long, red-varnished nails up and down his spine. Gleep shivered with delight and licked her in the face with his long tongue. He wriggled his forequarters, and a shower of scales rained down on the woman. She gathered them up and fondled his ears.

"Thank you! Oooh, he's so cute!"

"Gleep!" Gleep said, putting his head in her lap.

"Hey, back off!" the Deveel shouted at Gleep. "She's mine."

Picnick and I set plates, cutlery, and covered dishes on

the table for the couple. By then, I had sent a fingerful of magik around the room. Neither of these two was disguised, and no one else was hidden in any of the closets or side rooms.

"Happy to be of service," I said, backing out into the corridor. With one final swipe of his slimy tongue across the golden woman's face, Gleep thundered out after me.

Every time we made a delivery from our rolling tray, another load popped into being on yet another pristine white tablecloth, accompanied by brilliantly polished silver flatware and sparkling crystal glasses. Picnick tapped on the next door.

"If the food is sent here by magik, then why deliver it by hand at the door?" I asked.

"All our service is personalized, sir," Picnick said, beaming. "Our guests in these residences prefer us to bring their meals and arrange everything. It would be so unfriendly if we just sent the food in. Although we have a few visitors who don't want to see anyone else while they are here." His thin brows drew slightly together.

"Do you disapprove of that?"

"Oh, no, sir! It's not my place to judge one's preferences," he said, his white brows jumping up his blue forehead. "It would be easier to see if they are happy if they would allow us to make contact. We only wish to please."

"Do you think any of those anonymous visitors are the people who are trying to steal your guest files?" I asked.

For the first time Picnick looked angry.

"I hope not! I . . . I . . . I would refuse to bring them drinks!" He stopped, appalled at himself, and clapped a hand over his mouth. He spoke through his fingers. "Oh, sir, I hope you can find them! Our council is the most kind and considerate you can imagine. They are very troubled by the situation. It is worrying all of us. I hope you can bring back our magik!"

"That's what we're trying to do," I said firmly. I reached over the tray and rapped on the door. It swung open by itself.

Gleep galloped happily into the room. A family who looked like Klahds but with fine-scaled faces and long, flaming red tresses gathered around him and began to talk to him in an unfamiliar tongue consisting of hisses, whispers, honks, and roars. Gleep replied in the same language. I stared in amazement. I had never met anyone who spoke Dragon before. After we delivered their piping hot meals, I drew Gleep aside.

"Who were they?" I whispered.

"Wyverns . . . cousins . . . Dragons . . ."

"Really?" I glanced back at the door, tempted to go back and talk with them.

"Come on, sir," Picnick interrupted my thoughts. "We have fifty-four more stops to make!"

"How do you do that every morning?" I asked, slogging along next to Picnick as we returned the empty cart through a crackling magik portal to the vast kitchens for the last time. It was midafternoon and I had to use some of the energy I was hoarding to keep from falling flat on my face.

"Every morning and every lunchtime," Picnick said, cheerfully. "I love my job! I wish everyone were as happy as I am. Too bad you don't want to work here. I think you'd be great."

"Thanks." At first I thought he was being sarcastic, but I decided he meant it. "And thank you for your help. I hope my friends had more luck than we did."

"I do hope so," Picnick said, shaking hands with me. "I will keep a lookout for the young lady. None of my companions remember seeing her in the residences. All we have seen is our host of regulars. But, as you say, she might be wearing a disguise."

I went back to the Round Castle and reported to my friends. None of them had found a trace of a hidden magician, good or bad. The council had sent us a scroll. No one else had seen this Dorinda in days.

"We're sunk," Tanda said, her chin sunk glumly in her palm. Chumley patted her on the shoulder.

Bunny squared her shoulders. "I'll explain to Looie when he gets here."

"No," I said. "We're not sunk. Perhaps Looie was right about saving on expenses and this Dorinda goes home every evening after looking for the cup. That means we have to catch her in the act."

"But how?" Bunny asked. I shrugged.

"I don't know that yet. I need to think. Anyone want to go and have a drink with me?" I glanced at Bunny. "Just one."

"There's plenty of booze here," Aahz said, with a suspicious glance at me.

I shook my head. "I think better with a lot of noise around. I'm going over to the Rusty Hinge. I wouldn't mind some company."

"We'll find you later," Aahz said. He flopped into a solid armchair and slung his legs onto the footrest. "I've had enough of happy people for a while."

"What'll it be, Mr. Skeeve?" asked the attractive server in the Rusty Hinge. Since the day after we had won the Scavenger Hunt, my ban on entering the inn seemed to have been lifted for good. I was glad, because the inn was the one place I felt even a little at home in the lush resort.

"A glass of wine," I said. "Just one."

She poured clear, pale green liquid into a tall glass and set it in front of me. I sniffed it appreciatively. Even without the feel-good spell that was everywhere in Winslow, I knew it was good wine. I took a sip.

Where could I look next for the girl, or Servis, or the cup? What did we do next? I was tired and frustrated.

A card game was under way at the table near the door. I glanced up at them. The dealer caught my eye. I recognized Swush, the Landshark I had met in the employee canteen. So that was another staged game for the benefit of a gathering of visitors from other dimensions. He tipped me a playful salute and went back to openly cheating his companions. I sipped my wine and sat watching, wondering when one of them would protest against the Shark's clumsy card handling and miscounting of chips. Now that I knew what he was doing, I realized how much skill went into the appearance of inept dishonesty.

"Can I get you anything else?" the barmaid asked, leaning close. "You look lonely. Would you like some company?" She aimed a thumb over her shoulder. A couple of girls waved at me from a table near the back. I looked hastily away.

"Uh, no. Thanks anyhow. I just want to think."

The barmaid nodded and went off to serve the next customer.

I watched the employees for a while. They seemed as if they belonged in another dimension, a happy one where everyone loved their job and nothing ever went wrong. They were part of the way Winslow functioned. It was a different kind of life than the one I was used to. It wasn't a bad life, but I knew it wasn't for me. I liked my dimensions with a little more open dishonesty and the possibility of danger.

A few employees from the Activity Department came through with whistles and clipboards. They tried to get me interested in the contest or race of the day. I really didn't want to participate in any of the group activities. Looie was due to come and yell at us later. I actually felt sorry for him, not being able to solve his diplomatic problems. He was as out of his depth as we were. We still didn't have answers, or the Loving Cup. I was more frustrated than ever. And I had no ideas. I sipped my wine, trying to cudgel a plan out of my brain. I felt I was letting Bunny down.

A couple of empty seats separated me from the only other customer on my side of the central bar. I couldn't place the dimension he came from. He looked like a cross between a Kobold and an Imp—small of stature, with a pinky-orange complexion and little horns on his broad, almost bulbous forehead. He was playing with a series of little rainbow-colored metal links, making them dance around on the counter. With a nudge, they waddled toward one another and linked up in sequence with the colors of the rainbow from red through to purple. He gathered them up, shook them like dice, and they did it all over again. I watched with fascination for a while, until he looked up and smiled at me.

"Sorry," I said at once. "I didn't mean to stare."

"Not offended," he said. "I just learned this trick. It looks really complicated, but it isn't."

I was intrigued.

"Will you show me?"

"I'm Prob," he said, shaking my hand. "I come from Durk. Have you ever seen anything like this place in your life?"

"No," I agreed. "I'm from Klah. Winslow's about as far from my home dimension as they come."

"Durk doesn't have a lot of magik, but I have been training hard. I'm only an apprentice."

"Me, too," I said. "So, what's this?"

"A guy I met in here the other night taught me this little trick. Cute, isn't it? And it's a lot easier than it looks. The colors naturally fall into their place in the spectrum. You just have to nudge them."

Prob was right. It wasn't a hard spell to learn, and it took very little magik to make the cubes line up. We passed the time talking about our lives. He was the son of a vintner, he said. I told him about our business in Deva. I found myself laughing as we passed the time. I realized he was probably one of the local color who worked for the Winslow council, but I didn't mind. I had relaxed and was actually enjoying myself.

Before I knew it, I felt a tap on my shoulder. I glanced up to see Bunny standing beside me.

"Have you been here all this time?" she asked.

"I guess so. But I've only had one glass of wine."

I glanced through the windows. It was dark. I had been sitting there for hours without coming up with a single idea. Bunny could tell by the look on my face, but she didn't chide me for it. I knew she was still blaming herself. She gave me a sideways smile.

"Would you like to join the rest of us for dinner?" she asked. "I figure we'll enjoy one last nice meal before we go back to Deva in disgrace. Looie will be here later on, and we'll have to give back his expense money."

"I'm sorry," I said. "I wish I could have been more helpful." I noticed Prob gazing at her intently. People couldn't help staring at Bunny. She was so familiar to me that sometimes I forgot how beautiful she was. I hastened to do introductions.

"Bunny, this is Prob. He taught me this neat little magik trick. Prob, meet Bunny. She's the president of the partnership I belong to, M.Y.T.H., Inc."

"Nice to meet you," Bunny said, offering her hand. Prob clasped it gently.

"My lady." He stood up hastily and patted me on the back. "Well, Skeeve, gotta go! My wife's waiting for me. Have to take the sprouts to dinner."

Haroon wandered up to us and gave me a friendly sniff up and down my pants legs, then moved on to Prob. I started to introduce him, but he stopped dead then scuttled out of the room on his short little legs.

The next thing I knew, Tananda was standing there with a knife to my companion's throat.

It dawned on me that I knew what was going on, and why. I sensed the disguise spell and realized I had been had.

"You're not really on staff here, are you?" I asked. "I think we need to introduce ourselves. My name's Skeeve, and you almost got me killed."

"I know who you are," the man said with a sigh. The bulbous forehead and orange skin faded, leaving pale peach skin, long brown hair, and those breathtakingly beautiful blue eyes. Suddenly all of my friends were there surrounding us. None of them brandished armaments, but they never needed to. I ran, I remarked at that moment, with a truly formidable crowd. She, on the other hand, was the enemy. "My name's Dorinda."

"I know," I said. "We've been looking for you. You're really good at hiding."

Markie held out a palm. A tiny pink flame flickered into life in its center. The fire grew until it was a crackling ball larger than my head.

"Tell me why you shouldn't get to eat this right here," Markie said. She still looked like a cute little Klahd girl, but her eyes were as cold and fierce as an adult dragon's.

The girl's large eyes darted from one to another of us.

"I am so sorry," she said. "You surprised me when I was going through Meeger's room. I only meant to send you to a far dimension so I could go on searching in peace. I had no idea that you'd end up in Maire."

"Lie," Markie said, never changing expression. "No one can get past those dimensional defenses by mistake. I tried it myself after I got over the shell-shock. I bounced. I *could* get in because I have been there, but a random travel spell only gets you to the barrier."

"It was an accident!" the girl protested. She turned to me. When those lovely eyes met mine, I almost melted. "Please, won't you let me explain?"

"What about it, Skeeve?" Bunny asked. She flipped Bytina, her Perfectly Darling Assistant, a small red-shelled device, open in her hand and aimed toward Dorinda. Bytina's miniature magik mirror glowed with a brilliant light similar to the flames Markie wielded. I had no idea that the PDA doubled as a weapon.

"Come on," I said. I stood up and held out my hand to the other magician.

"Where are we going?" Dorinda asked. Her hand trembled as I took it.

"Our suite. We have a pretty good liquor cabinet and the chairs are comfortable."

"Do I have a choice?" she asked.

"No," I said.

CHAPTER THIRTY

"It's better if we work together."

—IAGO

Tananda and Chumley's room was the largest, so we went in there. Tananda hung the DO NOT DISTURB sign on the door and bespelled the lock closed.

"Would you like a drink?" I asked. Bunny had pushed Dorinda into the chair that had kept her from getting up a few nights before.

"No, thanks," the girl said, folding her hands together. "If I'm going to die, I would rather do it on an empty stomach."

"Why didn't you tell me who you were?" I asked.

"I was working up to it," she said, with an apologetic smile. "I wanted to apologize."

"Apology accepted," Markie said, rolling a crackling, silver lightning bolt between her hands. "Prepare to die."

I pushed in between her and Dorinda, risking electrocution. "Wait a minute. I want some information from her first."

"All right, it's your funeral."

Markie lowered her hands, but the ball of lightning bounced up and down by itself, as if impatient to cause havoc.

"What do you want to know?" Dorinda asked.

"Where's the Loving Cup?" I asked.

"I don't have it!" she exclaimed. "If I did, I wouldn't still be here!"

"You're not working with Servis?" Aahz asked. She turned to him.

"No! I've been looking for him for days. I've been everywhere. I've covered even more ground than you have, over and over again. I don't know where he is, either."

"Then he still has it. We need to find him and get it."

Dorinda looked panic-stricken.

"You can't have the Loving Cup! I need it!"

Bunny regarded her coldly.

"Who cares what you want?"

"I do," I said suddenly. "Looie hired you, too, didn't he?"

"Yes," Dorinda said. She held out her hands in supplication. "Look, I really need this job!"

"You're doing too many jobs, honey," Bunny said, folding her arms. "You hunt for missing persons, you retrieve valuable magik items, you hunt down blackmailers—Do you do birthday parties, too?"

"I would if I could!" Dorinda declared. Her nose turned red, and those beautiful eyes filled. She burst into sobs. I reached into my pouch for a handkerchief. I couldn't get the pouch open.

"No!" Markie said. She held her thumb and forefinger pinched together, and I assumed that it was keeping my pouch shut. "Let her cry."

But Dorinda had her own linen square, in a pocket inside her long sleeve. She didn't cry long. She shed a few tears, then pulled herself together. I had to admit, I was impressed by her aplomb, even when confronted by people who had every reason to be her enemies. "I'm so sorry. I usually have better control than this. I'm tired. I don't think I've slept in days."

I felt sorry for her, but I didn't know what to do. My friends had been teasing me for days about her being my girlfriend. I had not really thought of her in that light, until that moment, and then I couldn't get away from the thought. Her eyes fascinated me. I wanted to stare into them again.

"Are you from Klah?" I asked. She lifted her chin, and the sapphire irises met mine. I felt a quiver.

"No, but our dimensions are sisters. You find dimensions in groups and pairs like that, Wyv and Draco, and so on. I'm from Imbolk in Zaf."

I pulled up a chair and sat down beside her.

"They said you were a court magician," I said, trying to put her at ease. "I did that for a while."

"I know," she said, wringing her handkerchief in her fingers. "I know all about you. You've done some amazing things."

Bunny tapped her foot on the floor impatiently.

"Can we break up this little mutual admiration society? Why are you looking for the Loving Cup? Why have you been stealing missions from us?"

"Frankly," Dorinda said, "we need the money. The budget is tight."

"Doesn't everyone?" Bunny asked.

"Imbolk has money," Tananda said. "I, er, paid a visit there once."

"Yes, I know," Dorinda said, with a smug look. "That was before my time. You won't get in through that chimney hatch again. I had it bricked up and spelled shut."

"Shrewd," Tananda said. "But what happened to the rest of the gold?"

Dorinda sighed. "Imbolk is broke. Our current king has been on the throne for only two years. His father was widowed about five years ago and married a princess to ally with Haren, her mother's kingdom. He spent almost everything in the treasury to seal the alliance and impress his in-laws. He died heavily in debt. The new king really is trying to straighten out the budget, but everyone wants everything right now."

"So why are you trying to make up the whole shortfall by yourself?" I asked.

"It's not just me," Dorinda said. "Lord Ralf, the chancellor of the exchequer, is squeezing every budget to the last copper piece. He makes everybody who has any marketable talents take outside missions to defray expenses for each of our departments. He hires out our chefs for feasts at the guild halls, and our best scribes have been doing illustrated books for sale in foreign markets. Some of the departments have no useful skills outside the kingdom, so I'm trying to earn money for them, too. Things fall apart and they don't get replaced. I can't tell you how many potholes I skirt in the side yards. The stairs to my tower are coming to pieces, and there are holes in the roof, but I'm not as bad off as some of my friends. Lord Ralf keeps up the main courtyard and the king's audience and personal chambers so that His Majesty has no idea how really bad things are."

"What about all the regalia?" Tananda asked. "There was also a massive collection of fantastic magikal treasures, most of them solid gold and studded with gemstones . . . I mean, I've heard stories about them." Tananda fluttered her eyelashes innocently. "You could auction any one of them off and it would support the entire kingdom for a year!"

"That's the king's blind spot," Dorinda said, flipping a hand. "He won't let us sell any of them. He loves to go and visit them, and hear the old stories from the keeper of the treasure. He said they're the kingdom's patrimony. But things do go missing once in a while. That's my third job here," she added resentfully. "I've got to find a cursed item that disappeared from the treasury before the king notices it's missing."

Aahz pushed a palm toward her. "Don't tell me. The Nix Pyx? You didn't bring it here, did you?"

"No. Lord Ralf sold it, even though I warned him it was a bad idea to let that one go, but the king's mother-in-law was coming on a royal progress, and we had to have the visitor's apartments renovated, not to mention uniforms and supplies for the army. When I find it, I can destroy it and have a harmless, nonmagikal copy made."

"Sounds like our blackmailer," I said. "Who did Lord Ralf sell it to?"

"A magician named Meeger," Dorinda said. "He's from Haren, too. Frankly, he scares the Pixy dust out of me. No matter how carefully I ward my tower, I always find him sniffing around in there. He's been after the Nix Pyx for years. He finally made Lord Ralf an offer so high he couldn't turn it down."

"Did you know he was blackmailing the council here in Winslow?"

"It took me a while to figure it out. Looie hired me to find the Loving Cup. He said it was here. I hired myself out to the council as a freelance troubleshooter to afford the resort fees. Then things started to go wrong. I knew I wasn't handling the situation," Dorinda admitted, with a downcast look. "I needed help."

"So why didn't you come to us instead of undercutting us for minor assignments?"

Dorinda's eyes flashed when she turned to meet mine.

"Yes, I'm out of my depth, but without my fee for finding the Loving Cup I can't afford *your* services, either. You're pretty pricey, you know."

"Our rates are . . . negotiable," I said. "We can talk about that later."

"Skeeve, you're not thinking of helping her, are you?" Markie asked, horrified.

"I, er, um . . ."

I fidgeted as my partners glared at me. The truth was, I would have done anything for Bunny, but I wanted to help Dorinda. Something about her just appealed to me.

"The Loving Cup is ours!" Bunny said. "I need that on the books!"

"But we can both collect from Looie," I said. "There are six Loving Cups now, remember?"

"What?" Dorinda asked.

I explained what had happened the night of the Scavenger Hunt. Her lovely eyes widened.

"That's wonderful!" she cried. She threw her arms around my neck and kissed me. My friends exchanged glances, some satisfied; others, especially Markie, wary. Dorinda appealed to the rest of my partners. "Please, let me help. I'll do anything to show you how sorry I am."

"Where's Meeger now?" I asked.

Dorinda shook her head. "I have absolutely no idea. He's always been three jumps ahead of me. I just don't think that way."

"Well, we do," Aahz said. "And it doesn't really matter where Meeger is."

"Why not?" I asked.

"Because he might be steering the problem, but it's the Nix Pyx that is causing all the trouble. And I think I know where it is."

"Really?" I asked.

"Really. It's not what we see here in Winslow, but what we're *not* seeing that's important," Aahz said. I could tell he was working up to one of his long lectures. "What's missing from this place?"

Enlightenment dawned like a summer sunrise.

"Magik," I said. "This place ought to be awash in magik, and it isn't."

Aahz beamed. "Exactly, partner. We need to find out where it used to be."

"How do we figure that out?"

"We ask the council."

"Oh, no," Bunny said. "I'm not walking down that endless corridor again!"

"You don't have to," Dorinda assured her, with a wave. "That's just for disgruntled tourists. I can get you there in five minutes."

CHAPTER THIRTY-ONE

"So I may be a little difficult to work for."

—J. STALIN

Dorinda might not have been my partners' favorite person, but she kept her promise. We stepped through a portal near the entrance to the Round Castle and emerged in the dull gray corridor steps from the featureless office where the forbidding receptionist held sway.

"Hello, Kiki," Dorinda said, as we entered the gray room.

The receptionist's face broke into a welcoming smile. She rose and embraced the magician.

"Where have you been, sweetie?" Kiki asked.

Dorinda smiled briefly.

"Hunting. No luck."

Kiki grimaced. She gestured to the wall where the invisible door lay.

"Go on back. They're having milk shakes. I'll bring you some. Strawberry, right?"

"Right," I said.

They really did know our preferences. We really could not permit Meeger to get possession of their files.

"How did you know one of the force lines had vanished?" Olk asked, astonished, when Aahz asked him the question.

Aahz took a deep gulp of his milk shake, which had been served in an enormous silver pail.

"Your blackmailer, who is a guy called Meeger, must have cut you off when he saw how much magik you use in a given day. It was his way of putting the screws on you."

I sipped at mine. Though it was the middle of the night and I had had no sleep, I was wide awake.

"Meeger?" Savva said. She plucked up several threads from the tapestry and consulted them. "From Haren? We know him. He likes his meat very undercooked, almost raw, and he drinks coffee morning, noon, and night. He's stayed here several times, always on his kingdom's expense account."

"Nice work if you can get it. But that's how he figured out that you must keep records of everybody else's likes and dislikes. He had access to the Nix Pyx—I can't tell you how much that name irks me!—and he had motive."

"Motive? What motive?"

"He's greedy," Aahz said. "That's plenty of motive."

"Winslow is so vast and complicated that he couldn't cause as much havoc here without harnessing the force lines," I said. "I think that's where he's using the Nix Pyx."

"But how do we find that place?" Olk asked.

"Where do your force lines run? Do you have a map, or can someone show me?"

Mannurs pursed his lips. "I am afraid that I only pay attention to the magik when I need it. I rarely seek out the force lines. They've always been there. Everything runs so well by itself, we only need to intervene occasionally. Truthfully, it is the visitors who make the greatest use of the magik sources. What about you, Miss Dorinda?"

Our erstwhile associate and prisoner shook her head.

"The ones I've been using are the same as when I got here."

"That would have been after this Meeger began his insidious mayhem, I fear," Helfa said. "If you are right about what he has done to Winslow, then I have no idea where he or the N—" She glanced at Aahz warily. "—Where the evil cup can be."

"Have you got a historian or an archivist?" I asked.

"I'm afraid not. The engineers of the system are long gone," Olk said.

Nurgin raised a quivering finger.

"I . . . I think I remember. I used to lead visitors around our jewel mine. Everybody loves poking around the old stones. We always made sure there were gems to be found, sometimes quite valuable ones, I might add. We, er, salted the mine by using a line of force that came right up the middle of the main street from out of the countryside, well past the safari camp, I believe."

"I've seen that one," I said. "Blue and wavy."

"No, my friend," Nurgin said, with a smile, "that's the small one!"

"The small one?" Aahz asked, disbelievingly. "Where did the old one lead?"

"It angled off into the hills. Always thought of it as a magik river. Brilliant white, sparkly, refreshing to draw from. Eh . . ." Nurgin paused and put his bony forefinger to his temple. "I'm rather surprised I hadn't thought of it being gone. As you say, the blue line is quite vigorous. But I don't get out much anymore."

"White is spirit magik," Aahz said. "The rarest of the five magikal elements."

"How can you block a force line?" I asked. "I thought it was a natural feature."

"Same way you'd dam a river," Aahz said. "But I never met the magician who could do it. I knew a guy who wrote his dissertation on diverting or damming force lines, but the professors thought he was delusional. He got laughed out of the university. I felt sorry for the guy. He ended up selling sports equipment in a small town in Perv."

"The empty force line sounds like the place for us to start," I said.

"Can you stop Meeger?" Olk asked.

"I think if we find the source, we'll locate the enemy," Aahz said.

"Will you let me help?" Dorinda asked.

"I . . . I . . ." I found it hard to talk to her when I looked her in the eyes.

"Yes," said Markie. "You can help if you shut up and follow instructions."

Dorinda's lovely eyes sparked, but she shut up.

"All right," I said. "Nurgin, can you lead us to where the line used to run?"

The elder councilor rose.

"It would be my pleasure," he said.

To my surprise, once he was on his feet, the seemingly feeble Winslovak moved so swiftly I almost had to run to keep up. He took us through the nearby door that led to the spot near the Round Castle.

We emerged into the sunny morning. I stretched my arms to ease the tiredness in my back. I yawned. So did the others.

"Let me help," Dorinda said. She put her forefingers to my temples. I stared into her lovely eyes. To my amazement, the weariness fled. She turned to the others.

"No, thanks," Markie said. "I don't want anything from you."

"All right," Dorinda said, trying not to look hurt.

"Nice day for a walk," Aahz said. "Let's go."

"This way," Nurgin said. He began to walk up the main street toward the distant hills. We hadn't even passed our residence when an evil presence appeared in our midst.

BAMF!

Looie glared from one of us to another.

"Well?" he demanded. "Where's my cup?"

CHAPTER THIRTY-TWO

"There's more than one way out of a bad situation."

—G. GYGAX

Bunny lifted her chin. Hastily, I threw the seductive princess image on her. I not only lowered her neckline, but I hid the signs of our sleepless night behind magikal makeup. She strode up to Looie and looked him in the eye.

"We haven't got it. Yet. It's early! We weren't expecting you until later on!"

The little man clenched his fists and jumped up and down on the ground.

"Not good enough! I need it now!"

Aahz growled at him.

"Do you see a cup? It's not here. We still have to get it. Understand? We don't have it yet!"

Looie poked a finger into Aahz's chest.

"All of you are fired! I want my money back! The delegates are back at the table, and they're fighting just like before. Without that cup, my kingdom is doomed!"

"We have bigger problems than you right now," Aahz said.

"There is no bigger problem than me!" Looie yelled. His face was red, and his eyes bulged.

"This entire dimension is coming to pieces," I explained.

"I don't care! My kingdom may fall because all of *you*"—he swept an accusatory forefinger around in an arc, ending on Dorinda—"have failed me!"

"I am so sorry, Your Grace," Dorinda said. "I have put forth every effort and am still trying to fulfill your quest. Believe me!"

"And for nothing, it would seem! You're dismissed. Go on." Looie flicked his fingers at her. "Get out of here."

I was torn. We had promised Looie, but this dimension was at stake, and we were Winslow's only hope. I also felt sorry for Dorinda.

"Don't send her away. We need her," I said. "Your cup might be in the middle of the problem with Winslow. Dorinda brought us some valuable information. We think we know where it is now. We need a little time to follow this lead."

"I don't care! You've had four days to find it!" He waved an angry hand at Dorinda. "She has had far longer! You are *all* wasting my time. I will have to try other means to save my land." He turned to glare at Aahz. "My deposit, Pervert."

"I might have returned it if you had addressed me correctly," Aahz said, in a low, dangerous voice. "But now you can go scratch for it. Consider it the cost of doing business. We have better things to do for clients who appreciate us. You hired M.Y.T.H., Inc., but you never trusted us to do the job correctly."

"But I need the cup! I need it now!" Looie exclaimed. He jabbed a finger behind him. "I have a tableful of delegates who all hate each other deciding how to divide up my kingdom! The two ringleaders are already at one another's throats!"

"We can't give you what we haven't got," Bunny said.

Looie grabbed her by the wrist.

"Then *you* can explain it to my king," Looie said. He shook back his sleeve to reveal the thick bracelets on his wrist.

"Hold one moment, please," Chumley said, plucking the gem from Looie's arm. The duke stared at him.

"Wait, the purple toupee can talk?"

"Indubitably," Chumley said, straightening his pince-nez. "It seems to me that there are two problems here: the missing cup, and your diplomatic impasse. I believe we can solve your second problem."

"Who's *we*?" Looie demanded, glaring at the Troll.

"My little sis and me." Chumley put his arm around Tananda's shoulders. Looie looked from Troll to Trollop with disbelief on his face.

"What? Are you some sort of comedy double act?"

"Not since primary school. I am quite serious. Under my nom de paix, Lord Wat-es-et, I have been an emissary from Her Majesty Queen Suzal of the Kingdom of Aegis to other lands in the dimension of Ghordon.[7] Little Sis, if you could just pop home and get my credentials . . ."

"No problem," Tananda said, with a wink. She vanished and reappeared in seconds with a carved stone tablet. She tossed it to her brother. Chumley caught it and presented it to Looie.

"A testimonial to my skills," he said. Looie scanned the stone document, unimpressed. He threw it to one side. Tananda caught it before it hit the ground.

"So what?" Looie asked. Chumley cleared his throat.

"So, since you have had little success, I offer myself, as part of M.Y.T.H., Inc.'s comprehensive service in the cause of peace, to negotiate on your behalf until such time as the Loving Cup can be located. My sister is also an expert at

---

7. Have a glimpse into Chumley's sideline in *Myth-Fortunes*, a book as well as an Audible listening experience.

putting disparate individuals at their ease—or temporarily neutralizing them until I can deal with them."

Bunny put a silken hand on his arm and ran a finger down the side of his florid face.

"What about it, Looie?" she asked. She fluttered her eyelashes. "Chumley is really very skilled. He can tear their arms off if they won't negotiate properly."

Looie wavered visibly. He gulped.

"Whoo," Dorinda murmured to me. "She's good."

"The best," I said, with pride.

Looie didn't like it, but he was overwhelmed by logic and desperation. He threw up his hands.

"All right! But I'm staying here! I want the cup in my hands as soon as possible!"

Chumley was unconcerned. "Might go better if you're not there, what?" he said. "But you'll need to introduce us."

"All right!" Looie snatched the bracelet back from Chumley's large fingers. "Come on!"

BAMF! BAMF!

Looie, Chumley, and Tananda disappeared. In moments, Looie returned to the same spot alone. He glared at us.

"All right. Let's get my cup back!"

"Not you," I said. "You're not coming."

"What?" Looie asked. His eyes bulged out so far I thought they might pop out of their sockets.

Bunny undulated subtly. I made the silk dress in which I had clad her shimmer over her bosom and hips.

"You have to stay here with me," she said, dropping her voice to a low coo. "You're too important to put yourself at risk."

Looie glared at her, an ugly combination with the perpetual leer he wore whenever he looked at Bunny.

"Risk? This is a resort!"

Bunny leaned close to him. "I didn't want to say this where anyone else could hear, but you were wise to hire us. There's a rogue magician on the loose."

Looie's eyebrows rose.

"Powerful?"

"Powerful enough to keep us away from your cup all this time. But now that we have teamed up with one of your other agents, we know where to look and how to get it back. In the meantime, I made us a reservation at Le Snoot. They have a special table waiting for us." Bunny lowered her eyelashes suggestively. "It's very private."

"Hmmph!" Looie was temporarily mollified. He jerked his head toward the rest of us. "Are you sure they can get the Loving Cup now?"

"I promise you, the next time you see them, they will have the cup." Behind her back, Bunny crossed her fingers.

"Good. Then tell them to get moving."

Bunny fluttered dismissive fingertips at us. I didn't mind. I was worried about keeping that promise she had just made.

CHAPTER THIRTY-THREE

"I didn't expect to see you *here."*

—D. LIVINGSTONE

With a wave of his hand, Nurgin changed from his long robes into walking clothes. His blue pipestem legs stuck out like the points of a compass from his knee-length shorts, and his skinny neck barely held up his balding head. His feeble appearance was deceptive, though. He had led us several miles out of the manicured part of the resort and into a well-kept but steadily thickening forest. My energy was beginning to flag after the first five miles, but he just kept moving along at the same steady if slow pace. I firmly believed that my legs would give out before his did. Markie floated on air beside me, preferring not to walk.

"Aren't you worried about running out of magik?" I asked.

"I have enough to float all the way across this dimension and still fight sea monsters," she said. "My capacity to store magik is a little higher than yours, and I've been trained to use power a little more efficiently, from what I've seen of you in action. Not that you're bad for a Klahd. I'll come visit sometime and teach you a few techniques."

"I'd appreciate it," I said. I never thought about the difference in how large a supply one magician or another could retain. From what my friends said, it sounded like part of it depended on what dimension you came from, but part of it was training.

The forest was like the rest of Winslow: well maintained, slightly unreal, and beautiful. The trees arched over our heads in a canopy of green and gold. A hundred different kinds of colorful little birds flew from branch to branch, singing. Even the undergrowth looked manicured. Among the thousands of bushes and shrubs, I never saw a dead branch or thorns that could reach out and snag a rambler's clothing. As we went farther and farther from the main street, the plants grew more tropical in nature. The leaves broadened and thickened, and vines wound up the boles of the trees. The flowers went from forest pastels to vivid jungle hues. We were walking parallel to the footpath. I spotted a sign that stood about eye level for the safari camp. I heard trumpeting in the distance. I wondered what kind of animal made that noise.

"I remember the magik rushing underneath my feet like a river," Nurgin said to Dorinda, who was walking beside him, listening attentively. "I know it went through here. If you try, you might be able to feel the edges of where it used to be."

"How?" I asked, striding to catch up with him. "If a line of force is dead, doesn't it just disappear?"

"Not at all, partner," Aahz said. He stumped along behind Nurgin, while Gleep and Haroon ran up and back, sniffing the ground all around us. "Think of it like a streambed if the water's been diverted. Magik leaves a trace where it's been."

Dorinda wrinkled her nose and peered around. "I think

I see an edge on that side," she said, pointing at the ground. "A long way underground. But it's the opposite of what I thought I would see. There are faint touches of power outside the line, not inside it."

I tried to see, not with my eyes but with my mind. I thought I perceived what she was talking about. In fact, when we came upon a huge oval boulder in the middle of the path, I distinctly saw the "stream" part on both sides of the part of the monolith that lay buried, leaving a pointed delta behind the giant rock.

"I can follow that," I said. In fact, I had often hunted along empty riverbeds in Klah because the animals used them as roads. My fellow Klahds usually ignored them, but they were better paths than we made. "It's an absence of magik."

"That's right, that's what I see," Dorinda said. She raised eager eyes to me. "I think we've got it."

I smiled at her. I liked being with her. I only wish it hadn't been under those circumstances.

"Now, all we have to do is follow it to the blockage, whatever Meeger has set up to prevent the magik from flowing, and uncork it."

"If he isn't sitting there waiting for us," Aahz said sourly. "Any blackmailer worth the price of the stamp on his letters will set traps and alarms to protect his insurance."

Dorinda and I glanced at one another in alarm.

"We won't take any foolish chances," I said.

"I know," she said.

We walked along together, keeping an eye on the edges of the empty line deep underground. I kept trying to think of things to say to her. It was difficult. Half my sentences started with, *I still have nightmares because of what you did to us*, and the others with, *I haven't been able to stop thinking about you.* She was as pretty as I had remembered. When she smiled, those big blue eyes lit up like sapphires. She was taller and slighter than either Bunny or Tananda, with long hands that had square palms but thin fingers. Her long, light-brown hair waved over her shoulders. I admired the slender neck and the small ears that occasionally peeped out. Compared with Bunny or Tananda, her dress was modest to a fault. Her hooded robe was belted around a small waist, but its long skirt and long sleeves concealed everything in between.

A large white rabbit hopped out of the undergrowth. It had a bunch of flowers with tiny pink blossoms in its jaws. It padded up beside me and kept pace as we walked.

"Were your parents magicians?" I asked.

"No," she said, with a shy laugh. "My father's a blacksmith. My mother is one of the dowager queen's embroiderers. What about yours?"

"My mother's dead," I said. "My father is a farmer."

"So both of us are the first generation of magicians in our family. What does your father think of that?"

"I haven't been home since I started my training," I said truthfully.

The rabbit made a strange noise, as if it was clearing its throat. I glanced down. It tilted its head up to me as if it were trying to say something, but its mouth was full. I shrugged. It rolled onto its back and kicked me.

"Hey!" I said, glaring down. The rabbit jumped to its feet and held its head up to me. Feeling like an idiot, I took the bouquet from its mouth. The rabbit gave me a disappointed look and hopped away into the woods. Sheepishly, I offered the bouquet to Dorinda.

"Thank you," she said, with a shy smile. "Windflowers are my favorites."

"Uh, good!" I babbled. "I mean, I didn't know that. It's not me, it's Winslow. They're pretty amazing here for picking up on likes and dislikes. Um." I paused, realizing I had just given Dorinda a bunch of flowers. That was a courting move if there ever was one. Was I moving too fast? My mind blanked as I tried to think of something clever to say. ". . . Uh, do you like being a magician?"

"It's not the easiest path," she said. "But yes, I know it's my destiny. And you?"

"I'm better off than I would ever have been if I stayed home," I said. "I've had great experiences, and I have made the best friends any fellow could have."

"Gleep!" said my dragon, rushing up to shove his head under my hand. I scratched it, scattering green scales all over. He gave me confidence. I grinned down at him.

Dorinda's eyes went from Gleep to Aahz to Markie, who was nonchalantly pretending she wasn't listening.

"You're lucky," she said simply.

"I know."

"You make your luck," Aahz said, brusquely. "Smell that?"

I inhaled.

"Just the usual scents you'd come across in a forest," I said, puzzled. "Plants, animals, water, stone."

"Wrong, sonny," Haroon said, his large black nose in the air. "Sour. Old. Not just stale, but rotten. I never smelled anything like this here. Winslow always smells fresh and clean!"

"I can't smell any of that," Dorinda said.

Haroon regarded her with pity in his large brown eyes.

"Well, lass, you could if you'da been born Canidian, ya pore thing. Them's bad stuff up there. Still quite a ways ahead, but close enough to be spreadin' its poison."

"Sounds like we aren't far from Meeger's hideout. Did you ever come across a place where the force line surfaces?" I asked Nurgin.

The old Winslovak raised his palms. "If there was, I never found it. I always thought of the line as being under the earth, never above it. I was always able to draw magik from it by reaching down."

"Well, Meeger couldn't block it if he wasn't right in the middle of it," I reasoned.

"Haroon, this is where you come in," Aahz said. "We're

looking for a cave of some kind." He thrust out a forefinger. "Follow that smell!"

Haroon took a few deep breaths and shot off across the forest floor.

"Haroooooon!" the Canidian cried.

In moments, he was out of sight in the undergrowth. Gleep thundered after him, crashing among the branches and jungle plants. We ran along behind.

It would have been hard going if not for Gleep. I stepped over trampled bracken and flattened bushes and ducked below shattered branches that had not survived being crashed into by a dragon's hard head. A red spider the size of my foot glared at me out of its multiple eyes as I passed between the torn remnants of its web. I used magik drawn hastily from a narrow red force line that corkscrewed overhead to repel vines and plants that draped across my path. Dorinda and Nurgin stayed close to me. I lost sight of Aahz and Markie, though I could hear both of them swearing behind us.

"Where are you, Haroon?" Aahz bellowed.

"Harooooooon!" came the Canidian's cry, ahead and to my right. I thrashed my way over giant ferns and in between fleshy fungi twice my height.

Suddenly, the smell hit me. Haroon was right: It made me think of rotting, fetid meat—or Pervish cooking. The farther I went, the stronger it grew, until my eyes watered. I glanced back. Dorinda had a handkerchief over her nose and mouth. Nurgin blinked rapidly.

"You can go back to the resort," I called to him. "It could be dangerous."

"Not a chance, young man," Nurgin said stoically. "I'm here to help! I want my dear resort cleansed of filth like this."

The smell grew stronger. With tears running out of my eyes, it was hard to see the path. I walked straight into a palm tree. A hand grabbed my collar and turned me toward the left.

"That way," Dorinda said. "You're veering out of the streambed."

"Thanks."

To protect my eyes, I closed them. In my mind, I could see the edges of where the force line used to be and followed the image instead. Gleep's passage had stayed within the boundaries, so I didn't bump into anything solid. The air became thick with reeking moisture. I felt as though I were breathing soup.

"There you are, young'un," Haroon said in a low voice. "C'mon over here."

I pried my unwilling eyes open. It smelled as though I were standing in the midst of a field of dragon droppings, but it still looked like an ordinary tropical forest. I glanced around, both with normal vision and my mind's eye.

"The line runs over there," I whispered, pointing through a thicket of black-and-yellow flowers.

"Yeah, it does, but there's a cave over yonder. Never smelled like this in all the years I bin here." Haroon pointed his large nose in the direction of a rise in the ground. The rest of the group caught up with us.

"Why are we stopped?" Nurgin asked.

"Shhhh!" Aahz hissed.

"Why?" the old Winslovak asked in a much lower voice.

"Listen!"

Aahz's bat-shaped ears were far more sensitive than anyone's except possibly Haroon's. I strained to hear. I felt my eyebrows rise at the same time as Dorinda's when we heard a faint clanking and a distant voice wailing up and down the scales.

"What's that?" I whispered.

"I think we found Meeger," Aahz said.

"That's odd," Dorinda said, listening with a thoughtful expression on her face. "I would never have thought of Meeger screaming. He moves around our palace so quietly that I never know where he is until I can hear him breathing behind me."

"You don't know what he's like at home," Aahz said. "Maybe he sings opera while he's torturing lab mice." He held out his hands, talons up, and limbered up his fingers. "Get ready. I'd rather sneak up on him than die in some epic battle that will be sung by bards after we're gone."

"Gleep!" exclaimed my dragon. He took my sleeve in his teeth and tried to tow me in the direction Haroon had indicated.

"And you!" my partner said, detaching Gleep from my arm and grabbing him by the snout. He looked my dragon straight in the eyes. "You stay behind us and you do what I say. You make one sound, and I'll have a new dragon skin rug for my den!"

"Glff!" Gleep sneezed explosively into Aahz's hand. Disgusted, my partner wiped his hand down his pants leg. Gleep looked up at him lovingly and slurped his face. Then he set his haunches obediently on the ground, an all-too-innocent look on his face.

A faint yellow line in the distance was the only source of magik in the area. I let Dorinda go first to fill up her store. What power was free to glean was so sparse that I regretted using any magik on the way there. Markie went next. It took her only a few moments until she had what she needed. I had to wait until the straining force line had replenished itself enough so I could absorb its magik. The council was right to be concerned. Every line flowing into or through the resort was at capacity. When I sensed that my internal supply was full, I nodded to Aahz.

"Let's go," Aahz said. "Stay behind me."

I thought it was unnecessary for Haroon to have to sniff the ground. I could have followed the stench blindfolded.

Thick-leafed plants almost concealed the slit in the ground from which the cries and wails emerged. Markie whipped up a couple of spheres and held them in her palms.

Inside the translucent magikal shells, miniature tornadoes banged against their prisons, demanding to be let out. Aahz slipped into the opening first. We waited a moment. His hand emerged and beckoned. Dorinda went next, with Markie close behind her. Haroon and Nurgin followed. I went last, with Gleep at my side.

I blinked in the darkness. The cave was high enough that I could just stand upright. A faint globe of light appeared between Dorinda's palms. She held it above Aahz's shoulder to light his way. We walked for what seemed like endless hours along a narrow, twisting passageway. The moans and cries grew louder.

Roots tickled my head as we went down a slope. The damp ground had been worn into a hard path. Footing was solid. All I had to worry about was bumping my head when the ceiling dipped. A few dozen yards in, the cavern opened up to either side. A still pool filled most of the floor, leaving only a narrow arc for us to walk on. Gleep sniffed the water. Something jumped, breaking the surface.

BLOOP!

Gleep jumped. The thing, a sickly white creature with huge dark eyes, submerged again at once.

BLOOP!

"Stop it!" Aahz hissed. His voice was drowned out by a loud moan far ahead, beyond a dark spot in the rough wall that indicated the next cave entrance.

Dorinda doused the lamplight. We felt our way along, one hand on the wall, one hand on the shoulder of the person ahead. Gleep kept his nose up against my back.

"No!" came the voice in the distance. "This is not the way I want it!"

As we got closer, I could see a faint pinpoint of yellow light coming from the next chamber. A hand closed on my shoulder and dragged me forward into the midst of the group. Aahz's face loomed in shadow.

"This is it," he whispered. "Stay against the wall. Get as close as you can, and jump him with everything you've got! We get one chance. Ready?"

"Yeah," Markie murmured back. The rest of us nodded.

We sidled into the new cave. This chamber was infinitely larger than the first. The ceiling soared above my head. I could tell by the feel of the air and the occasional bright spot of luminous lichen.

Moss slimed against the back of my neck like Gleep's tongue as I slid sideways. We climbed over boulders and screes of tumbled rocks. Now I could see the glow of golden light at the far end of the tunnel. I could sense the enormous buildup of power behind it, surging against it like ocean waves. In front of it, a small, dark figure seemed to be bowing and dancing.

"Meeger!" Dorinda breathed. "Wait a moment, that isn't him!"

"No," I said, standing up.

"What are you doing?" Aahz growled, reaching for my arm.

"I know who that is!" I said. "Servis!"

CHAPTER THIRTY-FOUR

"And then there was one."

—D. MACLEOD

I broke away from the others and ran toward the bar of brilliant golden light set in the vast dark wall. The slightly built Winslovak was shoving objects toward it. They clung for a while to the bright outline, then clanged to the floor. In the shimmering glow, I saw what they were: the six Loving Cups.

"Servis!" I cried.

"No!" the Winslovak shouted. "You must not have bad service here! My clients need to be happy! Go away! Why won't you go away? Everything was good until you came here!"

"Me?" I asked. "What did I do?"

But Servis wasn't talking to me. He picked up the cups one after another and pushed them into the blinding glare.

"Take this! And this! And this!"

"Servis, stop!" I said. I dragged him away from the light. "That's not helping!"

He raised desperate eyes to me. I would not have recognized the neatly groomed, well-dressed employee in the ragged, disheveled figure. But he knew me. He bowed deeply.

"Mr. Skeeve! What can I do for you, sir?"

"Sit down," I said. He was much smaller and lighter than I was. I picked him up and swung him toward a rocky outcrop covered with thick moss.

"But I must stop that . . . that evil!" Servis said.

"Sit there. It's what I want! Please do it."

"Oh, sir, I hate to disappoint you, but it's my job to clear up messes and misunderstandings!" He kept trying to pass me. I dodged in front of him, and finally had to use some of my magik to fix his feet in one spot. "Please, Mr. Skeeve! Let me free! It's my job!"

"Not at the moment," I said. "It's mine. Sit down. Have you seen anyone else in here?"

"No!" Servis said. "Just that!" He pointed to the object embedded in the wall.

The others joined me then.

"So he did steal all the Loving Cups," Markie said. "He must have been here since that night. Poor fool."

"I have tried to dig it out of the stone," Servis said, weeping. Nurgin patted him sympathetically on the back. "I have tried to cover it. I have offered it food and wine and all the marvelous things I could find in the resort. I gave it all the Loving Cups and their most benevolent magik! Nothing works! I do not know what it wants!"

"You really want to help?" Aahz demanded.

Servis looked up at him with hope in his eyes.

"Oh, sir, it would be my pleasure!"

"Then sit down and shut up," Aahz said. "I can't think with you yelling your head off."

"Of course, sir," Servis said. He sat down and folded his hands.

"Better," Aahz said. "Now, what have we got?"

"Servis had the right idea," I said, surveying the beacon in the wall. "I can see why he thought the Loving Cups would help. It's kind of cup shaped."

"That's the Nix Pyx," Dorinda said, in dismay. "Meeger was smart. Block the force lines with its vile magik and Winslow falters."

"Do you know how to counter it?" Aahz asked.

"That's easy," she said. "We have to get it away from the force line. Once we do, the power will flow again."

Aahz gestured toward the golden light.

"Be my guest," he said.

I rolled up my sleeves. I could tell by the hot yellow magik that the Nix Pyx put out that it would be a tough customer to handle. I didn't want to absorb any of its power. Instead, I took the magik I had gleaned along our trek. Using Aahz's technique, I built a globe of force around it. Because the Pyx's aura was so large, it took a good portion of my magik. Once I had it surrounded with red magik, I made the globe press against the walls of the cave. I believed that once it popped loose, the force line would be free.

The Nix Pyx fought me. Like anything magikal, it had an affinity for power. It had a whole source behind it, but it absorbed mine as well. Sweat ran down my face as I strove to keep the Pyx contained. It was older and far stronger than I was. I built my globe thicker and thicker, but it ate through the layers.

"I'm running out of magik," I said, through gritted teeth.

"Just say where and when," Markie said. She raised her hands, palm outward.

"My spell's fading," I said. "I need to collect more magik. Contain the Pyx! Try to push it out of the wall."

"Got it." Markie clapped her hands together. The sound wave echoed off the ceiling of the cavern. Brilliant blue-white light augmented my spell. The globe turned into a massive pearl. I could barely see the cup inside, but I could feel it.

It was angry.

The blue-white pearl started glowing so brightly we could hardly look at it. It wavered and shrank until it was the size of a pea. We leaned forward to see what was going on.

BOOM!

The magik exploded outward. Markie threw up a shield of power to protect herself, but it wasn't enough. She was catapulted clear across the cavern. Nurgin ran to help her.

The golden light lanced out again. I fought to contain it, but I wasn't strong enough. I used every single particle of power I could amass to surround the Nix Pyx in an unbreakable shell. It beat at the shell with hot magik.

The pressure eased slightly. My red globe took on a gentler purple hue. Dorinda stood beside me. She pointed her hands, palms pressed together, directly at the Nix Pyx.

"Magik alone isn't going to dislodge that," I said. "Help me keep the force on it. I think I can get it out of there."

After long training with Aahz and on my own, I wasn't bad at doing two things at once. Rebuilding the shell with what power I had left, I started to climb up the tumble of rocks.

"No, Skeeve, don't go!" Dorinda shouted.

"What are you doing?" Aahz called to me.

"I'm going to pull it loose!" I called back.

"Wait a minute," Aahz said. "What does that thing do?"

"It negates magik," Dorinda's voice echoed behind me. "It removes spells, and turns good things bad."

"Hold on there, partner!" Aahz shouted.

"What? Why?" I asked. I was nearly up to the Pyx by that time. It gave off heat like an entire tree burning in a fireplace. I reached out for it, wrapping my hand in a thread of magik to protect it.

In a moment, Aahz had scrambled up beside me. He grabbed me by the belt and heaved me away. I tumbled down the slope and landed in a heap on the cavern floor. I jumped up and started up again.

"Don't you come up here!" Aahz snarled. "Just keep it contained!"

I started after him. This time Haroon grabbed me by my collar. Gleep took my ankle in his mouth and held on.

"Let me go!" I cried.

"No, friend," the Canidian said, calmly. "Do what Aahz says."

So I did. Dorinda held my hand. We concentrated on reinforcing the spell around the cup.

Aahz yanked at the Nix Pyx. It seemed to be stuck. He put one foot on the rock beside the gleaming purple globe and pushed. It loosened very slightly, then snicked back into place. Aahz swore colorfully.

"I can help!" I said.

"You come up here and I'll tear your head off!" Aahz bellowed. "Ow! Put another layer on the spell!"

I pictured a third layer of the orb surrounding the brilliant gold cup. Aahz put one foot on the rock beside the cup, put both arms around the globe, and heaved.

POP!

Like a cork in a bottle of effervescent wine, the orb flew out of its socket. Aahz went tumbling down the slope. Rocks, loosened by the explosion of power, tumbled down after him. Shards of stone rained from the ceiling. I threw my arms around Dorinda's head and face to shield her. When the rain of stones and sand stopped, I ran to Aahz.

"Are you all right?" I asked, helping him up.

Aahz shook me off. He rose to his feet and brushed himself off.

"Piece of cake."

"Cake?" I asked, looking around in puzzlement. "Where is there cake?"

Aahz groaned. I don't think it had anything to do with his fall.

Dorinda put out a hand for the purple orb.

"Don't touch it!" Aahz bellowed at Dorinda.

"What?" she asked. She extended a couple of fingers. The big globe of violet light floated over and hovered beside her elbow. "It's not stuck any longer. I can levitate it like anything else. Oh!" She turned, lifting her chin as though a breeze was blowing against her face. "Feel that!"

I certainly could.

With the Nix Pyx removed from its path, the white force line was no longer blocked. It ran over us like an undammed river. The magik that had been lacking since our arrival was free. I filled up my internal stores in less time than it took to breathe. I let it wash around me. It felt like a great hot bath and the best liquor I had ever drunk. Everything around me glowed like molten gold. Eventually the crest passed and the force line smoothed out. I waded in it waist high. It was an amazing sensation. I had never touched a force line directly before. The two of us laughed, splashing one another with pure magik. I turned to Aahz. He had an odd expression on his face.

"Are you all right?" I asked Aahz.

"I'm fine," he said.

"Why wouldn't you let me help you?"

"Because touching the Nix Pyx would have taken your powers away," Aahz said. "I don't have any at the minute, so it's no big deal."

Nurgin escorted Markie back to us.

"Be careful, Miss Markie."

"I'm all right!" she said. She sported a huge bruise on one cheek, but she seemed otherwise intact. "I missed all the fun." She looked up at Aahz with grudging admiration.

"Nice job, Aahz."

"Don't mention it, squirt."

I was horrified.

"But, Aahz! How can we get your magik back now?"

Aahz waved a hand dismissively. "I figure the effect will wear off one day, just like the joke powder Garkin used on me.

I've got plenty of time. C'mon. Get the Loving Cup. I want to get back to Deva."

"Right!" I said. I was still amazed and humbled by the sacrifice he had made for me, but he might still tear my head off if I made a fuss about it. His implication was clear: He had plenty of time left, but I was still only a Klahd, with a Klahdish life span. I turned to Dorinda. "Let's collect the cups! We can both claim the find from Looie!"

"That will be a pleasure," she said. She ordered the floating orb with the Nix Pyx, now the only source of light in the cavern, to accompany us. We climbed up the rugged slope.

The socket of solid stone where the Nix Pyx had been ensconced was still there, albeit shattered and blackened, but the cups that Servis had been offering it were no longer on the ground below it.

"Where did they go?" I asked. "Did he accidentally invoke all of them?" I groaned as I thought about having to trace the Loving Cup across the dimensions.

"They have got to be here somewhere!" Dorinda said, in alarm. She turned up the intensity on the violet globe. In its lilac shadows, we both started pushing aside stones. None of the Loving Cups were under them. Haroon waddled his way up to our side.

"If you'll just allow me, missy," Haroon said. He sniffed my hands and Dorinda's, then put his nose to the ground.

"Harooooooooon!" he howled, his voice echoing off what was left of the stalactites on the ceiling.

He ran across the stone floor through piles of debris that had been scattered by the explosion when Aahz pulled the Nix Pyx free. He stopped at a small heap of pebbles and nosed them aside. Dorinda sent the orb floating to hover over his head. The warm glow picked up the sheen of gold.

"There's one of them," I said. I put the first cup into her hands, then went to help Haroon dig.

There was nothing in the rest of that heap. I started pushing nearby stones aside.

"Where are they?" I asked, becoming more desperate by the moment.

"Ain't nothin' there, son. I'd'a smelled it."

"But where are the others?" I asked.

"Back there," Haroon said, nodding his big head toward the cup in Dorinda's arms. "Seems to me when we released your big magikal line there, it undid the spell that split yer Loving Cup into six pieces."

"Tough luck," Markie said, sympathetically. She plucked the cup out of Dorinda's hands. "I'm taking this back to Bunny."

"Now, wait a minute!" I said. "What about Dorinda?"

Markie fixed me with a stare that said I ought to know better. I had to choose between one of my friends for whom I felt deep responsibility and a girl I had just met. A girl who, as much as I liked her and as helpful as she had just been to us, had tried to have me killed. I hung my head.

"Sorry," I said to Dorinda.

"I understand," she said. She shrugged in resignation. "We'll make ends meet some other way."

CHAPTER THIRTY-FIVE

"I did it, but the other guy got all the credit."

—GOLLUM

The trek back to the resort took a fraction of the time that the trek out had. So much power flowed around us in the restored force line that we coasted in it, floated in it, and finally flew. Like Markie, I lay on the air and let the magik push me along. Dorinda and I held hands and laughed together like little children. Nurgin helped Servis spruce himself up. By the time we reached the main street, the forlorn Winslovak was restored to his previous dapper appearance.

News of our success had arrived much faster than we had, with the power flowing from the restored force line. Bunting and banners had been strung between the rows of buildings. The street was filled with carnival rides, balloons, live unicorns with rainbow-colored coats, and row after row of tables filled with food and drink. Every single visitor and employee crowded the pavement, dancing, eating, drinking, and making merry.

When they saw us approaching, they all began to cheer. A brass band, at least a hundred horns and three bass drums strong, marched out to meet us. I tried to compose a few words of appreciation in case they asked us for a speech.

The crowd opened a path, and the remaining seven members of the council emerged. They strode up to us. I straightened up and gestured theatrically to Markie, who was holding the Loving Cup in her arms. But they weren't interested in that.

"Servis!" they cried, embracing him one at a time. "Good old Servis! We celebrate good Servis!"

Nurgin threw an arm over his shoulder and led him forward.

"He is everything Winslow stands for! He has proven that he will go to any length to make our beloved visitors welcome!"

One held up his hands for silence.

"Let this celebration in his honor commence! All hail good Servis!"

The band struck up a lively march. Everybody surrounded the surprised Winslovak to shake his hand or pound him on the back. He wore an expression of dazed delight on his face.

"But . . . ?" I began. "But what about us?"

Aahz came and nudged me in the ribs.

"Forget public acclaim," he said. "We'll get a golden thank-you from Looie in a minute. In the meantime, I could really use a drink."

A pretty Winslovak appeared out of the air, bearing a silver bucket with a tiny umbrella balanced on the rim. Aahz accepted the cocktail and chucked her under the chin.

"I really need one of these waitresses in the office," he said. "It's faster than mixing my own drinks."

* * *

Bunny and Looie weren't in our rooms in the Round Castle, and the Rusty Hinge stood deserted.

"They are probably out celebrating with everyone else," Aahz said, accepting another pail of good cheer from a passing waiter. A line of Deveels hopped past us, laughing uproariously. "We'll find them when all the whoopee-making dies down. I plan to party my socks off. Anyone want to join me?"

"I'm in," Markie said, sipping from a tall glass of bright green foam. She floated on her back, the Loving Cup balanced on her stomach. "I can dance anybody in the house off their feet."

"I'll take a piece of that," Haroon said. "I'll sniff ya out the best party spots, believe me!"

"Gleep!" said my dragon.

I turned to Dorinda.

"That sounds really nice. Would you like to, er, dance? I mean, with me?"

She glanced at her feet, then back up at me through her long eyelashes.

"Well, I suppose. If you really want to."

Was I being too forward? I realized I probably didn't look too appealing, covered as I was with mud and dust from our travels. But, as Aahz sometimes told me, if you didn't ask, you didn't get.

"Yes," I said. "I'd really enjoy it if you would."

Dorinda smiled, and I felt as if my knees had just melted. "All right, then. I'd love to."

"Great!" I said.

"Gleep!"

Gleep put his head into my ribs and shoved me away from her. I stumbled into a nearby bench, interrupting a kissing couple.

"Uh, sorry!" I said, as they glanced up in surprise. I righted myself with the help of a handy bit of magik. Gleep pushed his face into mine. His breath made me gag. I swallowed my gorge.

"Don't be jealous," I said, pushing his face away. "It's just a dance. It's not like we're dating or anything. Exactly."

"Eyes . . . on back," my dragon whispered.

I froze.

I realized I sensed that scrutiny, too. I hadn't felt it since we had last been in the main part of the resort. I looked around to see if I could spot where the sensation was coming from.

"What's the matter?" Aahz asked.

"We're being watched," I said, looking around. None of the happy passersby paid attention to us. Where was it coming from?

"Can't smell anythin' new," Haroon said.

"I just feel as if something has its eyes on us," I said.

"Nothing new there," Markie said. "They're always watching you here."

"This is different," I said, trying to pin down the sensation. "It's not welcoming or helpful. Far from it. It's . . ."

BAMF!

"Annoyed? Malign? Disgusted? Were those the words you were looking for?"

A tall, gaunt man who resembled my Skeeve the Magnificent disguise appeared before us. His black cloak swirled around him. Dorinda gasped.

"Meeger!"

CHAPTER THIRTY-SIX

"Nothing is more important than good manners."

—E. POST

The hollow-cheeked magician fixed her with a gaze that was a cross between a leer and a baleful stare.

"You undid my magik, Dorinda," he said. "How close I was to getting what I wanted from the council—and you took my cup out of the force line!" He pointed at the Nix Pyx, floating beside Dorinda. It bobbed behind her as if taking shelter from his gaze. "Return my property!"

"Not a chance," she said. Crackling energy formed in her palm. It flowed over her shoulder to the golden chalice and surrounded it with magikal barbed wire. "It goes back to Zaf with me. You fooled our treasurer. I told him that the last thing that ought to be sold was the Nix Pyx, especially to you. I don't know what kind of spell you put on him, but it won't work again, you selfish maniac!"

Meeger planted an innocent hand on his chest.

"Selfish! You should be thanking me for my generosity!

How can you call me selfish when I left your treasurer with enough gold to pay the bills for the next three months?"

"Barely enough for that! And you stole the Loving Cup from the council's strongroom here in Winslow so I couldn't bring it back to the duke! I have spent weeks looking for it when I could have been home looking after the kingdom!"

"I left the Loving Cup for you in my hotel room," Meeger said, with a mean smile. "For a moment or so, anyhow. Why didn't you end up in Maire?"

I gawked at him. Dorinda was innocent! I knew it! That trap had been meant for her, not us.

"*We* took your little excursion," I said, nonchalantly, polishing my fingernails on my jerkin, "but M.Y.T.H., Inc., is stronger than you think. Maire was just an . . . inconvenience."

Meeger's narrow brows rose up his forehead.

"An *inconvenience*? You must be joking."

"How could I be joking?" I asked. "We're here, no pieces missing. Wince has a pretty good act, doesn't he? Maybe you ought to go and see him for yourself!"

I had been gathering up energy until I was brimful with white magik. Picturing Wince's stage set, I threw everything I had at Meeger. Maybe I couldn't send him to Maire, but it ought to bounce him out of Winslow.

The power knocked him backward, but he didn't disappear. Instead, three Trollops sharing an earthenware bottle of liquor with a Deveel vanished off the street. I gasped at him. His eyes narrowed.

"Do you think I came here naked and blind, Klahd? I am protected by my art!" Meeger taunted me. He grew four feet higher so he loomed over me like a nightmare. "If you hurry, maybe you can save those innocent people from torture. Or are you going to stand there like the ignorant fool you are?"

I was horrified. He had set another trap, and I had blundered into it.

"Who says I care about what happens to them?" I asked, though inwardly I was frantic. "I'm here to support Dorinda."

"Why do you care about this pathetic prestidigitator?" Meeger countered. "It's pointless to aid such an inept magician who should never have left her father's shop. She ought to be back in Zaf making the sun shine on the king's birthday!" He turned to her. "Return my property! If you won't, I will appeal to the Council of Wizards to have your license revoked!"

Dorinda set her jaw.

"Go home, Meeger," she said. "I'll bring countercharges that you've been blackmailing Winslow."

He pursed his lips.

"Tut-tut, my child, they can't trace anything back to me! You're the only one who thinks I am involved. And all because of a single artifact that I don't even possess any longer." He spread his hands out. "You must be responsible for the whole thing! Your association with the council has been one long con!"

Dorinda gasped at him. I took her hand and squeezed it.

"It's a bluff," I said. "He has nothing. We hold all the cards now. Get lost, Meeger. You're in the wrong place. Winslow's for happy people. Got any more cheesy tricks up your sleeve before I bury you in a bog?"

"Nothing special," Meeger said, interlacing his long fingers together and twisting his joined hands outward in a loud CRACK! "But I've always been partial to this!"

Hot orange fire lanced out from his fingertips. I jumped back to avoid the streak of flame, but it doubled around and came at me from behind. Gleep shoved me out of the way and opened his mouth. He swallowed the fire like a cat drinking a stream of milk squirted out of a cow's teat.

"Gleep!" he exclaimed.

Meeger snarled. He raked me with more fireballs. Gleep ran back and forth, happily leaping onto the streams as if he were chasing string. Not one of them came close to hitting me.

Haroon leaped into the fray. He ran up to Meeger and closed his powerful jaws on the magician's leg. Meeger aimed a forefinger at the Canidian. I couldn't let him hit Haroon with magik. I put a ball of energy between his arm and his chest and forced them away from each other. The jet of fire rocketed off harmlessly into the sky. Meeger kicked at Haroon.

"Let go, you mangy sausage!"

"Grrr! You bin causin' trouble here for weeks!" the Canidian growled. "Now, you gonna leave here, or do I have to drag you?"

"Drag away, fleabag!"

Meeger flicked a hand at him. Haroon went tumbling head over tail into the legs of the crowd. He scampered back. As many times as Meeger knocked him away, he returned to threaten the magician's ankles. Fire leaped from Meeger's fingertips. Gleep was there to defend his friend and eat every stream of fire. I fought to keep my spell intact. I just didn't know very many offensive spells. I tried lighting his robes on fire, but Meeger snuffed the flames effortlessly.

Dorinda pressed her hands together. She peppered Meeger with silver bubbles. As each struck, it left a round silver blob on his robes. I couldn't figure out what they were supposed to do, until they mounted in number. They weighed the cloth down until the gaunt magician's knees began to buckle. Meeger flicked his hands down his robes, but they wouldn't dislodge. One hit him in the side of the face and clung like a limpet.

"Nice trick!" I said. She smiled at me. But Meeger had obviously seen it before. He made a pass with one hand. First one, then a few, then all of the silver spots clanged to the ground. He raised his palms. Beams of pure magik shimmered on both.

"Is that all you have?" he demanded. "Party tricks?"

"Not even close," Markie said. "Here's one I learned at Elemental School!"

Lightning lanced out of a clear sky. It blasted the pavement at Meeger's feet, making him jump backward. Between the Cupy's hands, a dark gray sphere took shape. It escaped from her grasp and skidded over the stones, roaring toward him. Meeger threw spells like blobs of color at it, trying to kill it before it engulfed him. He backed up against a wall, trapped by the onrushing windstorm.

Suddenly, the tornado shrank to the size of a broomstick.

"What the—?" Markie exclaimed. She clapped her hands. The tornado widened to its original size, only to narrow again. And again. She threw back her head in frustration to shout at the sky. "Stop killing my storms! I need them right now!"

It was too late. With a wicked grin, Meeger whipped his forefinger in the air. Markie started spinning around so fast all I could see was her golden curls whipping in a circle.

"Stooo-ooo-oop meeee!" she cried.

Dorinda and I threw handful after handful of magik, attempting to deaden his spells and free Markie from the cyclone. Each chunk of power bounced off Meeger like so many soap bubbles. Aahz took a running start and tackled Markie out of the air. They tumbled over and over, landing at the feet of a marching band. With amazing reflexes, Markie lifted them both off the ground out of the way. They marched back to us. Aahz's eyes were bright ochre with fury. Markie created an ominous, dark red ball of power that balanced on top of her finger. Meeger tried to dodge away from her, but Dorinda, Gleep, Aahz, Haroon, and I had him surrounded. The Canidian bared his teeth.

"Leave now, Meeger," I said. "The council refuses to accede to your demands. Go away while you still can. Your only way out is to go under your own power."

Meeger sneered at me.

"You're having so much fun being an enforcer, Skeeve the not-so-magnificent! Have more fun!"

He raised one hand.

I braced myself for another onslaught of terrifying magik. Instead, he twitched the end of his forefinger in the air.

I felt hard points rasping against my ribs, over and over. Against my own will, I started to giggle. I clutched my sides. Dorinda started laughing. Markie dropped her ball of magik and threw her arms around herself, trying to keep her composure. Aahz grinned so widely that I could see all his teeth. Even Gleep was helpless against the tickling. He lay on the ground, chuckling and kicking all four legs. Though I fought it, I couldn't stop myself from laughing uproariously.

"Ha ha ha ha ha!"

"Hee hee hee hee!" Dorinda tittered.

"Ho ho ho!" To my astonishment, that was the noise Markie made.

"Eep eep eep eep eep!" my dragon burbled.

"Hark hark hark hark!" gasped Haroon.

"Do . . . some . . . thing!" Aahz choked out. "Ha ha! Haw haw haw!" He collapsed onto his back, gasping and hooting.

I drew magik up from the surging force line. But I couldn't concentrate. I couldn't even inhale more than halfway before the breath exploded out of my body again and again. I lay on the ground, laughter racking my body. My mind couldn't form a single coherent image.

"He—he—help me," I whispered to the people going back and forth around us. I put out an arm in supplication to a party of Imps conga-ing by wearing party hats. They glanced down and grinned at us, never ceasing their rhythmic dancing. They thought we were having a good time!

Still chortling, I dragged myself up to my knees and fought my way toward Meeger. Aahz, too, battled against the spell. We leaned on one another, crawling forward inch by inch. I could tell by the gleam in Aahz's eyes that if he could get his hands on Meeger, he would tear him to pieces. But Meeger had no trouble at all evading us in our weakened condition.

A few feet away, Dorinda dropped to the ground, her eyes half-closed, her chest still heaving helplessly. I didn't have very much strength left myself. My eyesight narrowed as the world started to go black. I fought to stay awake. My juddering ribs hurt.

"Glee-ee-eep," my dragon chortled weakly beside me. His wings were splayed out on the pavement. His legs kicked in the air.

Metal clanged off the stones near my ear. Meeger stepped over my body toward Markie and looked down.

"My, my, what's this?" he asked, with an air of false surprise. "Could it be the celebrated and much sought-after Loving Cup? What a nice surprise!" He stooped to pick it up. I could just barely see amid the tears of laughter as he stowed it in his belt pouch. Another clang sounded, this time nearer to Dorinda. The Nix Pyx! "And look at that, another magik cup!"

I willed him to bend down and take it in his hands.

Touch it! Touch it! Touch it!

But Meeger was no fool. He kicked it away.

"I won't be needing that just yet," he said, standing over me, his eyes glowing. "Now, all I need to do is to wait for all of you to die of laughter! It won't take long. Then I can force the council to do exactly what I want them to! Oh, I am going to enjoy this!"

"Pardon me," said an infinitely polite voice. "I believe you dropped this."

Through the haze, I could see a huge purple finger appear out of nowhere. It tapped Meeger on the shoulder. Surprised, the gaunt magician turned.

Looming over him from behind was Benjy. The Troll thrust

the Nix Pyx into Meeger's arms. Automatically, Meeger closed his hands on the metal cup. And realized his mistake one second later. His mouth dropped open in horror.

"Noooooo!" he wailed. He threw the cup away. It clattered on the paving stones and rolled to a stop beside a statue. Meeger dashed his hands together as if trying to get rid of the Pyx's touch.

Just as suddenly, the vigorous tickling on my ribs ceased. I lay gasping for a moment, then climbed to my feet. I offered a hand to Markie and Dorinda. Aahz struggled to hands and knees, and eventually his feet. We leaned against the nearest wall for support while we gasped for air.

Meeger gawked at Benjy.

"What have you *done*?"

"Just returning your property, sir," Benjy said, innocently. "I just heard you refer to that as 'my cup.' You dropped it. I retrieved it and restored it to you. We of Winslow always seek to be of service to our guests. It is our pleasure as well as our profession."

Meeger struggled to speak.

"No! I mean, but . . . ! My magik!" He tried to summon up power from the force line. His hands scrabbled fruitlessly at the empty air. I knew the frustration he felt.

Dorinda pointed at the cup on the ground and waved her finger. The Nix Pyx rose in the air, and a hot globe of glowing blue power grew around it.

"That has done enough damage for this century," she said. "I had better get it home."

"You!" Meeger shrieked, waving his arms at Benjy. "You monster! You have destroyed me!" He kept throwing handfuls of air at the Troll. If they had been filled with magik, Benjy probably would have been burned to a cinder. The more his attempts failed, the angrier Meeger became. He grabbed Benjy around the neck with both hands and tried to strangle him.

"Please, sir, calm down," Benjy said, removing the magician effortlessly and setting him on the ground. Meeger went for him again, this time trying to bite him in the side of the neck. "Please don't do that, sir. I'm afraid if you can't, I will have to take, er, more extreme measures."

"You don't have to throw him into a wall," Aahz snarled, sticking his face into the magician's. "It'll be my pleasure."

"My magik! I am going to kill you all!" Meeger shrieked.

"What with?" I asked. "Doesn't look like you have any weapons left!"

Meeger glared at me.

"This isn't over, Skeeve!"

"I've made worse enemies than you," I said.

"No, you haven't," Meeger raved. "Tell him, girl! Tell him what I'm capable of!"

"Is he delusional?" Markie asked.

"A little," Dorinda said. "But you'd be right not to underestimate him. He's dangerous."

"That's right! I'll restore my powers, and you all will suffer!" Meeger declared. "I will declare war on you! Everything you prize will become mine!"

A huge purple fist crashed down on Meeger's head. His eyes rolled up and he sank to the sidewalk.

"Oh, my, I am going to get in trouble," Benjy said, not looking at all repentant. "I have just been helpful outside my station. I am afraid I will be put on report."

"Thank you so much," Dorinda said, standing on tiptoe to kiss his furry cheek. "You saved us all!"

"How did you know to turn up just now?" I asked.

"Why, you asked for help, Mr. Skeeve," Benjy said.

"I . . ." I remembered trying to squeeze words out to the dancing Imps. "I didn't think anyone could hear me."

Benjy smiled.

"We all heard you, we employees. Thankfully, I was close by. I have been in and out of every portal in Winslow trying to find you. The Nix Pyx was added to our manuals just before the party began. It had a red spiral warning beside it so we would not confuse it with any other magikal vessel, especially the Loving Cup." He nodded to the goblet that Markie retrieved from Meeger's pouch. "So glad I could help you, my friends."

"Help!" I said, remembering my ricocheted spell. "We have to get to Maire and bring those people back!"

CHAPTER THIRTY-SEVEN

"Sometimes what you want isn't what you need."

—MIDAS

We beat Wince's minions to the partygoers by less than half a minute. With Markie and Dorinda running interference against the horsemen, I drew up a return spell and had the Trollops and the Deveel back on the main street even before their bottle ran out. I was glad to return from the darkness of Maire to the brilliant sunlight of Winslow.

A dance band played from a low dais just beside the Central Help Desk on the main street. Around the stage, thousands of happy people pranced and kicked in time to the music.

Blinking against the strong light, Aahz peered over the shoulders of the crowd and pointed toward the Central Help Desk building.

"There they are," he said.

I glanced in the direction he indicated. Bunny sat beside Looie on a bench just inside the archway, away from all the merrymaking. Both of them sat with their arms folded, looking grim. I waved my arm to get her attention. When she spotted me, her face lit up.

I tapped Markie on the shoulder.

"Let me take the Loving Cup," I said. "You all go enjoy the party."

"All right," she said. "But I don't think I ever want to laugh again."

A Titan came up and bowed to her. Markie let him take her hand and lead her into the midst of the dance. Aahz put his arm around the waist of a captivating young lovely with bright yellow skin and orange hair. Aahz led her in a shifting, sliding series of steps that soon had the crowd cheering them on. I had no idea he was that good a dancer.

I took Dorinda by the hand and pulled her with me through the crowd. Bunny left her perch and hurried up to me. I put the cup in Dorinda's hand and led Bunny aside.

"What happened?" Bunny asked. "It's been awful! My disguise spell stopped working just about the time the party started! Looie looked at me as if I had turned into a slug. He hasn't said a word to me since! As if anyone ever really looks like that."

"We ran into a problem," I said. I took her by the hand and guided her out into the sunlight. "Come and dance with me. I'll explain everything."

Though I was not the best dancer in the world, I swept her around the square. She clung to me. I held her close until her heart stopped racing and told her everything that had happened from the time we had left the main street.

"So Servis did have the Loving Cup!" she said.

"All of them," I agreed. "But he took it in a good cause. He really was trying to help. He apologized all the way back for discommoding us."

"Poor old guy," Bunny said. "I had it a lot easier than he

did. All I had to put up with was six hours of leering, followed by another of sulking."

Markie detached herself from a circle of five good-looking men from several dimensions.

"There you are!" she exclaimed. "Aahz! He's over here! Did Looie get the cup?"

I glanced over the heads of the crowd and spotted Dorinda standing near the entrance to the round building. She nodded to me.

"Yes, he did," I said. "He's gone."

"Well, thank the Elements for that!" Markie said. Aahz bowed to the yellow-and-orange girl and came over to us.

"When?" Bunny asked, looking back toward the Central Help Desk. "When did he get it?"

"Just now," I said.

"While we were dancing? Where's the money?"

"I let Dorinda give it to him," I said. "She got paid."

Bunny put her hands on her hips and turned to Aahz.

"Did you know about this?" she asked.

The corner of Aahz's mouth lifted slightly.

"No, but I could have guessed. You know the kid!"

"Why aren't you angry? She got the fee instead of us!" Bunny said, as if she couldn't believe it. I felt bad for her, but I nodded.

"Yes," I said. "Fifteen gold pieces."

She had opened her mouth to berate me, and stopped before a syllable left her lips.

"*Fifteen?* Not two hundred?"

"Nope. That's what Aahz negotiated for. She asked for twenty. Looie refused and beat her down. They settled on fifteen. That's what she got."

"Oh," Bunny said. Her bad mood melted away. "Now I feel so greedy."

"What's wrong with being greedy?" Aahz asked. "We

know what we're worth! You could have collected and paid her out of her share!"

"I know I could," I said. "But fifteen was really a fair fee for the job. We don't need it, and she really did. We forget sometimes what it's like to be the little guy. Most people aren't M.Y.T.H., Inc. They see less income as a good return than we do. I'm sorry I didn't tell you in advance, but I knew you'd understand. Markie, you contracted with us for this job. I'll guarantee your fee as if we collected the full amount."

Markie waved a hand.

"Forget it. You've been generous to me in the past, too. Call it even."

"Thanks."

BAMF!

Tananda and Chumley appeared in our midst, high-fiving one another.

"Oh, I say!" Chumley said, adjusting his gold glasses on his nose. "Very good to see you! You look more perky than when we departed."

"I'm fine," Bunny said. She had assimilated everything I had told her. I couldn't tell if she was still angry, but I was willing to take all the blame she threw at me. Aahz was more amused than mad. "It looks like it went well on your end."

"Indeed, yes! As I assumed, things went much more smoothly without Looie there. We met His Majesty, the king. A good ruler, really."

"Nice guy," Tananda said, running a thoughtful finger up and back along her collarbone. "Generous, too!" She showed me a huge golden ring with a glowing, multicolored gem in it. "He really appreciated our ability to settle a crowd and get some genuine discussions moving."

"Once I started threatening to break arms, that is," Chumley said.

"He did nothing of the kind," Tananda protested, with a

laugh. "He was gentle and persuasive. I was the one who threatened to break arms."

"How bad was the negotiation?" I asked.

"It simply wasn't that difficult," Chumley said. "There were several parties involved, all of the neighboring nations. Once they ceased posturing and brought out their genuine concerns, we were able to make rapid progress on settling them. It would seem that Looie, unsurprisingly, was the bottleneck that prevented them from agreeing upon a set tariff for cross-border trading."

"He wanted a cut of everything on top of the tariffs," Tananda said. "Which didn't surprise us at all."

"No, indeed, what? I had everyone write their ideal percentage in sealed envelopes and examined them in private. The numbers were so very close I was surprised that no accord had been met before. It took little time to handle that matter. His Majesty has asked us to return next month for further talks. I am reading the back correspondence on matters of water rights and harborage."

"I don't think you're going to have time to work here part-time as a bouncer," I said with a smile.

"Perhaps not," Chumley said, with evident regret. "Shame, that."

"Maybe Winslow can hire Looie to sit under bridges and annoy tourists," Tananda said. "He's a rotten negotiator. I think he is going to have to look for another job. Unless he can get the king to hold on to the other handle of the Loving Cup and make an appropriate wish. Too bad the cup disappears after you use it. That could have been a nice thing to have on tap for tough jobs."

"Yeah, about that," Aahz said, looking very innocent.

"Aahz, what did you do?" Bunny asked, her eyes wide with worry.

"Why do you assume I did something wrong?" Aahz

boomed. "I just bounced over to Whee-Don's Trick Shop in Deva and bought a miniature tracer spell. I put it in the base of the Loving Cup when we got back into town. I can find it again if we ever need it."

"I say, Aahz, good show!" Chumley said.

A waiter in a very fine white suit appeared beside us and offered a leather-bound book to Bunny.

"Madams and sirs, your most exclusive and special table at Le Snoot is ready for you."

Bunny looked at me. "I didn't make a reservation. Did you?"

I smiled slowly.

"I didn't, but I can guess who did."

"Her again?" Markie exclaimed. "Dorinda?"

"Do you mind?" I asked.

Markie thought about it for a moment.

"No. I suppose I don't."

"Neither do I," Bunny said, with a smile. "Not at all. Let's go."

CHAPTER THIRTY-EIGHT

"Is it still 'all's well that ends well,' if 'love's labour's lost'?"

—W. SHAKESPEARE

"I hope this is all right with you," Dorinda said to us, as we entered the small private dining room past a line of bowing waitstaff, sommeliers, and busboys. She wore a form-fitting gown in soft blue silk. A stiff collar stood high behind her neck, but the décolletage dipped in front to invite the eye to survey her modest curves. She patted the seat to her right and beckoned me over. "It was the least I could do, when you've all been so kind to me."

Where Winslow had been lavish in its hospitality before, it now did its best to sweep us off our feet. From finger bowls to oyster forks, the white-draped table was set with every utensil I had ever seen, and dozens I hadn't. Crystal glasses stood in ranks at every place like translucent troops. Immaculately dressed Winslovaks with white cloths draped over their arms swooped in and out, filling glasses, offering hors d'oeuvres, shoulder and foot massages, hot hand towels, pristine white napkins over the lap, and our own personalized menus with glowing print we could easily read in the subdued lighting of the dining room. I settled into a chair that embraced me like a long-lost friend and sipped a glass of wine while I read through the lengthy menu. I set down the empty glass.

"More, sir?" asked an august-looking gentleman in a tail-coat, appearing at my shoulder with a carafe of blue wine.

"Uh, no," I said. "One's my limit."

He leaned closer and gave me a meaningful wink.

"This is the same beverage you enjoyed the other night in the Rusty Hinge."

"Oh," I said. "Then keep it coming!" I held up my glass.

The food in Winslow was always excellent, but this surpassed anything I had tried before. Though I tried to be moderate, the servers kept plying me with delightful dishes. I tried to keep up with the conversation while I ate.

". . . I was a little taken aback at first that Skeeve let you take our fee," Bunny said to Dorinda, who sat on her right. "But Looie didn't ask for our advance back, so we didn't lose too much on this deal."

"I know it was presumptuous of Skeeve to speak for the rest of you," Dorinda said, eating daintily with a small silver fork. "You have no idea how much difference it will make in our castle! I am very grateful. So I took it on myself to ask the council to give you the same offer that they give me."

Bunny lifted her red eyebrows.

"Which is?"

"They let me stay here free of charge while I am working here," Dorinda said. "Haroon has the same arrangement."

"Right you are, little missy," Haroon said, lifting his face from the silver bowl the waiters had brought him. "I get to spend my whole vacation detectin', and I ain't out of pocket about it. Not that I got any pockets, but you get it."

"I certainly do!" Bunny said, beaming. "That's really sweet of you, Dorinda."

"And with the hundred gold pieces we won in the Scavenger Hunt," I said, pushing my salad plate to one side, "our bottom line is going to look pretty good this quarter. Isn't it?"

Bunny had the grace to look a little ashamed of herself.

"Yes, it is. I can show the books to Uncle Bruce without any problem. He can't try to reassign me for a while."

"Never," I assured her. "We won't ever let him."

"What are you going to do about the Nix Pyx?" Tananda asked, nodding toward the glowing blue sphere that hung in the corner of the room like a naughty child. "It's a pretty devastating piece of magik. I don't know much about things like that but if you ask me, it should never have existed in the first place."

"I'll have to take it to a specialist and have it despelled," Dorinda said. "Our treasurer isn't a magician. He'll never know that it doesn't work anymore. And there are so many fakes in the world that this will just have been one of them. The hype so rarely matches the reality."

"Destroy it," I advised. "There are plenty of jewelers in the Bazaar who can make you a good replica out of the metal. But you'd better stand by when they do it, or they'll keep the real thing and sell it out the back flap of the tent when you're not looking."

Dorinda glanced at the cup speculatively. "And if it's a little lighter than the original, well, the extra gold can pay the masons for a new oven for the castle kitchens. The old ones leak too much heat."

"Half-baked bread's only good for dragons," Tanda said.

"Gleep!" my dragon agreed, although he had a platter of meaty bones the size of a rug in front of him.

I was pleased to see how well everybody was getting along with Dorinda. Aahz even made a few side comments to me, comparing her favorably with some of my past girlfriends. Dorinda had relaxed among my friends, as I knew she would. Her beautiful blue eyes sparkled. The others were doing their part to make her feel at home. She was a good hostess, too, making sure everybody had what they wanted for dessert. I enjoyed her conversation as much as the blue wine. We all felt mellow by the end of the meal.

"Guess I'll cancel the contract I put out on you," Markie said, pushing her empty plate away at last.

"You didn't really do that, did you?" I asked, anxiously.

"You'll never know, Skeeve," Markie said, with a studiously blank look on her face. Dorinda looked nervous and apologetic.

"I'm sorry for all the trouble you had," she said. "I really thought Meeger had sent you. I always suspected he was connected with some shady characters. But all I wanted to do was send you somewhere else. I had Limbo in my mind. The only reason you ended up in Maire was Meeger's booby trap."

"I know that now," I said, eagerly. "We all do. Come back to Deva with us. Now that everything has been straightened out, I'd like to have a chance to get to know you. I have so many places I'd like to show you."

Dorinda touched my hand.

"I'd like that, but Meeger was right. I have no business spending time away enjoying myself when my kingdom is in such trouble. Besides, I have three other assignments I have to finish off so I can get paid. The masons won't start work on my tower stairs until I can give them money for the stone and their labor. Maybe one day."

"Maybe one day," I said.

"I hope so. I would love to see your home. And spend more time with you. All of you."

She leaned over and kissed me on the cheek, then rose from her seat.

BAMF!

She was gone. I was sad, but maybe just a little relieved.

I turned to see the others watching me curiously. I gave them a halfhearted grin.

"Let's go home," I said. "You know, you can have too much fun."

Robert Lynn Asprin

Robert Asprin was the author of the Myth-Adventures, Phule's Company, and Dragons Wild series. He passed away in May of 2008 in his hometown of New Orleans.

Jody Lynn Nye

Jody Lynn Nye lists her main career activity as "spoiling cats." She has published forty-eight books, including *Advanced Mythology*, fourth in her Mythology fantasy series (no relation); eight science fiction novels; and four novels in collaboration with Anne McCaffrey, including *The Ship Who Won.* She has also edited a humorous anthology about mothers, *Don't Forget Your Spacesuit, Dear,* and published more than a hundred and forty short stories. Her latest books are *Wishing on a Star,* part of the Stellar Guild Series, and *Rhythm of the Imperium*, third in the Lord Thomas Kinago series. She lives northwest of Chicago with her husband, author and packager Bill Fawcett, and their cat, Jeremy. Visit her on the Web at jodylynnnye.com.